PRAISE FOR ALINA BRONSKY'S *B*

D0446924

"Written by the intriguingly pseudonymous Alina Bronsky, *Broken Glass Park* is a vivid depiction of contemporary adolescence under pressure. After such a debut, it will be interesting to see what the author can do as her talents mature."
—Amanda Heller, *The Boston Globe*

"A very assured, sharp and funny book . . . Sascha is smart and tough and has a wonderfully tart, distinctive voice, ably captured by translator Tim Mohr."—*Minneapolis Star Tribune*

"In her riveting debut, Bronsky gives us Sascha Naimann . . . Sascha's hunger for life shines through her relentless fight to leave behind a painful childhood—a struggle complicated by an unexpected twist in the final act—making for a stark, moving tale of resiliency and survival."—*Publishers Weekly* (starred review)

"What a literary creation! No wonder this book was such a sensation in Europe. Sascha is alternately endearing and exasperating, compassionate and chillingly cold-blooded, always ready to use her budding sexuality as a weapon, never quite admitting even to herself what she's looking for with such avidity and violence. When she flips out and begins hurling rocks through her neighbors' windows, you realize how tenuous her grip on sanity might really be . . . Filled with rich characters, rapid-fire dialogue and an unforgettable heroine."—*Shelf Awareness*

"Old-fashioned storytelling at its best . . . Bronsky's writing and psychological understanding are persuasive and engaging. Sascha is an unusual character and her story a truly unique one that deserves to be read."—*The Quarterly Conversation*

"Bronsky's language is potent and vital. Brutality, rage, loss and trauma are expressed with candor. As a result, when Sascha's flashes of tenderness and vulnerability rupture the prose at unexpected moments, they hit the reader with as much force as her more violent impulses."—*The Financial Times*

"*Broken Glass Park* is, above all, fearless. The narrator is defiantly, unapologetically herself: female, but like no other female I've encountered in literature; still a child, but tasked with all the responsibility of an adult; angry, and unwilling to mitigate her anger with a nod toward likeability. But because of this she is likeable, and real, and complex."—*Tottenville Review*

"If an American had written *Broken Glass Park*, it might easily have been dismissed as a young-adult novel. That label would have been too simplistic. Teenage protagonists, with their underdeveloped frontal lobes and their raw emotions, are perfect submersibles for exploring our inability to connect . . . In a parallel literary universe, while Holden Caulfield wanders Central Park in search of a cause, Sascha Naimann dares to walk barefoot in a park littered with glass, searching for a future that will not cut her to pieces."—*The Nervous Breakdown*

"An achingly beautiful debut novel . . . *Broken Glass Park* is a captivating and unsettling read . . . With its delicate treatment of the existential complexities surrounding the perpetuation of violence and the salvation of acceptance, it is likely to garner much more critical acclaim."—Catherine Bailey, *Three Percent*

THE HOTTEST DISHES OF THE TARTAR CUISINE

Alina Bronsky

THE HOTTEST DISHES OF THE TARTAR CUISINE

*Translated from the German
by Tim Mohr*

Europa
editions

Europa Editions
116 East 16th Street
New York, N.Y. 10003
www.europaeditions.com
info@europaeditions.com

Translation by Tim Mohr
Original Title: *Die schärfsten Gerichte der tatarischen Küche*
Translation copyright © 2011 by Europa Editions

Library of Congress Cataloging-in-Publication Data is available
ISBN 978-1-60945-006-9

Bronsky, Alina
The Hottest Dishes of the Tartar Cuisine

Book design by Emanuele Ragnisco
www.mekkanografici.com
Cover illustration by Silke Schmidt

Prepress by Grafica Punto Print – Rome

Printed in Canada

For Stephan

"As in every language, there is no shortage of extremely crude expressions in Tartar. Understanding these vulgarities helps one read and manage a variety of situations. The following words, then, are not intended to be used but simply to aid the understanding of specific situations."
—From the chapter "Insults and Oaths in Tartar" in *Word for Word* (Travel and Knowhow Editions)

THE HOTTEST
DISHES OF THE
TARTAR CUISINE

The knitting needle

As my daughter Sulfia was explaining that she was pregnant but that she didn't know by whom, I paid extra attention to my posture. I sat with my back perfectly straight and folded my hands elegantly in my lap.

Sulfia was sitting on a kitchen stool. Her shoulders were scrunched up and her eyes were red; instead of simply letting her tears flow she insisted on rubbing them into her face with the backs of her hands. This despite the fact that when she was still a child I had taught her how to cry without making herself look ugly, and how to smile without promising too much.

But Sulfia wasn't very gifted. In fact, to be honest, I'd say she was rather stupid. And yet somehow she was my daughter—worse still, my only daughter. As I looked at her—her nose running, perched there on the stool with her back hunched like a parrot in a cage—I had mixed feelings. I desperately wanted to shout at her, "Sit up straight! Stop sniffling! Wipe that pathetic look off your face! Don't scrunch your eyes like that!"

But I also felt sorry for her. After all, she was mine. Somehow! I had no other daughter, no son, and for years my body had been hollow inside—as barren as the sands of a desert. This daughter I did have was deformed and bore no resemblance to her mother. She was short—she only came up to my shoulders. She had no figure whatsoever. She had small eyes and a crooked mouth. And, as I said, she was stupid. She was already seventeen years old, too, so there was little chance she would get any smarter.

I only hoped that her simplemindedness might prove attractive enough to some man that he wouldn't notice her awful legs until the two of them were already standing in front of a justice of the peace.

Thus far that hope had come to nothing. Sulfia had a few female friends on our block, but the last time she had spoken to a boy was probably ten years before, just after she started primary school. Yet, one day, there I was sautéing a fish in oil (it was 1978, and anthrax spores had just leaked from the huge lab in our city), and Sulfia put her hand over her nose and then threw up four times in the toilet.

Even that witch Klavdia, who lived in another room of our communal apartment, noticed something amiss. Klavdia worked in a birthing center as a midwife. That was her version, at least. I didn't believe her. She probably wasn't anything more than a janitor. There were two parties in our apartment. One party— our family—had two bedrooms; the other party—Klavdia—had one. We shared a common bathroom and kitchen. It was a nice old building, and very central.

Sulfia sat on the stool and in answer to my questions told me that her sudden pregnancy could only have come about from *dreaming* of a man at night, while asleep, and I believed her immediately. The streets were full of pretty girls in short skirts, and a real man would never come anywhere near Sulfia unless he was nearsighted or perverted.

I looked sternly at Sulfia, disappointment in my eyes, but she just stared down at her little feet. I knew such cases existed, cases of virgins having a dream and nine months later bringing a child into the world. And there were even worse cases. I knew of one personally: my cousin Rafaella found her daughter in the blossom of a huge exotic house plant of unknown origin—

she'd brought the seed from somewhere down south, she said. I can still remember just how baffled she was.

I looked at my daughter and wondered what I could do now for her future and my reputation. I had some ideas.

I went down to the pharmacy and bought mustard powder. Then I scrubbed the bathtub until it was gleaming and filled it with hot water. We were lucky that we had hot water just then, for it had been shut off time and again over the previous weeks.

I sprinkled the powder into the water and then stirred it in with the broken-off handle of a snow shovel I'd found on the street the previous winter and brought home with me because it looked solid. Sure enough, I'd already found a use for it.

I stirred and Sulfia stood next to me, watched, and shivered.

"Get undressed," I said.

She quickly climbed out of her dress and her white panties and looked at me.

"Get in," I said.

You always had to connect the dots for her.

She gingerly lifted one of her ugly, dark legs and braced herself on me. She dunked her big toe into the water and started moaning about it being way too hot.

"It's even hotter in hell," I said patiently.

She looked at me, tried to put her foot in, and cringed, jerking it back out.

I was losing my patience. The water has to be hot, not lukewarm, I explained. She looked at me with a wounded look, and then let herself drop into the bathtub. Water splashed onto the floor.

"Are you crazy?" I shouted and turned the tap back on *very hot*.

As I mopped up the puddles on the tiled floor, Sulfia whimpered in the tub: it was too hot, she was going to be scalded to death.

"Nobody has ever been scalded to death," I said, though I knew it wasn't true. When her whimpering stopped, I looked up. Sulfia lay in the tub with her eyes closed and her mouth hanging open. I lifted her up and ran cold water over her with the showerhead. Better a pregnant daughter than a dead one, I thought. Sulfia came to. Her skin was red, and she immediately began to complain.

I dragged Sulfia past Klavdia's curious face and into our room, put her in bed, and gave her cranberry tea to drink. She fell asleep. She slept for twenty-two hours, tossing and turning and groaning the whole time. I kept checking the sheet beneath her. It remained white.

After the mustard bath, Sulfia's skin began to peel, but otherwise nothing happened. So I went to the market and bought a large bag of bay laurel leaves from one of my countrymen. I boiled up the leaves into a brew and gave it to Sulfia. She drank it obediently, like a good daughter. She didn't even make it to the toilet before throwing up several times in the washbasin—in plain view of nosy Klavdia. She couldn't hold any of it down, so it didn't do anything.

I began to worry. I didn't want to send my daughter to the doctor, and I didn't want any idiotic chatter at the school where she'd been studying nursing since the beginning of the year. I hoped to avoid any additional hurdles for Sulfia, who was hardly popular as it was. And I also knew that at hospitals they treated stupid young girls in her condition like pieces of meat. I wanted to spare her that.

I never would have expected God to send help in the person of Klavdia, of all people—that stupid clucking hen. But after observing my increasingly desperate attempts, Klavdia took the initiative. She put a hand on my elbow in our shared kitchen and whispered that she had helped a few other people in her time and knew exactly what to do.

I listened to her and then nodded. I had no choice. The next day we went into Klavdia's room and pushed a big table into the middle. Klavdia brought in a washable tablecloth covered with a floral pattern of forget-me-nots and bachelor buttons. I went and brought in Sulfia, whose black eyes bounced around the room in panic.

I explained to Sulfia once again that though they could arise on their own, problems never took care of themselves. They had to be solved. She trembled in my arms for a while. Then she obediently climbed onto the table.

Klavdia said she couldn't work this way. With Sulfia shaking so badly, she wouldn't be able to find the right spot. I had to hold Sulfia down—if she jerked around in the middle of it, Klavdia might stick the needle into her gut. I threw myself across my daughter's midsection.

"Hold her mouth shut," said Klavdia. As I smothered Sulfia's suddenly rising scream, Klavdia pulled a bloody knitting needle from between Sulfia's legs with a quick motion.

Maybe she is more than a janitor after all, I thought, impressed with Klavdia's steady hand. Then I released my grip on Sulfia's clenched jaw. Her head lolled to one side. The frail child had passed out again.

I carried Sulfia to our room on my back. I laid a waterproof pad beneath her pale bum and wrapped her in warm blankets.

She came to again. Her eyes, dark and round like raisins, wandered around the room. She made a soft whining sound.

Her face slowly got whiter. My husband, Kalganow, came home from work.

"What does Sonja have?" he asked.

He didn't call our daughter by her Tartar name. He called her what the Russians called her because it was beyond their capabilities to remember a Tartar name, much less pronounce one.

My husband was an absolutist. He didn't believe in God; the only thing he believed was that all people were alike, and that anyone who claimed otherwise was still living in the Middle Ages. My husband didn't like it when we made distinctions between ourselves and others.

I told him our stupid little Sulfia just had the flu. He went to her bedside and put his hand on her forehead.

"But she's cold," he said. "Cold and moist."

Well, I couldn't get everything right. Sulfia moaned and tossed and turned.

Twins, so what?

That night I suddenly got worried that Sulfia might die on me. It had been years since I worried about her, and I didn't like the feeling. I lifted Sulfia's blanket. Things looked good. I cleaned her up, gathered the bloody stuff, stuck it in a plastic bag, and wrapped the bag in a newspaper. I quietly left our apartment and heard Klavdia turn over in bed as I did. I carried the bloody bundle through the dark, empty streets and stuffed it in a dumpster a few blocks away.

In the morning Sulfia had a fever. She was bleeding like a stuck pig. I pulled a jar of caviar out of the depths of my refrigerator—I'd been saving it for New Year. I smeared it thickly on four slices of bread and fed it to Sulfia. Caviar was known to be good for replenishing blood.

Sulfia's teeth chattered. She had the chills. Tiny translucent orange balls of caviar stuck to her chin. I poured a drink made out of sea buckthorn berries into her twisted mouth. I had a garden out of town, and I'd picked the berries there in the fall.

My hands had bled from being stuck by the thorns; it had ruined the skin on my fingertips. Afterward I pureed the berries with sugar, ten liters' worth in canning jars. That way the sea buckthorns kept through the winter. Now I mixed spoonfuls of the puree into hot water and gave it to Sulfia to drink so she'd get some vitamins.

She sniffled and groaned, but my labors paid off. After a few days Sulfia stopped bleeding and was able to get out of bed and make it to the bathroom on her own. After a few more days she went back to her nursing school. Klavdia gave us an official note saying that Sulfia had been out with the flu. For the next few months I had an easier time putting up with her, until I noticed her belly starting to get round. At some point it became blatantly obvious. But I noticed it rather late. It had just never occurred to me. Eventually even Kalganow, who normally missed everything, noticed.

"What's Sonja got in there?" he asked, pointing with his finger. "How did that happen?"

"She's just a growing girl," I said hastily. I put my hand on Sulfia's stomach and froze. The kick I felt against my hand spelled trouble.

God was mocking me. God or Klavdia.

"Must have been twins," Klavdia said, shrugging her shoulders. "So what?"

She said we'd paid her to take care of only one baby, and she'd done that. Since she knew nothing about a twin, she couldn't have gotten rid of a second baby. She just stuck the one closest to the exit.

In fact, said Klavdia, the survival of the second twin was evidence of her skill. Others couldn't even ensure the survival of the mother.

I locked myself in the bathroom and let the tears flow, silently, so no one could hear me and so my eyes wouldn't get red. Sulfia sat on a kitchen stool and stroked her belly, smiling, eyes wide, munching on slices of bread stacked with cheese and cold cuts, fresh pickles I'd bought at the market, sour pickles I'd canned the past summer, marinated tomatoes, apples, a piece of apple tart, one bowl full of yoghurt, and another filled with cream of wheat and raisins.

Because I knew my husband would never believe the story about being impregnated in a dream, I told him she'd been raped by the neighbor two floors up from us. The neighbor was related to my husband's most senior supervisor. After that Kalganow didn't say anything more, not to me, not to Sulfia, and not to the neighbor, and we began to prepare for the arrival of the baby, never losing the faint hope that some calamity—an illness or a botched medical procedure—might still arrive first.

The child

The child, a little girl, seven pounds, twenty inches long, was born one cold December night in 1978 at Birthing Center Number 134. I had a feeling even then that she would become the type of kid who could survive anything without batting an eye. She was an unusual child and screamed very loudly from day one.

My husband and I picked up the baby in a taxi when she was ten days old. Along with our daughter, of course.

The little child nestled in a folded knit blanket piped with pink. It was standard issue at the time. My husband took a picture of us: me with the baby in my arms, next to me Sulfia holding a bouquet of plastic flowers lent to us by the clinic to use in the photos—obviously there was no place to get fresh flowers in winter. The baby's face was barely visible, a little flash of red between the folds of the blanket. I had completely forgotten that newborns are so tiny and ugly. This one began to scream in the taxi and only let up a year later.

I held the baby in my arms and studied its face. I realized that the fatherless baby looked more like me than like any adult I knew. She was, despite my initial impression, not really ugly. Up close I could see that she was actually a pretty little girl—particularly when she was quiet.

At home we unwrapped her and laid her on the bed. The baby girl had firm little muscles and strong reddish skin. Her tiny arms and legs writhed around and the bed shook beneath her. And she screamed nonstop.

Klavdia's curious face peered around the doorframe: "Oh, how cute! Already home? Congratulations! Have you fed that baby? The screaming's unbearable."

Sulfia sat in a comfy chair and smiled deliriously. My husband leaned down and frowned at his first grandchild. I had the feeling there was something he didn't like about her. Perhaps he was looking for traces of his supervisor in her little face.

"What's his name?" asked Klavdia from the doorway.

"It's a girl!" I cried so loudly that the baby stopped screaming for one brief moment and looked up at me, surprised. "A girl! We have a granddaughter."

"Okay, okay. What's its name?" Klavdia asked.

"Aminat," I said. "Her name is Aminat."

"What?" said Klavdia, who had always insisted on calling my daughter, whom she'd known since she was a baby, Sonja, and me Rosa, which was at least derived from my actual name, Rosalinda. We had beautiful names that nobody else seemed to be able to deal with.

"That is, Anna, Anja," my husband corrected. He always wanted to be like everyone else.

"Aminat," I repeated. I didn't think it was so difficult to remember. My granddaughter would be called Aminat, just like my grandmother, who'd grown up in the mountains. Even if I turned out to be the only one, I would always call her by her real name, and who cared that in daycare, kindergarten, school, university, and then in whatever profession she entered she would soon become just another Anja. For me she would be Aminat, and I immediately began to pray that someday she'd be able to live a life where people didn't automatically butcher her name.

"Her name is Aminat Kalganova," I said, and Klavdia's disapproving face disappeared from the doorway.

My husband put his hands over his ears and said, "That really is unbearable. Is she going to keep that up?"

My daughter Sulfia awoke from her trance and said, "I'm so hungry, mother."

The baby girl I named Aminat, after my grandmother who had been born in the Caucuses, turned my life upside-down. Everything changed. Sulfia took the birth of her daughter as an opportunity to sleep nonstop. And she ate nonstop, as well. She liked to hold the baby,—she spoiled her that way, in fact—but she was otherwise good for nothing. She even proved useless whenever the new baby was hungry. During the night, Sulfia slept so soundly that she didn't hear the miserable yelps of loneliness or the irate screams of hunger.

I lay on the other side of the wall and listened to the baby girl cry. I knew exactly what she needed. After the first three days I could distinguish the sounds. Eventually I couldn't take it any longer and brought the crib into the room I occupied with Kalganow.

I liked the way she balled her tiny fists and rubbed her eyes when she was sleepy.

Mornings I sent Kalganow to the milk dispensary for baby formula—after all, someone had to make sure the baby got enough to eat. She drained every bottle in the shortest time, much more quickly than other children. My husband tried to protest when I asked him to go; the line of unshaven young fathers at the milk dispensary made him uncomfortable. But I determinedly sent him every morning. This was about his own flesh and blood. Kalganow said he wouldn't treat his own grand-daughter any better or worse than he would any other child because all mankind were of equal worth. I called him a fascist.

After a few months, Sulfia returned to her nursing program and I registered little Aminat for daycare. We all had to get on with our lives somehow. Aminat cried bitterly. I had to pry her fingers from my skirt every morning when I left.

My granddaughter Aminat was lucky. She hadn't inherited any of the sluggishness or ugliness of her mother. She had my dark, almond-shaped eyes, my gently wavy black hair, a slender nose, and a bright look on her face. With some people, you can tell from the moment of birth whether they're smart or not. I had been able to tell with Sulfia—and had been proved cor-rect. Maybe it had something to do with the fact that Sulfia had been conceived in bed, with my husband, rather than by a stranger in a dream.

Aminat was nonetheless a troublesome child. She didn't want to go to daycare. She would start to scream as soon as we got there and I had to swat away the fingers she clawed into me. But I couldn't keep showing up late for work.

When I went to pick her up each evening, I could hear her screaming from the street. I felt embarrassed. I didn't like the fact that my granddaughter was disturbing the whole school. In fact, I felt I had to explain to the caregiver that Tartar chil-dren are usually well behaved. For the most part better than Russian children, though of course I didn't say that. I didn't want to sound arrogant.

Aminat fought all efforts at child rearing. I even caught myself referring to her as Anja in front of the kindergarten teachers because I was so ashamed of her. She was such a handful that I didn't want to make things any more difficult for the teachers by also insisting on using an Arabic name. I could be so thoughtful at times.

My daughter Sulfia meanwhile forgot she had given birth to a daughter. She finished her vocational training and began working at a surgical clinic. But she hadn't passed her exams, so she had to work as a nursing assistant instead of as a nurse. She performed the lowliest duties and nothing of importance. Still, I thought it was for the best for everyone.

I was just happy that despite her limited capabilities, my daughter had become a productive member of society and had even given birth to a daughter of her own, and a surprisingly fabulous one at that. Sulfia was out of the woods, leaving me time to see to raising my granddaughter. It was an important duty for a woman like me, and not such an easy one with a child like Aminat.

Very slowly I stopped paying attention to Sulfia. I no longer noticed when she came home or what she did when she was home. As a result, I was totally unprepared when I came home one day and found a note on the windowsill: *Dear Mama, dear Papa, I'm moving out and taking Anna with me. Please just leave me alone. Kisses, your Sulfia.*

Next to the note was the key to her room.

My heart beat loudly against my ribs as I threw open the wardrobe she and I shared and found it half empty. Sulfia's neatly hung dresses and skirts were gone, her underwear was gone, her pantyhose were gone. Some much more important things were gone, too: Aminat's rompers, socks, and sweaters, as well as her stuffed animals and bottles, her cloth diapers, and her favorite cup, the one with the yellow rabbit on it.

Traitor to motherhood

I didn't give myself much time to wallow in depression. I took action, as was always my way. I opened the tin can where we kept the petty cash and took out a few banknotes. I hurriedly threw on my coat and ran out to the street. I stood on the curb and put out my thumb. Not nervously fidgeting the way some people did it, but unambiguously, with dignity. That always worked.

A small, dirty car stopped immediately. I always looked younger than I was, and people were happy to be able to help a woman like me.

It was impossible to tell what color the Lada was beneath the filth, but the car got me to Aminat's kindergarten within eight minutes. The driver wouldn't take any money, and I didn't insist. He was understandably proud to have had a woman like me in his car. But I was too late. Sulfia had already picked up Aminat from kindergarten. She had planned everything.

Aminat's cubby in the entry hall was empty. Her indoor shoes and her smock were gone. The worm she had kneaded out of modeling clay during arts and crafts was gone as well. Aminat wasn't coming back to this kindergarten anymore, said one of the teachers, with an unusually official look on her face. Aminat's mother had moved to the other side of town and put her child in a kindergarten that was closer to her new residence.

"Where?" I shouted.

She was unable to be of further assistance, said the bespectacled hag, clearly taking pleasure in my distress.

I have to say I wasn't just distraught. I was surprised. For ages I'd thought that Sulfia had about as much drive as a garden slug. The fact that she was able to undertake such a Nacht und Nebel–style operation, to snatch Aminat away, register Aminat at a new kindergarten, and—perhaps most shocking— find a new apartment for two, without a peep to me or her father, did not fit the image I had of Sulfia.

"Say something," I pleaded with my husband as he sat there in the kitchen chewing stuffed cabbage that evening.

"We have to make sure they don't take away our second room now that there are two fewer people here," he said.

He had no idea where she could have gone. For the first week, I kept waiting for a call from her, or at least from the police. The telephone was in the foyer, where all the inhabitants of our apartment could use it. I was the first one there every time it rang, but Sulfia didn't ring and neither did anyone else.

By the second week I began to feel sick. I dreamed of Aminat, hungry and half-frozen, sitting in her crib and crying. Of how it wouldn't register with Sulfia because she would be doing some stupid task or other while Aminat suffered.

"You have to call Sulfia at work," I demanded of my husband as he gnawed on a chicken leg one evening. "You have to find out where she moved."

My husband said our daughter was an adult.

"But Aminat's not!" I shouted, and he looked up from his plate.

A week later I put on my maroon dress, let down my hair, made up my eyes and lips in the mirror, and took the trolley to the surgical clinic where Sulfia worked. I prayed she still worked there. I took up a spot in front of the entrance where a few poor, sick people in gray hospital gowns were also standing around breathing in the fresh air. I waited.

God rewarded me and sent Sulfia out after just two hours. She had on the old blue jacket that she'd been wearing since her school days and was carrying a mesh bag. In the bag I glimpsed five shriveled potatoes. It had always been impossible to send Sulfia shopping, especially to the green grocer. She let the worst, most rotten things be foisted on her without ever noticing.

When Sulfia saw me, her eyes opened wide, darkened, and took on a purplish hue. It made her eyes the color of overripe plums. She tried to retreat, but I made a beeline for her and grabbed the sleeve of her wretched coat.

"Where are you going, you turd?" I asked her with a friendly civility only I could muster in such a situation. "Where have you taken Aminat, you traitor to motherhood?"

She squirmed in my grip.

"Anja is *my* daughter," she squeaked.

"Since when?" I said, my voice rising.

The poor, sick people followed our conversation with intense interest. Sulfia made it difficult for them, however, because she mumbled so much it was impossible to understand her. I had always told her: you must speak clearly and articulate. She murmured that I had alienated her child from her. That I had tormented her. That she was so happy to be free of my tireanny. ("Tyranny," I corrected her.) That she'd rather live under a bridge than under the same roof with me.

"WHERE IS AMINAT?" I raised my voice a little more.

Sulfia began to talk as if she were crazy: she was the mother of her daughter, she didn't recognize me anyway, had never seen me before in her life, she had no idea who I was, I should leave immediately, I shouldn't come near her or her child, it was enough that I had ruined *her* life.

"You've found a man!" I realized, now genuinely surprised.

The sick people craned their necks and one whistled appreciatively.

"Finally!" I shouted. "Good! But where is Aminat?"

At this point Sulfia pulled herself free, opened her scrunched mouth into an irregular oval, and screamed: "Help! She's going to kill me!"

Shocked, I let go of her sleeve.

Sulfia broke off her steam-whistle cries and ran. I watched her go. I could have gone in, found her workstation, and asked her colleagues for her new address. But who knew what Sulfia, sneaky as she was, had told them about me. I put my hair up into a sober bun with four hairpins and slowly got going.

My stupid daughter walked ahead and I followed. Her blue coat pointed my way. When she climbed onto a tram, I got into the second car. As usual she didn't notice anything. Through the window of the trolley car I saw how she slumped into a seat with a blank look on her face.

A few stops later she stood up and got out. I hopped off behind her.

I followed her a few steps behind. Then she turned and went through a squeaky door and into a gray high rise. I recognized it immediately. It was the dorm for rural students who came to the city to train for hospital jobs and look for work and, first and foremost, for a husband. This was where Sulfia had moved, and no wonder. Even a much smarter person could not have found a real apartment in the city so quickly, and Sulfia wasn't smart—she wasn't even clever. She was a danger to herself and others. But she was a half-nurse, and somebody had obviously taken pity on her and assigned her a bed. Somewhere in this stinking dump was my beloved grandchild.

I asked the woman who guarded the entryway for the room number of Sulfia Kalganova. I said Sulfia had kidnapped a child. The woman readily took me to my destination, up many flights of stairs, down long, dark hallways. Along the way she told me stories from her mess of a life. I listened and offered halfhearted responses so she would continue to lead the way.

The room was small and dirty. Aminat sat in a crib and looked at me. Her face and body were covered with green spots. She had chickenpox; I recognized it right away. I knew children's diseases well, along with so many other things. Sulfia was sitting on her bed with her hands over her face. Her shoulders trembled. And all of this because she hadn't listened to her mother.

When Aminat saw me, she grabbed the bars of the crib with both hands and began to rattle them. Sulfia sprang to her feet, aghast, but I shoved her away. She bounced off my elbow and fell over. That's how awkward she was.

I pulled my little girl out of the bed, grabbed the tattered blanket, and wrapped it around the child. Aminat clasped my neck.

I carried my priceless bundle out of that hellish building, flagged a private taxi, and rode home. A grandmother who had just rescued her grandchild. I didn't have anything against my daughter Sulfia. I was happy to live as a family in our two rooms. Mature parents, young inexperienced daughter, little grandchild. It all fit. I was a fundamentally generous person, and I valued the interchange between generations. Helping support Sulfia in raising my grandchild didn't bother me at all. Neither did drawing Sulfia's attention to her own frequent mistakes. All I ever wanted was for her to improve herself.

What had happened now, however, was just not acceptable. Sulfia had endangered the child. She had left her alone and sick and had gone off to work. Of course she hadn't been able to find a new kindergarten for her. She had infected Aminat with chickenpox she probably brought home from the clinic—despite her medical training she didn't understand basic hygiene.

My mission was to save Aminat from squalor. Nobody else was going to do it. To every other person on earth, Aminat was nothing more than a neglected, unkempt little snot. It wouldn't have been long before she had abscesses and lice.

As far as I was concerned, there were no two ways about it: Aminat would stay with me.

For a while after I'd saved Aminat, Sulfia didn't have the heart to come by our place. She just called constantly and sobbed into the phone. Eventually she quit saying anything at all, but kept on calling. The phone would ring and all I'd hear when I answered was crackling. It disturbed Aminat's afternoon nap, so I unplugged the phone.

I sent Kalganow to re-register Aminat in her old kindergarten, but it turned out to be difficult. It was only possible with the consent of the mother, as she had the right to custody. I thought about ways to relieve Sulfia of this right. It would certainly have been better for all parties—better for her, for Aminat, and, of course, for me. But Kalganow said a trial like that would hurt both me and him professionally, as everyone would then find out what an awful daughter we had produced. I gave Kalganow a big bouquet of gladiolas from my garden and told him to give it to the principal of the kindergarten and to compliment her. The obstacles to registration evaporated.

Stethoscope, my sweet

Almost as soon as I saved Aminat from the dorm, I took up the fight against her chickenpox. She had big pustules on her face and body where she had scratched the chickenpox sores and caused secondary infections in them. She was basically one single pus-dripping pustule, and she had been such an attractive child.

I treated her sores with a concoction of boiled oak bark, taking it in stride when the compress ruined two entire sets of sheets—the bark left behind brown stains that couldn't be washed out.

Her sores quickly healed thanks to my treatments, and the bark poultice fell away in flakes and revealed the extent of the damage. I could see some deep pits in her skin left behind by the pustules. It filled me with great sorrow. And it took awhile before I was once again sure she was the best-looking child in the world.

It was important to me that Sulfia not sneak off with her again. So I told the kindergarten principal that Aminat's mother had sustained brain damage and was no longer allowed

THE HOTTEST DISHES · 31

to look after Aminat on her own. The principal wanted to see some sort of certification from a doctor. I went to our live-in neighbor Klavdia. She got me papers certifying that as a result of an insect bite, Sulfia had difficulties with routine tasks, adding that anyone who came into contact with her was obligated to offer help. This doctor's certificate was pure gold: from then on, everyone avoided coming anywhere near her.

She turned up one day and stood with her face pressed against the chain-link fence that surrounded the schoolyard. She watched the children swinging and playing in the sandbox. She never said a word and remained on the outside of the fence, but one of the teachers grabbed Aminat and took her inside. I had guaranteed that response with careful planning— and gladiolas.

When Sulfia called shortly afterward, I told her that if she ever got near Aminat again, she'd better have her things packed and ready because I would make sure she landed in the loony bin. And coming from me, it sounded extremely convincing.

At first Aminat lagged far behind in verbal skills. I had even begun to worry whether she might be slightly retarded. I kept repeating words to her, but she just ignored everything until one day her little mouth opened and out came an entire sentence: "When is stupid grandpa coming home from work?" From then on, she never stopped talking. At all. She talked day and night. And said peculiar things.

I was a good role model for her. She paid attention to the way I spoke, and to the fact that no Tartar words ever slipped out of me. Aminat needed to speak perfectly. She looked Tartar. She didn't need to sound Tartar as well. I didn't have any family left, but with Kalganow's country relatives I'd seen what could happen. First you start saying a few Tartar words, then you forget the Russian equivalents, and the next thing you know you're illiterate. That wasn't going to happen to Aminat. She was going to be the best, the prettiest, and the smartest. A Soviet child without any ethnic or regional identity, said Kalganow proudly. In a rare instance of accord, we both wanted the same basic thing for our granddaughter—even if our reasons were different.

Each day after kindergarten I talked to her about how her day had been, correcting her grammar as we spoke and trying to expand her vocabulary.

"Electricity, my dear," I told her when she tried to stick a nail file in an outlet.

"Communism, my dear," I said when I managed to get hold of a bunch of bananas for her and let them ripen on the windowsill, giving her just one each day so they'd last for a while.

"Gravity, my dear," I told her when she fell down yet again. It happened often; Aminat was incredibly clumsy during her first few years. For a long time, she couldn't distinguish between left and right or stand on one leg. Spinning gracefully in a circle, like other little girls, was beyond her capabilities.

I took her to ballet lessons at the Center for Youth and Culture. They didn't want to admit her at first. Until I let slip where my husband worked. Aminat got a spot.

We got a lot from ballet. Aminat slowly learned to straighten out her pigeon-toed walk. She fell down less frequently. When she sat down, she no longer automatically hunched her shoulders. Less and less often did I have to drill my finger into her back between her shoulder blades to make her sit upright.

A year went by, followed by another.

Aminat was going to be five and we decided to celebrate her birthday.

I spared no time or effort, and the resultant Napoleon cake would have been suitable for a state dinner. I had a way with puff pastry, as with so many other things. After four hours I had ten crispy cake layers that I slathered with custard and stacked into a marvelous structure every bit as light and sweet as I imagined Aminat's future life would be.

My husband got hold of some balloons and blew them up with puffed cheeks and eyes reddened from the exertion.

We didn't invite any children. We had just bought new furniture imported from Yugoslavia. We invited two of my husband's colleagues, Klavdia, and my cousin Rafaella. I unplugged the phone so the constant ringing wouldn't disturb us. I put Aminat in a frilly pink dress I had made myself, and combed her black curls.

She played with the balloons, hummed, and laughed like the happiest child on earth. She was given coloring books and felt-tip pens, tights, oranges, and a toy doctor's kit. She opened the kit up immediately and began to sort through the instruments. Watching her warmed my heart. And I could tell as soon as I saw her playing that my granddaughter was going to be a doctor one day, and quite a doctor at that.

I laughed joyfully at this thought. A doctor was something missing in the family. Since Kalganow had become chairman of the union he'd finally become useful. In a pinch, Sulfia, when she still lived with us at least, could administer shots. But having a real doctor in the house was important, especially as you got older. It was a respectable profession, and it would win me the appreciation of all my neighbors and colleagues, since, like me, they would all get sick and need shots, doctor's notes, and medicines.

"Stethoscope, my dear," I said, immediately expanding Aminat's vocabulary. "Intravenous drip, my dear. Tu-ber-cu-lo-sis."

I shouldn't have mentioned tuberculosis.

Mantoux tests were administered at Aminat's kindergarten. The children received shots on their forearms, and green dye was used to highlight the skin around the injection site. If the child had been exposed to TB, the injection site would get infected and swell. If, on the other hand, there was no reaction, everything was fine.

In Aminat's case, the swelling didn't just exceed the green line drawn around the injection site. Her entire forearm swelled up and looked like a big red pillow. Right in the middle was the now misshapen spot of green dye. When I saw this, I grabbed Aminat, wiped her nose, quickly ironed her striped pants so she looked presentable, and ran with her to the local clinic.

The doctor in charge of our district looked at Aminat's arm as I shoved it in front of her face and shook her head. She'd never seen *anything like it*, she said, not in her whole life. It could be helpful to repeat the test on the other arm. Aminat received a second shot.

By the next morning the swelling had reached her shoulders. The pediatrician shook her head disapprovingly and pulled out a stack of forms. Aminat would have to provide urine and feces samples, as well as have blood drawn and X-rays taken.

I was busy for the next few weeks. I collected Aminat's excretions at the prescribed times, took the full glass jars to the lab and passed them through an oval window, washed Aminat's neck, and took her in for her examinations. The doctors did their honorable work, and I did mine. I became a master urine sample collector. It sounds easier than it actually was.

I was happy about the many demanding tasks that fell to me because it gave me less time to spend worrying. With her red cheeks, Aminat looked resilient, but even resilient children sometimes keeled over dead with no warning or developed full-blown tuberculosis. I couldn't sleep at night. I chased images of a child-size coffin from my head and prayed ardently. I reminded God how good I had always been to Sulfia. Now I was even prepared to reconcile with her, to give her a chance to put all the ill will behind, but only if Aminat grew healthy again. I lay with my head on my pillow and whispered to myself.

Kalganow turned his back to me during those nights and

clapped his hands over his ears. He didn't like it when I talked to God. He didn't believe in God and found it embarrassing that I did. Most of all he didn't want anyone else to find out I believed in God and even talked to him. There was nobody here in our bed except the two of us, I assured him. Or rather, the two of us and God.

Kalganow was hypersensitive through this entire period. A phrase like "thank God" would make him cringe. Even worse was when Aminat would use the word "tykryk" instead of "alley" or call Kalganow "Babaj" instead of "Papa." He would scold me for smuggling these words into the house and denying Aminat the opportunity to grow up like a normal Soviet child. But I was innocent, as these words certainly never came out of my mouth in Aminat's presence. Maybe they were just there in her Tartar blood. Still, I didn't make an issue of it. Whenever it was possible, I kept my view of things to myself. After all, Kalganow was just a man and had weak nerves.

Aminat's pediatrician laid the results of all the tests and exams out on her desk. Aminat's leukocytes, thrombocytes, erythrocytes, antibodies, some sort of suspicious proteins, pigments, and rods were all tallied and recorded, some multiple times because the initial tests had been contaminated or botched. Aminat's EKG was lying next to her X-rays, to which the patient reacted enthusiastically: "Look, a skeleton!"

I didn't smack Aminat even though she wrinkled my skirt. I just looked straight at her doctor. This overweight woman with a derelict bird's nest where most people had hairdos was supposed to give us a verdict now—whether my little girl would live, and if so, under what conditions.

I looked at her. She shook her head. I could feel my hands begin to shake.

Aminat hopped out of my lap and stood next to me. She began to play with my gold earring but I didn't have the strength left to give her a lesson in good behavior as the doctor finally began to speak.

I listened to her for while. She spoke at length and I stared at her face, which reminded me of a poorly cooked crepe. I understood that Aminat wasn't going to die. At least not now. That she was even healthy. But possibly not. One never really knew precisely. The results could be interpreted in different ways. Perhaps the swelling of her arms had just been an allergic reaction. Perhaps she had indeed come in contact with the bacteria first identified by Robert Koch. In any event, a sanatorium for children with lung conditions would be just the thing.

I lifted my eyes to the cracks in the white clinic ceiling and thanked God.

Sanatorium for children with lung conditions

I didn't tell Aminat that she'd be spending three months in a sanatorium for children with lung conditions. Saying too much often hurt as much as it helped. On the prearranged day, I packed Aminat's underwear and clothes in a backpack and dressed her warmly. The sanatorium was in an old villa in a pine forest—the villa had at one time belonged to the enemy class. We had to take a train two hours north and climb out at a tiny, forgotten station.

It was very cold. Aminat held my hand. We walked for half an hour through the woods before we reached the gates of the sanatorium. I always managed to find the shortest route wherever I went, even when I didn't know the area. I never got lost, not in the city, not in the forest. I also always knew when and where buses went, and could feel them coming toward a bus stop before they were in sight.

"Why is it so horribly quiet here?" asked Aminat.

"Because," I said.

I knew these new surroundings must have seemed very unfamiliar to Aminat. She was a city kid born and bred. I'd never taken her to a forest before, just an occasional visit to the park. She'd never seen trees like this, packed so tightly together. For her entire life, the smoking chimneys of factories had decorated the horizon. When she lay in bed, traffic noise lulled her to sleep.

Aminat looked around. Her eyes had narrowed to slits, a sure sign that she did not approve. And she didn't even know yet that she had to stay here for three months, all by herself, among strangers, without her grandmother.

I opened the gate, climbed a stone staircase to the door, and entered a dark vestibule where children's jackets hung from a row of hooks. The walls were covered in a faded ladybug print. Something clanged in the distance.

"Let's go home," said Aminat adamantly.

I freed my hand from her grip, took her by her collar, and led her down the long hallway to a glass door, behind which children with blank looks on their faces sat around little tables eating from metal dishes—which explained the clanging. I handed over Aminat, her backpack, and a note from her doctor to the first member of the sanatorium staff we ran across.

The woman wore a gray smock that had faded from repeated washings. She had the face of a supervisor. She read the doctor's note through and said, "Aminat Kalganova? Ah, yes."

She took my Aminat by the hand and led her away. Aminat went with her obediently, like a good little girl, but kept turning around mid-stride to look back at me. It went much more smoothly than I'd feared. Though I suppose Aminat must have thought that when she returned, I'd be there to take her back home. Oh well.

I waited until the two of them were out of sight and then quickly left. I didn't manage to get out of hearing range quickly enough, though. Out on the forest path Aminat's desperate, angry screams reached me.

Three weeks later I got a call informing me that Aminat had contracted scarlet fever and had to be picked up. I took the train to the forest station and followed the path I now knew back to the sanatorium.

Aminat was sitting in a glass cell with a bed and nightstand in it. Here she could be kept away from the other children, explained the director of the sanatorium. She was ready to hold me personally responsible for the outbreak of scarlet fever that would have resulted if Aminat had managed to infect the other kids.

Aminat sat on the bed in a t-shirt and tights and peered through the glass wall at all the people going past her. At first she didn't recognize me. Her black eyes passed over me and then the director of the sanatorium. Then her eyes returned to me and began to sparkle.

Aminat threw her entire body against the glass pane. I saw her white teeth as her mouth formed a hopeful smile, pressed flat against the wall. The blotches on her face I noticed only later.

We entered the glass cell and Aminat jumped on me, wrapped her arms and legs around me, and squeezed so hard I could barely breathe. I patted her on the back, saying, "There, there."

I tried to put her down.

"So?" said the director triumphantly.

Without another word the director sat down on the bed, clamped Aminat between her legs, and lifted up her t-shirt.

Suddenly I was looking at countless tiny red bumps that formed constellations and whole galaxies on Aminat's back. I put on my glasses and bent down. Among the many things I knew was that scarlet fever looked very different from this.

"She's just had a reaction to something she ate," I said. "That's not scarlet fever."

"Do you have medical training?" asked the director.

She had medical training but couldn't distinguish scarlet fever from hives. Or she didn't wish to distinguish them. I suspected that already. Aminat was not an easy child to deal with at home, and probably not here either.

"Take her to your district clinic," she said.

"You're going to hear from us," I said as we left.

I carried Aminat's backpack. The paperwork with the doctor's assessment that the Kalganova child was suffering from a highly infectious disease that threatened her life, and that she must be quarantined, I ripped into pieces and let flutter off between the pines.

Aminat held my hand and skipped through the snow. Her smile spread across her entire face and she recounted her three weeks in the sanatorium.

It was grim. She had to sleep in a room with fifty other children. For the first few days she had been unable to eat from the metal dishes because they made such a shrill noise when the spoon scraped across them. Before bed, all the children had to wash their feet together. The towels were always folded a certain way: longwise, longwise again, longwise one more time and then crossways. One of the staff members constantly told horror stories. Almost every morning Aminat woke up in a strange bed next to another child and didn't know how she'd gotten there. She never, ever wanted to hear stories again. They got shots every day with needles so long they could have gone all the way through their arms and out the other side. Any children who wanted to go to the bathroom at night had to use a chamber pot that was emptied only the next morning. Aminat had just yesterday made her first friend, a girl who had received a package of candies from her parents and shared them all with Aminat. In the middle of the night she had begun to feel itchy, and in the morning Aminat had been asked whether she had ever had scarlet fever. That was the happiest moment of the entire three weeks for her because I soon came and picked her up.

We reached the forgotten little train station and sat down on a bench. The train that would take me and my little girl out of the forest and back home wouldn't arrive for an hour. The sun peeked over the tops of the trees and a few anemic rays brushed our cheeks. We held our faces up to the sky.

"Aminat, be quiet," I begged. I was getting a headache from all her jabber. I'd forgotten over these weeks just how much she talked.

"We had buckwheat porridge almost every night," Aminat continued.

"Should I tell you a story instead?" I interrupted.

"No," she cried.

I have rarely seen her as happy as she was on that day. But as far as stories went, it was clear: she wanted nothing more to do with them.

Traitors everywhere

Two days later the bumps were gone. But I didn't take her back to the sanatorium. She looked healthy. At every meal I gave her a piece of bread and a clove of garlic and showed her how she should rub the garlic on the bread crust. Aminat set the bread aside and ate the garlic clove whole. I was sure she would not get sick anymore: there were lots of vitamins in garlic. I sent her back to kindergarten. One evening three days later I arrived to pick her up only to learn Aminat had already been picked up.

I was barely able to keep myself from punching the teacher who told me. I wanted to punch her right in the chest—right on the nametag pinned to her white smock. The smock was new and so was the teacher. I'd never seen her stupid face there before. She was very young and must have just finished her training and certification. You could see she hadn't learned much from the pedagogical training. I had worked at a teacher's college myself and knew how they worked. I knew the type of girls who came through those schools. They all thought of themselves as fond of children but were for the most part just lazy, interested only in boys. And they had stupid faces.

"Her mommy already came," lisped the new kindergarten teacher chirpily.

I sat down on a low bench where the children sat to tie their shoes.

"What?" I hissed.

"Her mommy picked Anja up. Anja was so happy that today she wasn't the last one picked up."

I closed my eyes to collect myself.

"Her mommy is mentally handicapped," I said calmly. "Her mother is an evil psychopath. Are you not aware that you're not even to let her mother *set foot* on the premises?"

The idiot straightened a garland hung from the doorframe, a decoration for the national holidays celebrating the Soviet Army.

"No, I don't know anything about that," she said placidly. "I wasn't given any instructions like that."

I left without another word. Bitterly I realized that she was right. The protective wall I had erected around Aminat was built of paper, and it was just a matter of time before it collapsed. I had to admit to myself that I'd been too naïve, too goodhearted. At the end of the day this was fair punishment.

Except that Aminat didn't deserve it.

I went home. Kalganow was already there. He was eating some of the meatballs I'd made the night before and left in a dish in the refrigerator. They were stone cold but heating them up would obviously have been too much for his meager abilities.

"SULFIA!" I shrieked, running to the phone.

I dialed the number of her dormitory.

"Sulfia Kalganova," I shouted into the phone. "She kidnapped a small child."

I could hear jovial voices in the background. They were celebrating.

"Lady," said a voice, "Sulfia Kalganova hasn't lived here for ages."

I hung up the phone and staggered back into the kitchen. My husband had folded his hands across his stomach and sat staring out the window.

"When was the last time you saw Sulfia?" I cried.

He gasped with surprise.

"Two weeks ago, I think," he mumbled. "When she, um, how should I put it—when she got married."

I couldn't believe it. I couldn't count on anyone: traitors were coming out of the woodwork. Now even Kalganow, that amoeba, that spineless creature, that venom-less jellyfish, had dared to deceive me. And once again I'd been so unsuspecting.

Now it came out: he had secrets. He had gone to see our daughter Sulfia and told me only now when there was no other choice. You simply couldn't count on anyone in this world.

"Why didn't you tell me, you animal?"

"Because she asked me not to," he mumbled. "Because she's afraid of you."

"Afraid? Of me? Who could possibly be afraid of me? Nobody should ever be afraid of me. I only want what's best. Put those plates in the sink, you tyrant."

An hour later we left our apartment together. I wanted to know everything. I wanted to see everything. I wanted Aminat back. I wanted to make sure nothing bad had happened to her.

Even my husband could understand that. After I explained everything to him, he agreed and took me to see the restaurant where Sulfia had held her wedding reception. Astonishingly, it wasn't a bad restaurant. Then we took the bus eleven more stops so he could show me the street where she lived now.

He knew everything! The only thing he didn't have was a telephone number, he said. They didn't have a phone line yet; it was a new building.

Sulfia's husband, Kalganow explained, was a former patient of hers. He had been hit by a car and was patched back together in her ward. She had nursed him back to health. On the day he was released, he asked her to marry him. His name was Sergej.

"Sergej," I snorted disdainfully, and, dragging my Kalganow behind me, started down the street between the endless rows of newly constructed nine-story apartment buildings.

"Not so fast, Rosie," he begged.

"Aren't you at least sure which street she lives on, you tarantula?"

He squinted. It was snowing, and snowflakes clung to the black eyelashes I had so loved twenty-five years ago.

"I think so," he said.

"You think so? You only think so? You don't know for sure?"

"I don't know," he said. "I don't know anything. What does everyone expect from me? There's nothing I can do."

I punched him between the shoulder blades. My fist sank into the expensive leather of his two-year-old shearling coat. I made sure he dressed well. He was after all my husband—and he also had an important position at the workers' union. I left him standing there and walked on ahead. He grabbed me and I hit him again. He was a turd, but he was the husband I was stuck with.

Then I forgot about Kalganow for a second because somewhere a child started to cry.

"Do you hear that? Do you hear that? Is it her?"

"What?" My husband stood there looking around.

"That. A baby crying."

My husband strained to hear. I had the impression that beneath his fur hat his ears perked up to hear better.

"I don't hear anything," he said.

"You're deaf."

We walked up and down the street a little more.

I looked at the buildings, the balconies, the windows. Skis and skates sat on the balconies. Bags of deep-frozen meat hung from the windows. Inside on the windowsills were houseplants and cats. A few of the balconies were piled with dilapidated furniture, worn-out shoes, and empty bottles. These people had just moved in and had already created such pigsties. In the window boxes fresh snow covered dead flowers. Here and there I saw old Christmas trees draped with tinsel.

My husband swore that Sulfia hadn't given him her address. She had probably suspected he wouldn't be able keep mum.

"I don't know the address, Rosie, scout's honor," he said.

Several thousand people lived in the buildings here on this street. I tried to figure out how long it would take to go into every building and ring every doorbell.

Just then a woman came along pushing a stroller with a snotty little brat in it. I wasn't fooled for a second: the child was too small and ugly to be Aminat.

My husband's nose was running. Tears began to trickle from his eyes. It was extremely cold and he looked miserable. Why was I, of all people, stuck with someone like him at my side? At least he wasn't complaining.

"We're going home," I said.

"Really?" He was as happy as a child. He lacked perseverance and just wanted to get warm, drink a cup of tea, eat meatballs.

"We're going back to the bus stop, for your sake, you snake," I said, turning toward the bus stop and walking off.

I went back five times, alone. I walked up and down the street at various times, day and night. I stopped people coming out of buildings and asked them whether they knew a Sulfia Kalganova. Nobody knew her. I asked them whether they'd seen a scrawny Tartar woman holding hands with a pretty little girl. Nobody had seen them.

Three weeks later I finally ran into her.

It was both of them. Sulfia held the hand of my little girl. I could see immediately that Aminat was carelessly dressed. She didn't have a scarf on, and her hat had shifted so that her ears were exposed to the biting cold. Her black hair hung in her face. Her nose was red. She definitely had a cold, and no wonder with this mother.

I took a few steps to the side and hid behind a dumpster. Sulfia and Aminat walked past me hand in hand. I watched them turn toward a building and saw which doorway they entered. I hurried after them. I listened to the elevator go up for a long while, up to the top floor. Somewhere way up above I heard a door close.

It smelled good in the foyer of this building because it was still new. The scent of paint and chemicals hung in the air, a very clean smell, but I knew it wouldn't last long. A year from now the freshly painted walls would be covered with scribbling, drunks and cats would have pissed in every corner, and it would be lucky if even a hint were left of the hope for a better life that was built into every new house.

A short time later I stood on the ninth floor, just beneath the roof of the building. There were four doors on this floor. Behind one of them I heard the warbling of a child's voice I recognized.

I didn't ring Sulfia's doorbell. Not yet. Stepping lightly I descended the stairs, went outside, and breathed in the cold, watermelon-scented winter air. Hope filled my lungs; I could have floated off like a balloon.

To talk about atoms?

"What does Sulfia's husband do? This guy Sergej?" I asked Kalganow as he sat in the kitchen cutting up meat-filled *blini* with a fork.

He mumbled something. As always, his mouth was full.

"Some kind of physicist," he said finally, a leftover piece of onion between his teeth.

"Aha," I said pensively. "Not bad."

I didn't really believe it. What would my daughter Sulfia, who wasn't bright enough to read before the age of nine and who to this day had trouble with numbers, want with a physicist? And more importantly, what would a physicist want with her? To talk about atoms?

One morning at nine I finally rang the doorbell of Sulfia's apartment. I had on my nice long fur coat, a fur hat, heels, and tasteful lipstick. And I had a box of chocolate-covered meringues under my arm. The candy was a bit old—I'd been holding on to it for an important occasion. And now that occasion had arrived.

At first all was quiet behind the door. Then I heard rustling, coughing and cursing, and bare feet on linoleum. The door opened and for the first time I glimpsed the living, breathing man who actually lived with Sulfia—my son-in-law.

My first impression of him made me doubt even more that he really was a physicist. He looked scatterbrained. But he must have been some sort of academic because he didn't have to go to work on time. He was apparently home alone late in the morning. Big as a bear, with hair the color of wheat at harvest time, long, curly, mussed. The hair on his chest was somewhat darker. His legs . . .

With a start, the man hid himself behind the door.

"What is it?" he asked, with just his head peeking out now.

"I'm Rosalinda," I said, putting on a sweet smile. "It's nice to finally meet you."

"Ro-sa . . . lin-da?" he said, pronouncing each syllable. Yes, I did have a pretty name, like something out of a foreign romance novel. I wasn't just another Katja or Larissa.

"Rosalinda . . . " he mumbled. "You must be . . . "

"I'm sure you have heard a lot about me from my daughter!" I said, placing one of my high heels across the threshold.

He reacted quickly; perhaps he was a physicist after all.

"Oh, how awkward. You are healthy again?"

"Healthy?"

As I answered his question with a question, I pushed the door open with both hands. It was difficult, as he was standing behind it. I must have bumped something, because he let out a stifled cry. He let me into the apartment and begged my pardon a thousand times.

I nodded majestically as he dashed around the corner. At his size and stature, it wasn't a given that he could move like that. His underpants were new and clean.

Kalganow needed some new underwear, I decided.

"Please make yourself comfortable," called my apparently well-mannered son-in-law from the depths of the apartment. "I'll be right back."

The apartment had a living room, a kitchen, and at least one bedroom. I took off my jacket but decided to keep my heels on. I went into the kitchen and sat down on a stool.

The kitchen was nice—it must have been 100 square feet. The table was new, as was the plastic tablecloth on top of it. Next to a couple of plates set out to dry was Aminat's cup, the one with the rabbit on it. The stove wasn't too clean. Glasses of water sat on the windowsill with onions sprouting in them, the green shoots straining toward the ceiling. Sulfia learned that from me: it was an inexpensive way to get vitamins in the winter.

Vitamins, I had learned, were the most important things in life. Seeing those onions put me in a peaceful, tolerant frame of mind. I decided to bring Sulfia some of the tea fungus I had cultivated in my kitchen. The fungus produced a very flavorful, healthy drink that tasted like kvass. And it was certainly better for you, since the kvass you could buy from street vendors was definitely unhygienic. Even so, in the past I had bought kvass once in a while for Kalganow or even Aminat. But these days, head held high, I walked right past the kvass vendors along the sidewalks with their barrels, the women in dirty aprons filling jugs or plastic bags with the foamy yellowish liquid that, especially in the bags, looked like urine. I far preferred the tea fungus I'd received from a co-worker. All you had to do was feed it regularly with tea and sugar, and you could be sure the drink made from it was clean.

My son-in-law reemerged, this time wearing a greasy bathrobe. I still wasn't sure what to make of him. He poured me a bit of cold tea with the tea leaves swimming in it, and then filled the cup with hot water. As he did so, he asked whether my heart was doing better and how it had been at the sanatorium.

Now I understood everything.

Sulfia, the little dung beetle, had hidden me from him. She'd banished me by assigning me diseases and various places of residence. It certainly wasn't a solution that showed much foresight.

My heart beat steadily, slowly, and dependably, and had been doing so for years. For the most part it was other people who got sick. But I decided to play along with Sulfia's lazy game.

"It's doing well again," I said. "And did you enjoy the wedding?"

"Oh yes, very much," said my son-in-law with glazed eyes. "You know, we're very happy at the moment. Since little Anja finally came to live with us, Soja has absolutely blossomed. It's so wonderful you supported my wife in difficult times, but now she wants to handle things on her own. She wants our child to be with us. Any normal mother would want to have her child with her, isn't that right?"

I breathed in and then exhaled. Since when was Aminat "our child"? Since when was Sulfia a "normal mother"?

"But Anja misses her grandmother very much," my son-in-law told me. "Recently they had chocolates in kindergarten for one of the children's birthday. Anja brought her chocolate home and said we should cut it into three pieces. One for her, one for Soja, and one for grandma. She wanted to save the piece for grandma. Obviously we didn't do that—it was just a few crumbs."

"Soja?" I said, taken aback. He'd already mentioned the name, but I didn't really understand who he meant.

"Yes, Soja, my wife."

"Ah, right." I said. So it's Soja now.

It turned out they had two bedrooms, not one. All to themselves. Just the three of them. This wasn't some foreign paradise. Who here had a huge apartment for three people? Not even Kalganow, who was chairman of his union. But that was really his own fault: he didn't want us to live better than others, and so he did far too little to make our lives easier. If not for me, he'd probably still be living in a room full of bunk beds in some institutional building.

I looked closely at my son-in-law. How had Sulfia managed to land someone like this? Had she put something in his IV drip?

"When I awoke from the anesthesia and saw Soja, I thought she must be an angel," said my son-in-law, answering my silent question. He lifted the bottom of his robe and stuck out his leg. Fresh scars as pink as a piglet glistened between curly hairs.

"I understand," I said and was happy when he hid his limbs again.

"Come visit us on Sunday," I said. "I'd like to have you over for supper, the whole family, all three of you. I cook really well. We're Tartars, you know?"

My son-in-law blinked. "Sure, it would be a pleasure."

The sun clung to his wheat-colored eyelashes.

They didn't come on Sunday. I was just about to start cooking. I had thought a lot about what to make. Preferably a typical Tartar dish, something my son-in-law had never tried before. The problem was that I myself had not been raised on Tartar cuisine. After the heroic death of my parents in 1945, the last year of the Great Patriotic War, my brother and I had landed in an orphanage, and there we mainly got barley soup. Of course, I could cook well despite that—I taught myself later. But there was no grandmother to introduce me to the fine points of our culinary tradition. I never saw my grandmother Aminat. I just heard about what a tenacious and proud woman she had been. There was Kalganow's family, some of whom still lived out in the country, but what showed up on the table there made me sick to my stomach because it was so unhygienic.

I decided to improvise. In my student days I had shared a dorm room with two women, one an Uzbek and the other a Bashkir. I still remembered the two of them and the things they had sometimes cooked. I hit upon an idea—and I'd like to see somebody try to tell me it wasn't proper Tartar cuisine.

I had bought rice and mutton at the market. Back at home I made dough for *chak-chak* for dessert. The phone rang. Ever since Sulfia's disappearance, Kalganow had disliked answering the phone. But I yelled to him. My hands were covered with flour. He picked up the phone.

"It's Sojuschka," he called from the foyer. "You'll have to come."

I held my hands under the faucet and dried them on a hand towel. Then I went to the phone and took it from my husband. It still wasn't clear to me who was on the line. I just couldn't get used to Sulfia's new name.

"Yes?" I said into the phone.

"I'm not coming," the phone whispered in Sulfia's voice.

"Too bad," I said. "I'll have your husband take something home for you."

"*We're* not coming," rasped Sulfia's voice in my ear. "I just can't. We can't. I don't want to."

"What is 'I don't want to' supposed to mean?"

"Over my dead body. Forgive me." She began to sob and I pulled the phone slightly away from my ear.

I could hear cars driving past at Sulfia's end of the phone. She was obviously calling from a public phone.

"Is your husband perhaps nearby?" I asked.

"No!" she yelled. "Don't talk to him!"

"You listen to me, daughter," I said. "We are a family. We need to act civilly to each other."

She hung up.

I invited Klavdia to eat with us since we had extra food. We had mountains of it, and Klavdia had a mighty appetite. We hoisted our glasses and toasted. Sooner or later she'll come, I thought to myself.

I called my son-in-law at his office the next day. He apologized for Sulfia's behavior. He said that sometimes she acted totally irrationally, and that he was helpless in the face of it. When she heard that he had accepted my invitation to Sunday dinner, she had started to sob and tremble. Then she had run out of the apartment.

I repeated my wish for a civil relationship. I said we were still a family. I told him I was counting on him.

He said he would do what he could.

No manners

I barely recognized her.

Sulfia was still scrawny. But she had on a pretty black dress with white dots. Not the kind of dress women like her usually wore. More something for women like me.

She had on a wool hat like the ones old ladies wear when they have to wait in the cold at a bus stop. She took it off and her hair fell onto her shoulders, long, black, straight—had her hair gotten thicker?

"Greetings, mother," said Sulfia.

My son-in-law stood behind her with a bouquet of frozen carnations in his hand. He'd probably just bought them in a subway station. He smiled proudly. It hadn't been easy. Together he and I had overcome resistance, appealing to Sulfia on two fronts. He evidently had a lot of influence over my daughter. I think it tickled Sergej to have such a graceful swan like me as his mother-in-law, especially given that he had married such an ugly duckling.

The most important thing, however, was Aminat. It was all I could do not to grab her in my arms immediately and kiss her beautiful little face.

"Please come in, my dears," I said graciously, and took the bouquet of flowers from my son-in-law's hand.

"Don't be so shy," I said. That was for Sulfia's benefit; she was standing there as if turned to stone.

Aminat peeled off her hat and her white fleece jacket in a single motion, let both fall to the floor, wrapped both of her arms around me, and pressed her face to my stomach.

I casually put my hand on her head. I wasn't going to show what a happy day this was for me.

We had covered a big table in one of our rooms. For such an occasion, we didn't want to sit in the kitchen. This was the room in which Sulfia had grown up, as a child, as a girl. Later she had shared it with Aminat, and then for a time it had been Aminat's room. Since I'd lost Aminat it had sat empty. The furniture was still in it, cold and unused, but I had not been able to breathe life back into it, even when I bought a few new children's books and a puppet. So I had packed them away; they were stuffed into the depths of my wardrobe biding their time.

This empty room served as the storeroom for my tea fungus, which was doing so well that it took up more and more space. At first I had kept it in a five-liter jar, where it looked like a dozen crepes stuck together and dropped into slimy liquid. But it kept growing and the drink it produced kept getting more and more flavorful—at some stage it got too strong. I separated the individual layers and moved each into its own new jar, where they could continue to grow. I lined up the jars on the broad windowsill in Aminat's old room. I was more comfortable with it there, too, because I worried that Klavdia would secretly put bits of trash into the jars if they were left unattended in the kitchen much longer.

It wasn't easy to get hold of so many empty jars. Canning jars were a valuable commodity, and I had to get them from all over. I asked co-workers for them, searched for lids that would fit the jars I did find, and never threw anything away.

Now we had our big table set up in the middle of the room. I was the best hostess you could possibly imagine. I had spread out a starched white linen tablecloth and decorated the table with a vase of magnificent red roses. I'd been given the roses by the parents of a girl who was on the verge of being kicked out of the school where I worked for skipping class. The parents mistook me for the director of the school because I carried myself like one. When they realized they'd given the bouquet to the wrong person, it was already too late and they were too polite to ask for the roses back.

The frozen carnations brought by my son-in-law I left in the kitchen; putting them side-by-side with the roses would surely have been embarrassing for him. I had brought out our best silverware. There were glasses for wine and water. I had cooked a *shulpa*—delicate beef broth with pieces of meat—in a clay pot. Then came the main dish, a rice pilaf with mutton and raisins.

We sat down at the table. If Aminat hadn't chattered the

whole time there would have been silence throughout the meal, in which case I would have to have made conversation. Actually it would have been my husband's responsibility, but he was never any good at it. He liked to eat in peace. But Aminat was stuffing her mouth full and speaking for five. She asked questions and answered them herself. She had no manners. She had completely forgotten everything I'd taught her.

"My child," I reminded her with deep affection, "we don't speak with our mouths full."

She stopped talking and stared at me, seeming not to understand what I meant. Table manners were apparently not a topic of discussion at Sulfia's. In my eyes, denying a child a proper upbringing bordered on abuse.

"Why not?" said Aminat, half-chewed meat visible in her sweet little mouth.

"It just looks disgusting, my dear. And you are pretty—you shouldn't look disgusting."

Aminat chattered on and interrupted every timid attempt by the adults to converse with each other. Sulfia continued to say nothing, leaving me to do what was necessary.

"Sweetie, be quiet for a moment. The adults are talking right now."

"Who is? Nobody's saying anything."

Aminat turned her head happily from one silent face to the next.

"That's because you keep interrupting everyone. Good children don't do that."

She fell silent and pouted. But it didn't bother me. I knew children needed to be treated like a beet garden. When you eliminated weeds from their character, you got a better harvest.

"How are things at your job?" I asked my son-in-law as he was noisily slurping his soup.

"The work doesn't do itself, that's for sure," he said and guffawed. Once again I didn't know what to think of him. He ate enough for three and kept pointing out to Sulfia that she didn't serve Tartar dishes as tasty as mine. He told Sulfia that she should make *schulpa*. Or any kind of soup at all.

"She was never particularly interested in cooking," I said.

"I've noticed," said my son-in-law.

He laughed. Aminat laughed with him. I gave them both a stern look. Laughing at Sulfia was something only I was permitted to do.

"She had other interests," I said. "I encouraged her to do other things . . . for instance . . . "

I looked at Sulfia and thought about what talent could justify her household deficiencies. Nothing occurred to me. She had always been miserably lazy, just like her father.

"So how are things at your job again?" I said, turning back to my son-in-law.

At that moment, Aminat knocked over her glass of sea buckthorn berry drink and I sent her to stand just outside the door of the room so she'd feel a bit ashamed. After ten minutes I let her back in and gave her dessert. She sat still on her chair now, looked at me out of the corner of her eye, pushed the nut-sized balls of dough of the *chak-chak* around on her plate, and said not a word more. Handled properly, she could still possibly grow up into a well-bred child.

Nobody could see what sorrow or joy was in my heart at any given moment. But in Sulfia's colorless face you could read every thought that flitted through her head.

I had tried to teach her that nobody should be able to see when you were scared. That nobody should be able to tell when you were uncertain. That you shouldn't show it when you loved someone. And that you smiled with particular affection at someone you hated. I worked so hard with Sulfia, but it was all for naught. She had no talent, not the slightest understanding of what I meant. It had repercussions to that day:

over dinner Sulfia was for some incomprehensible reason very unhappy, and anyone who wished to could see it.

My son-in-law liked me. It was understandable. I was a handsome woman. In my late forties I still looked as if I were in my mid-thirties at most. My skin was firm and radiant, and I made myself up every morning before I went anywhere—even if it was just to the kitchen. I wore only red and black. I could pull it off.

At the first meal with our new extended family, I wore a simple black dress and black nylons. I had nicely shaped legs and made sure not to let them get too thin.

I always wore high heels. Sulfia never did. Today she had things on her feet that looked like a cross between an indoor slipper and a sneaker. She said my son-in-law had brought them from America. From America! Did people really wear that kind of crap over there, or had these shoes just been really cheap? If my husband had given me shoes like that I wouldn't have let him into our bed for weeks.

Admittedly, my husband had never been sent on a professional trip to America. Apparently I succeeded in getting a few important things across to Sulfia, since she had a man who made such trips.

All in all it was a lovely Sunday.

We said our goodbyes civilly in the foyer. My son-in-law was charming. He complimented everything: the food, the atmosphere, the effort, and the grace of the hostess. If I hadn't stopped him he would have complimented my hairdo and legs as well. He was the type of man who noticed those things in a woman. I had a dark feeling that I'd learn more about that.

Sulfia couldn't get out of our apartment fast enough. She was probably counting on not coming over again until the day we had to organize a funeral reception for Kalganow here. But she had neglected to include Aminat in her calculations.

Aminat threw her arms around my neck and bathed my pearl necklace in tears.

"Grandma, I want you to come with us," she sobbed.

I took her hands from around my neck, put her down, and patted her head. She dug her fingers into my dress. Her face contorted into an ugly grimace.

"MY GRANDMA!!! I DON'T WANT TO BE AWAY FROM YOU!!!"

Sulfia went pale. My son-in-law didn't know what to say. My husband acted as if he were somewhere else. I stroked Aminat's hair.

"We'll see each other soon, dear," I said.

Sulfia winced. Aminat stop crying immediately. She lifted her little face, puffy from crying, and looked at me.

"Mama doesn't want that," she said.

"Ach, such nonsense," said my son-in-law loudly.

Sulfia remained silent.

"Your mother will surely allow it," I said firmly. "I'll pick you up from kindergarten on Wednesday, alright?"

Aminat turned around and clutched the end of Sulfia's scarf.

"Mama, grandma will pick me up Wednesday, alright?"

"Wednesday works well," said my son-in-law, winking at me. He mussed Sulfia's hair as if she were his little sister.

"Right?" he said, and it sounded menacing.

Sulfia's eyes were dark and dull. She nodded.

A civilized family

We were a civilized family.

The first time I picked up Aminat from her new kindergarten, she screamed with joy and jumped around in a circle. I told her to put on her coat. She kept celebrating and dancing.

A teacher interrupted: "Anja, you're disturbing the entire group again."

Aminat stuck out her tongue.

I spoke to her sternly.

"Get your things on, you Satan."

Aminat stopped screaming, sat down on the bench with a dreamy smile, and held her feet out to me. I put her feet into her boots and wrapped the scarf around her skinny neck. It was all so casual and normal. As if the time when I thought my heart would rip apart from the sorrow of not seeing her had never been. I hadn't forgotten what it was like without her. I hadn't forgotten one bit.

I pulled Aminat's woolen mittens over her fidgeting hands. She looked me straight in the eyes. Sulfia never did that. Sulfia's gaze had always shifted around, and still did. But Aminat never looked away, regardless of who she was looking at.

I took her by the hand and led her to the bus stop. Aminat stomped in the puddles and splashed water all around. I hardly reprimanded her, though, because my own heart was celebrating. Winter was fading; the snow was shrinking into itself and turning gray. The air was warming and filling with scents. The trees were still bare, but their branches had a new vitality.

We boarded the bus that would take us home. Aminat sat at the window, laughed, and pointed at the many things that caught her attention. Spring was at the doorstep, and my heart beat with love.

We were a civilized family and got along well with one another. I often picked up Aminat from kindergarten in order to help the young couple, who had to work a lot.

I asked myself what they had done before, without me. Without my advice, without my help. I often took Aminat home to my place because it was cleaner there and I had everything she needed. Sulfia preferred it when Aminat stayed in her apartment;

when Sergej also asked me to do that I granted his wish. From then on I looked after Aminat in Sulfia's apartment, even though it was less practical. We played, I read to her, we painted together, I told her instructive stories from my life and from the lives of others. She listened, but not very attentively. At some point her thoughts would wander and she would begin to hum to herself.

I considered it my duty to bring up Aminat properly, to teach her right from wrong. I hadn't studied pedagogy for nothing. Around me she didn't eat with her mouth open or grab serving bowls meant to be shared. I smacked her face or her knuckles when she did things I had for good reasons forbidden, like picking her nose or scratching herself between the legs. I cursed at her in Tartar, calling her "Satan" and "donkey"—but affectionately. And anyway, she didn't know what it meant.

I took on Sulfia's housekeeping, too. Someone had to do it. I cleaned up in the kitchen, in the foyer, and in the bedroom. I vacuumed up dust, mopped the floors, and scrubbed the toilet. I didn't want Aminat to grow up in filth, with her stepfather's intestinal bacteria on the toilet brush and his herpes virus on the cloth handkerchiefs he left lying around everywhere. I gathered them—from between the sheets and pillows in their bed, from under the couch—and washed them in a bowl, hung them to dry, and then ironed them. Just as I did with all the other laundry.

Sulfia was, as always, ungrateful. All she said was, "Just leave it, mother."

She even screamed at me. That was after I straightened out her wardrobe. I sorted and folded the underwear, bras, and leggings, and repaired the holes in them by hand. I did all this despite the fact that I would rather have been watching TV or reading the paper. But she shouted at me so loudly that Aminat came to the door of the room and asked, "Mama, are you crazy?"

Up to then Sulfia had never shouted. She had just helplessly exclaimed, "Mother, why? Just leave it, mother. Mother, please don't touch that."

I let her scream. Everybody needed to scream once in a while in his or her life. But after a few minutes I also thought enough was enough.

When I decided she had gone on long enough, I picked up my boot and hit Sulfia in the face with it. She put her hand on her cheek. Aminat jumped on me, pulled at the boot—which I was still holding—and bawled: "If you hurt my mama again, I won't love you anymore!"

I was stunned. Love was an enduring theme in our family. We always knew that we loved each other. We told each other often, particularly Aminat and I. I let the boot drop. Aminat did not run off, though. She didn't even turn away. She stood there belligerently, like a little construction worker, and looked with her black eyes straight into mine.

"What did you say?"

"If you hurt mama again, I won't love you anymore. At all."

"Why would you say that?"

"Because I don't want to have an evil grandmother," said Aminat, hopping away on one leg.

Am I an evil woman?

I always listened closely to everything Aminat said. One of the reasons she seemed so ill mannered was that she could say very perceptive things. I battled her instinct to say whatever occurred to her because her frank observations often hit the bull's-eye, making people uncomfortable. Aminat had no patience for foolishness and could point out the flaws of others very precisely. Naturally this couldn't continue, and I worked hard with her on self-control. But I listened closely to what she said.

On the day Aminat told me she wouldn't love me anymore, I took my boot without a word and left my daughter's apartment without even saying goodbye. I took the bus home. Aminat's voice echoed in my ears for the entire ride: "I don't want to have an evil grandmother, I don't want to have an evil grandmother."

Was I an evil grandmother? I looked at my reflection in the dirty window of the bus. Is that what an evil grandmother looked like?

At home I stared at myself closely, this time in the polished full-length mirror.

I didn't look anything like a grandmother at all. I looked good. I was pretty and young looking. You could see that I had vitality and was intelligent. I often had to mask my expression to keep other people from reading my thoughts and stealing my ideas.

I went into the kitchen, where my husband was eating a vegetable casserole, and asked him whether I was an evil woman.

He choked and began to cough. I waited patiently. He coughed some more. His round eyes were petrified. I waited. He continued to cough and I hit him on the back.

"So," I insisted, "am I an evil woman?"

He speared a piece of eggplant with his fork. I snatched it away from him before he could stuff his mouth again.

"Am I an evil woman?"

He looked at the floor. The thick black eyelashes I had once so loved fluttered like a little girl's. My heart warmed; I thought of the hungry years of my youth. Too bad Sulfia hadn't inherited those lashes, I thought. But at least Aminat had them.

"So," I said, "am I an evil woman?"

"Why would you think that, sweetie?" stammered my husband. "You're really, really wonderful. You're the best. You're so smart . . . so beautiful . . . and you cook so well!"

"But none of that has anything to do with whether or not I'm evil," I insisted. "I could be a terrific cook and still make everyone around me suffer."

"No, no, my little squirrel," said my husband, using a term

of endearment from our early years. "Nobody suffers . . . nobody suffers because of you. You're so good to all of us."

"Even Sulfia?"

"Sulfia . . . ," My husband thought for a moment.

I waited.

"Sulfia," said my husband, "is your only daughter. You always wanted the best for her."

"I still do."

"Yes, I know."

"Do you think Sulfia knows it, too?"

"Of course. Though perhaps she didn't realize it earlier. It's normal for children not to value their parents. But now she's grown up, and I think she knows how much you love her."

I listened carefully. I was surprised my husband had thought about it so much.

"Are you sure?" I said.

My husband turned and poked at the casserole on his plate, then looked over at me with his eyes narrowed, as if afraid I was about to take away his food.

"Very, very sure," he said. "You're the best, the most beautiful . . . and you have such a good heart."

If my husband saw me that way, it couldn't have escaped Aminat. So she couldn't have meant what she said. She was just being fresh.

Five days later I came home and found a letter from my husband on the windowsill. In the letter he wrote that he loved another woman and wanted to live with her from now on. He thanked me for our years together and begged me to leave him in peace.

There was nothing more.

Apparently there are women who break into tears at such news. Their legs buckle and they sink to the tiled floor of the kitchen, with its checkerboard pattern, and other people must step over them in order to get to the refrigerator. I wasn't one of those women.

First I made a cup of tea, following all the rules of the art. I warmed the teapot and then poured boiling water over the tea leaves. If there was one thing I hated, it was poorly made, low-grade tea. I drank my excellent tea in small sips, ate homemade gooseberry jam, and thought things over.

I tried to imagine what it would be like to come through the door and not hear someone noisily chewing in the kitchen. Someone who annoyed me by eating the food—which I made in advance—cold because it was beyond him to warm it up. Food in general: I could almost completely abandon cooking now. I'd have oatmeal in the morning and make a salad in the evening. I'd be able to save so much time! And with that time I could read, watch TV, or do gymnastics.

I continued to think. I wouldn't have to talk to anyone when I came home from work. I started to count the number of shirts I would no longer have to wash and iron each week—not to mention the socks, pants, and underwear.

Shopping! I wouldn't have to carry home heavy shopping bags anymore because I'd need so much less food. I would have much less filth to clean up, as I myself didn't make any. I could talk to God as much as I wanted. I would get upset much less, since there was nobody there I constantly needed to get upset at. And I could meet men. New, younger men who would pay me compliments, then leave to go home to mommy, or to their girlfriend, for all I cared. Men who would make me feel like a woman again. Because I have to admit that it had been a long time since I had liked to be touched by Kalganow. When he accidentally brushed my leg in his sleep, I recoiled in disgust. He hadn't touched me intentionally in ages.

Of course the letter on the windowsill wasn't all for the good. Nothing in life came for free. I would have to pay for my freedom. For instance, I was now a woman who had been left.

That wasn't exactly an envious status. I had to live with the fact that people would look at me funny. But, God willing, everything else was in my own hands.

My husband was a coward: he left it to me to tell his daughter and granddaughter that he had left.

I decided not to show my lack of sorrow. I figured this episode would make everyone forget the earlier friction and the boot and the unpleasant words. Before I set out for work, I left a letter for Kalganow on the windowsill. "We should behave civilly with one another. I wish you all the best, and good health to boot. Please leave me your telephone number so we can wrap up everything. Your Rosa."

I knew he'd come by again to pick up his things, and he'd make sure he did it at a time I wasn't there. If he avoided me during better times, he certainly wouldn't risk running into me now.

That evening I took the bus to Sulfia's. She opened the door and her face looked tired and distant.

"Mother? Come in."

I hadn't worn any lipstick, and had only a dusting of powder on my cheeks and forehead. I had on my plainest dress, one I normally wore only when I went to our garden outside of town. I did, however, wear my boots with heels.

"Is everything alright?" asked Sulfia when she finally looked me in the face.

"Don't you know?"

"Has something happened to Papa?"

"You could say that," I said.

Now she was frightened. "What's happened?"

"Your father left me."

She leaned against the wall. Her face fell.

"What?" she said. "What did you say?"

"YOUR FATHER LEFT ME."

"No . . . He? . . . You? . . . No."

"It's true," I whispered.

Sulfia sank to her knees.

"Mama," she said imploringly, "Mama, don't."

She must have thought I was crying.

I covered my face with my hands so as not to spoil that impression. She stood up quickly and put her hands on mine. I flinched. It had been a long time since we had had physical contact.

"Mama," she said helplessly, "please don't be sad, mama."

"Leave me alone," I said. Sulfia's lips began to quiver as if she, not I, had been left.

"It's not as if anyone died," I said, in case she had misunderstood.

"Would you have preferred him to die?

I thought for a second.

"Yes, that might have been better."

Sulfia didn't ask any more questions.

I was a role model

The departure of my husband had, as I mentioned, its advantages. One of them was that Sulfia began to like me. It seemed as if it occurred to her for the first time what an amiable person I actually was.

She began to speak to me. She called me every morning to ask me the same question. It seemed she was worried I might have hanged myself overnight. I responded to her feelings attentively, giving her a not altogether happy portrayal of my current situation.

Then one day she called me and said, "I know who she is—papa's new woman."

I was polishing my nails. I'd bought the polish at a bazaar. It was supposedly from Germany. It was cherry red. I held my left hand in the air with my fingers spread. I held the phone with my right. The nails on the right hand were already polished. I made sure not to smear them. The polish dried quickly; it was much too old. I noticed as I applied it that it was too thick. I had paid four rubles for the bottle and I'd been taken. This wasn't German, it was rubbish.

"So?" I asked angrily.

Sulfia's voice quivered over the phone. She didn't know about my nail polish disappointment. She thought her news had upset me.

"Please calm down," she pleaded. "There's no way to undo things."

Perhaps some things, I thought. But I could take back the dried-out nail polish, throw it in the vendor's face, and demand my money back.

I could also put a few drops of acetone into the bottle, which would make the polish fluid again.

"Ach, you don't give a damn," I said and hung up.

An hour later she was standing at my front door. Aminat hopped around her in a circle. The peephole distorted my daughter's face in a particularly ugly way. Her nose was huge and her eyes abnormally small. "Hello, hello," sang Aminat. She threw off one of her boots and hopped around our foyer in one sock.

"Hello, my dear grandma, hello, my dear grandma, Anja is here, Anja is here."

She disappeared into her old room. A moment later the second boot flew out the door and bounced off the wall. All the work I had put into this child, and still she was so ill behaved. It was time that I got close to Aminat again before it was too late. I had room in the apartment now, and time, too.

Sulfia picked up the boot and put it on the shoe rack. Then she came over and hugged me.

I froze.

My God, was she short. She was scrawny, always had been. I had given her food nonstop, I made her clean her plate. When she was still at school I set out a sumptuous breakfast for her every morning—meat with a side dish or else a nutritious soup. She was never allowed to leave the house with an empty stomach. But she never got taller or heavier

I did everything possible to make her stronger. I painstakingly tried to teach her to swim, even though I myself didn't know how. But the cold river water got to her. She shivered, her lips turned blue, and soon after, presto, she came down with a bladder infection that lasted for several weeks. God knows how much effort I put into her, and it was always for naught.

I pushed her away and went into the kitchen.

Sulfia served me in my own home now. Naturally she couldn't make a decent cup of tea. The water wasn't boiling, she used too few tea leaves. The brew had no aroma and looked unappetizing. I drank what she put in front of me anyway, as I didn't want to discourage her.

Then she sat down opposite me, folded her hands, and said, "Mother, the woman is your age. Actually . . . she's a little older than you."

I looked at her silently. She was uncomfortable.

"Mother," she said, "I met the woman. Turns out she's sick. Her heart. Papa called me and asked me to introduce her to a doctor from our clinic. She's very sick."

She looked away, embarrassed.

"I feel so bad," she said. "I saw her. She's really not doing well. And I . . . I'm supposed to help her. And I . . . I don't have any sympathy for her. Because it's her fault that things are going so poorly for you."

I thought of my God. I knew he would allow me the right to wish every ill in the world on this woman that Sulfia was talking about so oddly. But I didn't wish her ill. I didn't want her to die, though I also didn't care whether she lived.

I was just a tiny bit curious.

"Keep talking," I said.

The woman, Sulfia explained, was named Anna, and worked as a teacher of Russian and literature. She dressed in gray clothes, wore her hair in a bun, had red veins in her cheeks, needed glasses, and had a sweet smile. She was divorced and had no children. She had met Kalganow in a park as he was sitting on a bench thinking about death.

"He initiated the conversation with her?" I said suspiciously.

"Apparently, yes." Sulfia looked unhappily into her teacup.

What do you know, I thought.

Sulfia had her address and phone number, and to prove it she said them both aloud. I asked myself what she expected from me now. Was I to call the number straight away and demand the release of my spouse? Or go knock on the teacher's door with a half liter of hydrochloric acid? What did Sulfia think I should do now? Everything I did was significant: I was a role model after all.

One day I opened the bedroom window to let in some spring air. It was still sealed for winter. I ripped off the paper strips I had used to seal it shut in the fall and pulled out the wadding I'd stuffed into the cracks. I destroyed the results of hours of labor: it was miserable work to prepare the window in the fall so there wasn't a draft that chilled the room. Klavdia left the insulation in and kept her window closed over the summer just to spare herself the work. But I wanted fresh air.

The room filled with the sound of motors, voices, and the jingle of the trolley bell. I stood at the window and took a deep breath. Yes, this was really spring. There were stands selling flowers and ice cream. The thick winter jackets and brown fur coats had disappeared. People were wearing light jackets and bold colors. Their steps had bounce. Many had left their hats at home. I saw hair again.

On the sidewalk, beneath a streetlamp, stood a man who also wasn't wearing a hat. From above I could see the sun gleaming on his bald head.

It was Kalganow, my husband.

He stood at the foot of the streetlamp and looked right up at me. I hid behind the curtain. I felt caught off guard.

His light, round face remained tilted up toward me. I could see it through the cloth of the curtain. What did he want? Why wasn't he with his teacher of Russian and literature? Had he lost the key to his new apartment? Gotten lost? He wasn't thinking about coming back to me now, was he? I panicked. A little.

Kalganow was always good at that: ruining my mood. His presence could cast a shadow over any otherwise splendid moment. The spring day was beginning to fade. The wind no longer felt caressing, but rather treacherous. I closed the window and drew the curtain.

I sat down in my armchair and picked up my knitting needles. I was knitting a scarf for Aminat. Obviously not just an ordinary one. I was making a kitten pattern. To take such a basic thing as a scarf and make it as unique as possible—I had a knack for that kind of thing. I concentrated on counting stitches.

Perfect spouse

That night I dreamed of Kalganow for the first time. It was strange. In the dream my husband was still young. He looked the way he had when we first met. I was sixteen, and he was a friend of my brother. Five years older, a grown man. Three years later my brother jumped from the twelfth floor of a high rise. He was always a peculiar person.

Boris, I thought. Boris was my husband's first name. I had never called him that, though. I had my own names for him. I remembered how I opened the door for him one day when he came to visit my brother. I had just left the orphanage and moved in with my brother. He was my only close relative, and now that he was in his early twenties he was grown up and responsible. I remembered how suavely Kalganow said, "Hello cutie." And how amazed I was that a man could be so handsome. Yes, my husband had been handsome at one time. I had completely forgotten that. I was so attracted to him that I immediately thought to myself, If I married somebody like him, our children would be lovely. Not exactly, as it turned out.

We got married shortly after my eighteenth birthday. He'd had a girlfriend in the meantime. She was neither attractive nor smart, but I was still sick with jealousy. I had secretly kneeled down in the bath and prayed to God for assistance. Actually, I just wanted to make sure my future husband didn't decide to marry this other girl before I was old enough. But God overdid it a little. My future husband's girlfriend died suddenly of tuberculosis.

As far as Kalganow was concerned, there was no God. He was with the Communist Union of Youth, which I thought was good. It was also clear that it opened horizons. I embraced his political fervor.

Though it was obvious at first glance he was Tartar, he never wanted to talk about it. He used to say it was all arbitrary, the categorization of people as Russians or Ukrainians, Jews or Gypsies, Uzbeks, Bashkirs, Azeris, Armenians, Chechens, Moldavians . . . or Tartars. He was born in Kazan, but he never liked the place. He had a dream: that all people would mix together, stay far away from their ancestral homes, and cast off their cultural roots as they would so much dead weight. He was of the opinion that all these various people were discriminated against.

In our first few years together he spoke a lot about that. I listened to him—I knew how a wife had to behave. The most important part was not to point out to the husband what stupid things he said. A woman's tolerance in this area was key to a stable marriage. I understood all of this in theory, and then passed muster in practice. I was the perfect spouse.

We were a nice couple at the beginning. Both of us handsome, slim, healthy, with sparkling eyes. Back then I got pregnant constantly; it was a problem. We had no money and no apartment, despite his job. He was a communist idealist, not one who made sure to look after his family. In his opinion we shouldn't be any better off that anyone else. I stopped counting the number of innocent souls I sent back to heaven as a result. But it wasn't any more than anyone else.

At some point my husband brought home condoms. My influence on him was having some effect: slowly but steadily he began to build a career. He started as a simple worker, then he became active in the union. His ambition grew, he continued to climb and be promoted, and he had access to things other people hadn't even heard of.

Like these condoms, for instance. They prevented children reliably. In fact, they prevented the act that led to children. They were rare and valuable. After use I washed them and hung them to dry. I let them dangle from the clothesline in our room. I had the feeling that the longer they hung there, the less frequently my husband made advances on me. Back then I was tired and gaunt, I was studying pedagogy and working nights as a janitor in an all-day kindergarten. My enthusiasm for the marriage slowly but steadily dwindled.

Then came the prospect of our two rooms in the communal apartment. The next soul that knocked on my door, I would let live. It was Sulfia. I never asked myself what would have become of the children I sent back to heaven. God forgave me. He gave me Sulfia, and that was something, I suppose—he could have given me a complete cripple.

When Sulfia was born, my husband remained unmoved. He didn't like her Tartar name. Unlike me, he had a large family full of Tartar names. I had nobody except my cousin Rafaella.

Kalganow wanted to name our daughter Maria. But no Maria was going to enter my house. There were flocks of little Maschas wandering around, populating the kindergartens and the playgrounds.

My husband didn't show much interest in our daughter, especially after I named her Sulfia. And when he did things with her, for the most part he made mistakes. He nearly dropped her when he held her. And with Sulfia, it was clear that if she were dropped even once, it was over. She was scrawny and weak. She could spend hours on end just staring into space doing nothing. I'd never seen a child like that.

"What's wrong with our daughter?" I asked my husband.

"Leave her alone," he answered. "Maybe she's thinking."

"Thinking?" I said. "That's not an activity."

That's not to say I never thought about things. But to do so I didn't need to sit down, fold my hands in my lap, and put a faraway look on my face. It was something I did alongside other things. I had to work and raise my daughter. Nobody helped me.

I didn't want to work with kids; Sulfia was enough for me. I didn't want to work with students at a vocational school, either. They had nothing in their heads. I found a good position at the teachers' college. My work was very important: I collected information on all the latest scientific developments in pedagogy and archived the material. I put Sulfia in a boarding kindergarten. That is, I took her there on Monday and picked her up again on Friday—coughing and sniffling because Sulfia was so unremarkable that she often went overlooked. It seemed to me the kindergarten teachers fed and washed her only because they were afraid of me.

God only knows how much I tended to this child. Every summer we spent a month in the country with distant relatives of my husband who made their own sausages instead of buying them in a shop.

Kalganow's relatives were devotees of *qaziliq*, the horsemeat sausage. First they soaked the meat in pots they left standing around. Then they turned animal intestines inside out, washed them with cold water, and scrubbed the slime off the intestinal walls. Then they turned them right side in again and sewed one end shut. They filled them with meat and fat, tied off the open end, and hung them out in the sun for several days. The sausages hung around, gently swinging in the wind with fat dripping onto the ground through holes poked in the casings. After a few days the sausages headed down to the basement for a few months, but in the evening I found cooked *qaziliq*—cut into thick discs—on my plate from an earlier batch. I didn't touch it: these relatives never washed their hands.

It was awful, but I clenched my teeth. They were very simple people. They spoke nightmarishly bad Russian. I spoke Tartar with them because otherwise they wouldn't understand. I had nearly forgotten the language because I'd lost my family early and Russian was spoken in the orphanage. I dredged the words out of the depths of my memory and was surprised how well it went.

With their constant grins and twinkling teeth, Kalganow's relatives even got Sulfia to smile. First she started to imitate their speech, mumbling *tyr-pyr-myr*. Then she started to say words and phrases she'd picked up, not all of which were nonsense. I didn't do anything to encourage her. I was proud of my flawless Russian, especially now that I realized it wasn't a given.

Fortunately they had goats. That was the main reason we went out to the country—and only secondarily for the good country air. Though I far preferred the fumes of my city to the smell of cow shit I had to breathe in the country. But I endured for the sake of my child. I had heard that goat's milk made you strong and healthy, and Sulfia was so scrawny.

Every morning and every evening Sulfia got a glass of freshly milked goat's milk. Obviously boiled, because everything out here was full of germs. I boiled it myself using a cast-iron cauldron built into their earthen stove.

Sulfia made a rueful face whenever she saw the full cup. She didn't like the taste. I told her it was a vaccination against stupidity. Sulfia sniffed the cup, disgusted, unhappy. She looked at me. My gaze was enough to make other people jump out of a window. So it was child's play to make Sulfia drink her goat's milk. The first time she gulped it down. Then she grabbed her stomach. When you drank it so quickly, naturally you got a stomachache. Sulfia's pathetic expression drove me nuts. Then she suddenly put her hands over her mouth, ran out, and threw up into the raspberry patch outside. She was a brave little girl and would never have made a mess on the floor. After she had regurgitated the goat's milk, I gave her a second cup and made sure she drank it very slowly. I'm not sure she would have survived to school age without this milk. I sacrificed myself for her betterment.

I myself didn't drink any goat's milk. I did taste it once, out of curiosity, after Sulfia complained about its bitterness—she never complained about things otherwise. I took a sip and instantly dashed out to the raspberry bushes. Yes, this milk was not enjoyable stuff, and I was happy I wasn't the one who had to drink it.

Other things to worry about

During the initial period without my husband, I filled the empty hours with thoughts. I thought a lot. I conducted a thorough evaluation of my life. It was clear that not everything had gone smoothly. But I had always made the best out of every situation. In my late twenties, for instance, I had to get a new passport because my old one had been stolen. For that I needed my birth certificate, which I no longer had. The orphanage where I spent the bulk of my childhood had burned down, and all the records destroyed. The passport-issuing authority had to take my word—so I made myself seven years younger, which seemed about right for me anyway.

I had always tried to make up for the failures of others, whether through advice, action, or my own good will. That's a notoriously thankless job.

Occasionally I interrupted my reflections and walked to the window. Often I saw my husband standing next to the lamppost. Sometimes at night, too. I asked myself what this meant. I didn't open the window because I didn't want him to think I was going to ask him to come up. He never did anything; he just stood there looking wretched.

But I had other things to worry about.

I'd seen my son-in-law downtown with a young blonde.

They were sitting at a café, at a little round table in the sun—like something out of a foreign movie. They were eating ice cream from glass bowls. Sulfia never did that kind of thing, sitting in a café eating ice cream. The stranger laughed like a lunatic. My son-in-law smiled and looked at her. Now and then he took her hand, which she would quickly pull away to gesture wildly in the air. She was a very fidgety young woman.

I hid behind the Lenin monument. With my eagle eyes I could see everything. How he paid the bill and helped her into her coat. A light green one, a daring color. I knew every style that had been in stores during the last five years—could rattle them off by heart—and this coat was not among them. It looked suspiciously like something from America. My son-in-law had obviously not brought slippers back for this woman.

They walked together to a trolley station. They kissed each other in front of everyone. How shameless. Couldn't they at least find a building entryway or an empty spot in a park?

I carefully considered my options.

One of them I rejected, namely to run up to the slut in green and shove her under the oncoming tram. I would take another path. I had no doubt there were other options. I just had to figure them out—and to judge by what I'd seen, I had very little time to do so.

Soon I had a good idea. I waited for Sulfia in front of the entrance to her surgical clinic. She worked a lot and had managed to repeat her training and become a proper nurse. When she finally came out of the building—loaded down with five mesh bags stuffed with the groceries she'd spent her lunch break buying at the market, like any normal married woman—she reacted calmly.

"Mother?" she said. "What's the matter?"

She looked at the package I had in my hand and her eyebrows gathered.

"I'm not even going to try it on. Save yourself the trouble, please."

A little while back I had tried to help her dress better. Now that I saw her more frequently, I just couldn't stand it. Always a pair of pants that sagged in the knees and the behind, and a sweater from her husband's dresser. It was really no wonder she was in her present predicament. So I had begun to bring her things offered for sale by friends and co-workers who had managed to get hold of them through labyrinthine channels only to find out they didn't fit. They were nice things, not like the nightmarish clothes made of execrable materials that hung in the shops. I'd already offered Sulfia a cream-colored blouse with big golden buttons. And a dress that went to the knees and accentuated the bust—even if it was lacking, as in her case. All sorts of dresses, blouses, pants. But Sulfia refused to wear any of them. She didn't so much as try any of them on, and even I was incapable of persuading her.

This time I had an extraordinary treasure in my hands. A light wool jacket in a subtle pink color. With her raven-black hair, she would have looked like a princess in it. I told her that. She shook her head, stubborn as a mule. Here I was trying to save her marriage, and all she could do was shake her head.

"You haven't even seen the jacket yet," I said.

"I don't need a jacket," said Sulfia. "This one is fine."

"But, my daughter, that one is already ten years old."

"So? It's still like new."

"Sulfia, listen to your mother."

"Mother, we could save ourselves a lot of time if you would stop bringing all this stuff. I have enough things of my own."

"I see that."

"What I wear needn't be to your liking," said Sulfia.

And what about Sergej, I almost answered in the face of her cheekiness. I suppose it needn't be to his liking either? Well, don't worry then, because he doesn't like it! If he could choose between a woman who looked like a mangy old crow and one like a spring breeze incarnate, I'll give you three guesses as to which one he would choose!

"I'm tired, mother," said Sulfia. "Can we possibly get together another time? I slept so little."

"Wait," I said. "I have to talk to you."

Sulfia stayed put. Her bloated mesh bags, filled with potatoes, red beets, and cucumbers, knocked against her legs.

"Come to my place," I said. "I have to tell you something."

"Another time, mother, yeah? I'm going home."

"It's important," I said.

"Then tell me now," said Sulfia, looking over my shoulder at the bus that was just pulling away from the stop.

"I can't tell you now. At least not here."

"Then leave it for another time."

She just didn't want me to help her. She was keeping me from saving her marriage. She always resisted whatever I did. The good times between us were apparently over, just like the good times between her and Sergej.

"Mother, I'm so tired I'm about to fall over. Let me go, alright?"

I took her by the arm and looked directly into her eyes.

"Sulfia," I said, "you need to get pregnant as soon as possible."

Sulfia began to blink.

"What?" she said. "What do I need to do? In your opinion?"

"Get pregnant."

"What?"

"Have a child."

"What?"

"GET PREGNANT, SULFIA! God damn it!"

"But how?"

I sighed. It occurred to me that I'd never told her how it worked. At first I had thought she was too young, then I thought there was no need. Then Aminat was born. These days I figured that she wouldn't need any explanation.

Sulfia looked at me affectionately.

"Mother, you've had a hard day. Shall I take you home?"

"But you didn't want to a minute ago."

"I think it would be better if I go with you."

We went back and forth like that for a while. She offered to take me home, I turned her down. I just kept telling her that she desperately needed to have a baby. That it was her only path to happiness. Sulfia tried to put her cool hand on my forehead. I insisted on a new baby. I told her that Sergej could certainly produce a handsome son.

Sulfia's pale cheeks blushed. But she didn't contradict me. She took me by the arm and led me along the street. I let her do so—it gave me more of a chance to get my message through to her. I was sure that if I said it enough times, it would sink in. I just had to be persistent, and that I could be.

Sulfia opened my apartment door, helped me out of my coat, led me into the bedroom, and sat me down on the bed. I realized she thought I was having a nervous breakdown. Maybe she thought it happened to people who got left.

"When a man has a child, he's not so quick to run off," I whispered. "If he's half decent, then he comes to his senses. Then he's duty bound. Sergej would not leave his child in a lurch."

I looked at Sulfia: she was very pale again.

She's an Angel

Sulfia didn't have enough time to put my plan into action. One month later Sergej called me. It was early in the morning and I was about to head out to work. He said I needed to come over because Sulfia wasn't feeling well and he didn't have time to look after her and Aminat.

I immediately took a private taxi. Strangely enough, I somehow had more money since Kalganow had left and taken his salary with him. It defied all logic, but it was pleasant.

Sulfia lay on the couch in the living room, her head hanging down and her hair touching the floor. She had thrown up on the carpet. Now she was snoring loudly. Next to the couch was a vodka bottle. It was on its side, its contents spilled on the floor. I picked it up and stood it upright, but there was nothing left inside.

I heard a strange snuffle. Aminat had squeezed herself under the little side table, despite the fact that she'd grown quite tall recently. Her long uncombed hair hung in her face. Her black eyes peered at me through the strands of her hair. She sniffled louder now that there was someone to hear it.

"Come out of from under there," I said. Aminat crawled out on all fours and stood up. She had on a nightgown I'd patched the elbows on.

I dried Aminat's face with my lacy handkerchief.

"You have no reason to cry," I said sternly. "Nobody has died. Rosa will take care of everything."

Aminat looked up at me. She didn't believe me.

"You look bad. I'll speak further with you only after you clean yourself up. Take a bath, brush your teeth, comb your hair, get dressed!"

She ran out of the room and I attended to Sulfia.

My daughter never drank alcohol. No vodka, no beer, no Crimean champagne. None at all, ever, not even on New Year.

I placed Sulfia's head on the couch. Brought a moist towel and wiped her face. Got a rag and cleaned the floor. Put up her hair. She groaned and her arms and legs twitched. She smelled like a homeless person. I spread a down coverlet over her.

Aminat returned—wearing her brown school uniform with a wrinkled skirt, and with her hair braided into two pigtails. The part she had made snaked sloppily across the top of her head. I took the hair bands off her pigtails, combed her hair, and then parted and braided her pigtails again. I gave Aminat her fleece jacket along with her hat, gloves, and knapsack and shoved her toward the door.

I poured cold water over Sulfia's head until she came to. Then I made her a strong cup of coffee with lots of sugar and lemon, and scrambled her an egg. I convinced her to get into her bed. I fluffed the pillows. Tears streamed down her face in torrents that soaked through the fresh nightgown I'd put on her.

She was sick. She had a headache and had to throw up. She was totally unaccustomed to alcohol. She thought it was made to dull emotional pain, not knowing that you should never drink when you were heartbroken—alcohol amplified everything, unhappiness as much as happiness.

"Why didn't you get pregnant?" I asked.

"How?" said Sulfia. I sighed.

She fell asleep later. I called Sergej at his job.

"Come home and look at this," I said.

"I've already seen it," he answered dryly.

"You know you're going to hell for this?" I asked, realizing immediately that it was the wrong approach. Sergej didn't believe in hell: he was a physicist.

"I'm sorry," he said.

"You deserve to die." This was also below my usual standard for insults.

He was silent.

"She's an angel," I said.

"I'd prefer a woman," said Sergej.

"Coward," I said, and hung up.

He came by again to talk. Fortunately I was there at the time making cream of wheat for Aminat. Sulfia stayed in bed all the time. I heard Sergej unlock the door and heard his steps in the depths of the apartment. I decided not to interfere. Spouses should resolve things between themselves. I stayed in the kitchen, until Aminat tugged me toward the living room by my skirt, saying, "Mama is crazy."

It looked as if she were right. Sergej was packing books into his suitcase. Sulfia lay on the floor holding on to his ankles.

"Get up!" I roared.

"You see?" Sergej said unhappily to me.

It was as if Sulfia had lost her mind. Now she was trying to hold on to his sleeve. He kept ripping himself free of her. I held Sulfia back by force.

"Get out of here," I said to Sergej while I wrestled with Sulfia.

"I'll expect you tomorrow afternoon at one in front of the Lenin monument. We'll talk there."

"I can't make it then," said Sergej.

"I wasn't asking. Now get out."

He took his suitcase hurriedly to the elevator. Sulfia was hanging in my arms like a puppet; I let her sink to the carpet and went and slammed the door behind Sergej. The more prolonged the breakup, the more tears, I thought to myself. A waste.

I showed up half an hour late to the Lenin monument. I was still a woman. Sergej was already there and appeared to be alone. He had a pair of American sunglasses sitting on the bridge of his nose and his hair was longer. I hadn't noticed that yesterday.

"Buy me a cup of coffee?" I asked.

We sat at the same café table where I'd seen him with his new girlfriend. The server made us wait—we still had socialism, after all. I said nothing; I wanted Sergej to be the first to talk. But he leaned back and looked . . . I couldn't actually tell where he was looking because he still had on his sunglasses. We sat in silence for five minutes, and then ten.

"And now?" I said.

He shrugged his shoulders and folded his hands in his lap.

"I'm sorry," he said.

"Aren't you ashamed?"

"Yes," he said. "Very much."

"She's physically ill from grief," I said. "And it's all your fault."

"But you're there with her," said Sergej.

"I'm going to curse and damn you," I said.

He sighed and looked off into the horizon.

"She's keeping the apartment."

Sergej showed the first sign of emotion.

"Excuse me? And where am I supposed to live? That place

is much too much for two people. We're going to offer it in a trade for two smaller places. One for me, one for her."

"That's not what you're going to do. Sulfia is going to stay in the apartment with Aminat. You can move in with your new girl."

"She still lives with her parents."

"Your problem."

Now he looked genuinely distressed. I knew that the scarcity of apartments could really put a damper on romance. What good was passion when behind thin walls the in-laws were watching TV and little nieces and nephews could storm into the room at any moment? Sergej would never again have it as good as he had had it with Sulfia—at least I would try to make sure of that.

He finally took off his glasses. His eyes were red.

"I have nothing more to say to you," I said, standing up.

"Get in touch if anything comes up," said Sergej. Without the glasses, his face reminded me of a dog's snout.

"Oh, I will," I promised and walked away in my high heels.

Getting the apartment was a clear-cut victory, one that had been oddly effortless. If Sergej had balked (and if I'd been in his new girlfriend's position, I would have made sure in advance that he had arranged an apartment trade), I didn't have much to fall back on: Sulfia and Sergej were both registered occupants, and it would have been entirely legal for him to divide it or trade it for two smaller places.

But I didn't have time to savor this triumph. Sulfia fell apart completely. She just wouldn't follow the example I had given her.

She stayed in bed all day. Aminat began to set the alarm herself. When the alarm rang, she got out of bed and walked down the hallway barefoot to say good morning to her mother and to see whether she was still alive. Aminat's biggest fear was that Sulfia might die.

Sulfia just rolled over silently. Aminat went to the kitchen and made herself toast with butter. Then she took her knapsack and the apartment keys and left for school in a wrinkled school uniform, with dirty fingernails, and with pigtails that disintegrated into tangled strands during the first class.

I went every day and tried my best to keep things in order and bring some life back into the household. I pulled off Sulfia's covers, but she didn't stir. A few times I dumped cold water over her, but that didn't have any effect either. She was a difficult case. I had to work, and couldn't spend days on end sitting at her bedside watching her do nothing. Before I left I put a cup of tea and a few slices of bread and cheese on her nightstand.

After work I went shopping and rushed back to Sulfia and Aminat. Sulfia lay in bed and she hadn't touched her breakfast. More and more often Aminat wasn't there. I would go out to look for her, call her name, check behind the garages, in the basement, and among the shrubs. Aminat would always turn up when I was looking in the opposite direction and call out behind me, "Here I am!"

"Where were you?" I would ask, yanking hard on one of her messy pigtails. She would smile at me and answer, "Taking a walk."

"With whom?" I would ask sternly.

"Alone!" she would laugh.

It was obvious that the time had come to keep a closer eye on Aminat.

She was only seven years old, a first-grader, but she'd grown four inches the previous summer. She had gangly legs now and looked like a fawn. Her knees were bony and scratched. There was something hard about the look in her eyes, something even frightening if you looked right into them. She squinted a lot. I warned her not to, because it caused permanent wrinkles.

In the weeks while Sulfia lay senseless in bed, I didn't manage to supervise Aminat the way she needed to be. I was too busy running two households. Cooking food and trying to get some of it into Sulfia. I brought in doctors, first from the local clinic, then from private practices, for which I paid out of my own pocket. One said Sulfia needed to snap herself out of it, another said things would get better on their own. A third prescribed cupping therapy and vitamin injections.

Sulfia didn't take part in the speculation. She just stared out the window or dozed. She didn't even do the crossword puzzle I left next to her bed in the hope of teasing a little life into her.

But I didn't worry. To my knowledge, nobody had ever died from lying in bed for too long. Then one day Aminat came home, opened the door, tossed in her school things, and left again. On the floor were her knapsack and her red cap. She was gone, without even a word. I realized I'd neglected my granddaughter—and that once again it was Sulfia's fault.

I immediately began to straighten up. I opened her knapsack and turned it upside down. Out came a few greasy notebooks, a couple of sunflower seed shells, and a flood of five- and ten-kopek coins. I stacked and counted them. Seven rubles and ninety kopeks: a lot of money!

Fearing the worst, I picked up Aminat's school journal, a record of her homework assignments, grades, and teachers' notes. I should have looked much earlier. Aminat hadn't logged any homework assignments in months. There were countless entries written in red by the teachers: "Aminat disturbed the class," "Homework not completed," "Must do additional reading at home," "Parents requested to schedule teacher meeting," "Disturbed class again," "Aggressive," "Urgently need to talk to parents." Page after page.

No, I wasn't shocked. It was fitting. If you didn't support and look after children, didn't raise them properly and teach them right from wrong, they'd grow up badly. This child was out on her own all the time, and obviously stole money. It was also no coincidence that sunflower husks fell out of Aminat's bag. That meant she was hanging around with the old ladies who sat in front of the market and sold things from their own gardens—potatoes, wild garlic, and lilies of the valley. They had a huge open sack of sunflower seeds and for ten kopeks these uneducated women would fill a cup with seeds and dump them into a baggie made of newspaper or directly into the jacket pocket of the buyer.

In our early years together Kalganow had also bought himself sunflower seeds, but I quickly broke him of the bad habit. There was nothing more peasant-like, crude, and unhygienic than putting unshelled seeds in your mouth and then spitting out the husk the way old women did, sitting around gossiping on stoops or on warped park benches, dirtying the ground at their feet. I used to root around in all of Kalganow's pockets looking for a seed that would betray him, and now, so many years later, I would have to do the same thing with my grand-daughter. To let things like this go could be disastrous—I knew that from my pedagogical training. It was also partly my fault; I'd let myself get too distracted with Sulfia.

I went into Sulfia's room and ripped off her covers, grabbed her by her bony shoulders, and shook her hard. Sulfia let out moaning sounds, but her eyes sprang back to life.

"Get up," I said. "Start cleaning up."

I let go of her, picked up my pretty new handbag, and went out to look for Aminat. I was angry that she, too, was making things difficult for me.

I looked for nearly two hours, asking children on the street, looking into random entryways, pushing through branches to look in the shrubs that ringed buildings and playgrounds in the area. I ruined my nylons. Finally I found Aminat—with God's help and my intuition—in the moldy basement of a neighboring high-rise apartment building. She and a girl I didn't recognize were squatting in front of a tattered basket in which multicolored balls of wool were writhing.

At first I thought they were rats. Then I saw they were kittens, two weeks old at most, their eyes just opened. They made soft noises, and Aminat was listening to them so intently that she didn't hear my footsteps on the concrete floor as I approached. She turned around only when I wrapped her pigtail around my wrist.

"Grandma!" she shouted.

It was a wonder of self-control; instead of fear and guilt, her voice expressed only joy.

"Look at how cute the kittens are, Grandma! As soon as their mother is no longer nursing them, we'll take one home, okay?"

I dragged Aminat out of the basement by her pigtail. The hair pulled at her scalp, but after an initial wail she fell silent. And she remained mute as I took her out behind the garage, dropped her pants, and thrashed her with Kalganow's old leather belt, which I had packed in my pretty new handbag as a precaution. After that I took her home. She didn't say another word. She just kept wiping her face on her sleeve until I forced her to stop because it might get dangerous germs in her eyes and nose.

A clean girl

It was the simple truth: the best thing a woman could do for her family was to provide clear and firm guidance. They didn't need coddling. When I entered the apartment with Aminat, Sulfia was standing in the kitchen washing up.

I pulled the petulant Aminat past her and into the bathroom, where I filled the tub with warm water and dribbled in some fragrant bubble bath Sergej had brought back from East Germany in a pretty bottle. You couldn't buy bubble bath here, and we used it exceedingly sparingly. Aminat watched the mountain of foam rise as the water streamed into the tub. She didn't move until I ordered her to undress. She took off her dress and threw it sloppily to the floor. I pushed it aside with my foot.

"Get in," I said.

"Too hot," said Aminat, after she dipped her big toe into the water.

"It's hotter in hell," I said.

Aminat hesitated, took her foot out, then put it back in and let it disappear in the foam before letting herself drop into the tub, splattering me from head to toe with water and bubbles.

"Watch what you're doing!" I shouted.

Aminat dunked herself under again and again. Foam adorned her head like a crown. She blew the foam and laughed.

I didn't let her enjoy her bath for too long. She didn't deserve to. I told her to stand up in the tub and I scrubbed her from head to toe with a sponge. I wanted her to be really clean again. She put on a sullen expression that reminded me of her mother. I washed her body thoroughly with the sponge, all around and in every crevice.

I told her to kneel and I washed her hair twice. It was much too long. I got her out of the tub and wrapped her in a bath towel. She had red streaks on her skin; the sponge was old and hard.

"Now you are a big girl instead of a filthy pig," I said.

I cut the nails on her fingers and toes. I cut the nails so short on a few of her fingers that they started to bleed. But she didn't complain. I took her into the living room, spread newspaper on the floor, set a kitchen stool down on the papers, and had her sit down.

"Close your eyes," I said, and she obeyed unsuspectingly.

Only as the fifth bundle of hair fell to the floor did she figure out what I was going to do.

"What are you doing?" she cried, trying to jump off the stool. I pushed her back onto the seat.

"Stay seated or I'll cut off one of your ears," I said. She slapped at my hand. I grabbed her wrist.

"You saw how sick mama was, didn't you?" I whispered in her ear.

Aminat looked at me out of the side of her eye, frightened, and nodded.

"And do you know why she was so sick? Because you've been such an ill-behaved child. You have been, haven't you?"

Aminat now sat silently on the stool. Yes, she'd been bad, and she knew it. She had always had a clear idea of herself and the world.

"And you want mama to get better, don't you?" I asked, cutting another clump of hair.

Aminat's eyes followed the strands of hair as they fell to the floor. She nodded, turned her head, and caught her ear on the end of the scissors.

I took my handkerchief and wiped the blood from the blades.

"Then you should always do what I tell you," I said. I could tell my words were being planted in fertile soil.

I had succeeded in breaking her resistance. The hardness disappeared from Aminat's face. She blinked, she grimaced, and she began to cry silently as I walked around her with the scissors and continued to shorten her hair down to a few inches so she'd look like a clean, neatly groomed girl.

To be honest, she now looked like a boy, a pretty one with short hair. When I allowed her to stand up, she ran into the hall to look at herself in the mirror. She stayed there suspiciously long while I gathered up her hair. It was a substantial mound of glistening black hair. I couldn't resist taking a lock, wrapping it in newspaper, and putting it in my pretty handbag. The rest I wrapped in a double layer of newspaper and carried to the trashcan. As I did, I went past Aminat, who was still standing in front of the mirror apparently unable to move. It must have appalled her—what little girl wanted to look like a boy? But a little outrage could do this child good.

I was wrong: Aminat was thrilled. She thought it was great to look like a boy. She decided to be one. If I'd realized the haircut would have this effect, I would have had second thoughts.

But there was no time to reconsider at this point. Now I had to deal with her work habits.

The first thing I did was visit her teacher. She was a short, round person with large glasses and her hair in a bun. I watched for her after class ended and the children came out of the classroom one after the other. I saw Aminat push a boy in the back with both hands so hard that his nose landed between the shoulder blades of the child in front of him. Surely the boy had started it.

Aminat was so busy she didn't notice me. That suited me. I waited until the throng had headed off in the direction of the school cafeteria and then entered the classroom. I had on slightly shiny black pants that emphasized the nice shape of my legs. In my heels, I towered above the little teacher, and she looked up at me with shock as she continued to shuffle through some notebooks.

"I'm Aminat Kalganova's grandmother," I said, smiling pleasantly. "Please allow me to offer you this small present."

I put a box of chocolate pralines down on her desk. I had found them at Sulfia's; she often received gifts from patients. You had to wonder how these sick people managed to get their hands on chocolates and cognac, just the sorts of things that were beginning to vanish from shops. I had picked out a medium-sized box. Sulfia had never thought to give something to Aminat's teacher. Unlike me, she didn't understand how to establish a good rapport.

At first the teacher said she couldn't accept them; then she said it wasn't necessary; finally she thanked me and covered them with the notebooks, so they would no longer distract us.

We sat down together at a school table. The teacher was an insecure person. She said she had just taken over the class from a sick colleague. She talked her way around the obvious topic for a while. This type of woman made me impatient. It took forever to tease out any useful information. The pralines did not fail to have their effect, however, as the teacher restrained herself from unleashing a curse-filled tirade about my granddaughter. So she could be bought cheaply, too. I had already figured that I'd have to buy her goodwill with a pair of winter boots the next time, but I had overestimated the price of her good grace.

The teacher didn't think Aminat was bad, just tomboyish (and I had cut her hair only a few days ago!). Yes, sure, Aminat disturbed class a lot; she was able to kick and throw wads of paper at anyone sitting within six feet of her. Yes, she failed to do her homework. Still, in class she often managed to answer correctly even when you thought she wasn't listening. She also spent many hours sitting on the heater in the hallway as punishment for these disturbances. And she ruined her classmates' appetites in the cafeteria by comparing the food to excrement.

I clucked my tongue. For some reason this teacher was scared of me. She tapped her fingers on the tabletop and said that Aminat displayed the defiant demeanor of an intelligent but neglected child. And she liked to sing.

"We often have broken families here," said the teacher.

I interrupted her. Aminat's mother, my beloved daughter Sulfia, has been sick, I said. During this time I would have expected the school to follow through on its responsibility to educate, but this hope was not fulfilled. I let slip where Kalganow worked. I promised her that Aminat was going to become a completely different person now. And as far as her being fresh—no child had ever dared be fresh with me, I said.

I asked the teacher for her telephone number. She looked more and more lost. Then she ripped a piece of lined paper out of a notebook. I hoped it wasn't Aminat's notebook. She wrote her number and her name—Anna Nikolaewna. I stuck the paper into my bag. I should have brought a much smaller box of chocolates.

I kept my word. Aminat became an upstanding young lady. Sulfia was still on sick leave, though she wasn't really sick—just lazy. I fought that. I made her pick up Aminat from school every day. I wrote out a weekly schedule for Sulfia to follow. At home Aminat was allowed to play for half an hour and then had to start on her homework. I came over in the evening. I ate Sulfia's pan-fried potatoes, which were always either burnt or raw, and looked over Aminat's homework assignments. And for every sunflower kernel I found in Aminat's vicinity, she had to write "I do not want to be a country bumpkin" twenty times in a notebook reserved for that purpose.

Aminat couldn't recite a single grammar rule but she wrote everything correctly. Good spelling was in her blood: she never made mistakes. But she made up for it with smudges and grease spots. Her handwriting was also terrible.

She didn't notice any of that and always presented her homework to me proudly—she had quickly gotten accustomed to me checking it. She also got used to me ripping the dirty paper out of her notebook and making her write everything over again. There were a lot of ripped out pages at first, until she figured out what I was expecting. She improved quickly.

Aminat was amazed the first time she brought home a five—the highest grade possible. She had never earned one before. The next day she got another five. After two weeks she got a four—and was disappointed. That afternoon her homework was flawless the first time through. She didn't want to perform poorly anymore.

Sulfia started going to work again. I stopped visiting every day. Everything was running smoothly, and I wanted to savor the final years of my youth and beauty.

I was actually rather inexperienced

I decided I was ready. I would let men initiate conversations with me on the street. Up to now I had always put on a face that discouraged it. Even the stupidest man could see that I wouldn't answer him. I was pretty, but not something for him. One day I flipped the switch.

The first man spoke to me on the bus. He stood up to offer me his seat (men constantly offered me their seats when I used public transportation). Earlier I had always just nodded and forgotten about them immediately. This time I looked directly into the eyes of the man who gave me his seat. He had somewhat dilated pupils and a burst vein in his left eye. It was dark in the bus, but maybe he'd been aroused by my gaze. I estimated his age at thirty-seven or thirty-eight years old. He had on a wedding ring that was thin and probably didn't cost much. His fingernails were cut short, something I welcomed in men. Though in his case they were cut angularly. The first thing I'd teach a man like that would be to use a nail file.

I exited the bus just to test him. Naturally, he followed me out. The bus was full. Rather than elbowing people out of the way, he kept repeating in a loud voice: "Excuse me, please! I need to get out! Excuse me, please!"

The other passengers cursed at him and called him an idiot. I agreed with them in principle. He finally extricated himself just as the bus doors were closing.

I waited until he had gotten out, then began to stroll slowly along Lenin Avenue. Almost immediately he was by my side. We walked a few steps together. He said nothing and didn't look at me. I lost my patience and began to walk faster. He picked up his pace, caught up with me, and put his hand on my elbow.

"Take your hand off me," I said gently. He looked at me. His pupils were the size of pins because the sun was shining directly in his eyes.

"You are the most beautiful woman I've ever seen," he said ardently.

I found him charming. With a few subtle hints, I let him know that I wouldn't consider it beneath me to eat an éclair with him at a café. We sat down and talked about my beauty and my thoughts about Shakespeare. We discovered the first thing we had in common: we both loved springtime. We talked a little about his marriage. I finished my coffee and could feel a sad look lingering on my back as I walked away from him.

He appealed to me. Two days later we saw each other on the bus again. It was something I knew would happen. He beamed when he saw me. This time he couldn't offer me his seat because he was standing, holding on to a pole with one hand. He smelled of soap and nervous sweat. When the bus braked, I leaned against him as if by accident and felt his heart beating with excitement.

I was excited, too. I was actually rather inexperienced, at least about the logistics of these things. I suggested we go to my place. He didn't say another word.

Klavdia wasn't home. I asked the man to wait in my kitchen, locked the door, and dialed Sulfia's number. I told her to call me in an hour. If I didn't answer, she should call the police. The man looked harmless enough, but I wanted to be sure. What I liked about Sulfia was that she always did whatever she was told, and didn't ask any gratuitous questions.

While the man waited in the kitchen, I went into the bedroom. I decided to take off all my clothes. I was really out of practice. I didn't need any strange, nervous fingers on my hooks and buttons. As I pulled the nylons from my legs, I was enraptured by the form of my calves. I freshened up my makeup, slipped into bed, pulled the covers up to my chin, and called loudly to my new acquaintance.

He fumbled his way down our long dark hallway until he found the right door. Then he entered. I had practiced my seductive smile in the mirror. He took a running start like a long-jumper, threw himself on me, and began to kiss me. You could tell he hadn't cheated very often. He couldn't kiss well and his hands felt clammy.

My excitement faded. He peeled off his shirt and simultaneously kicked off his pants. I thought he was funny but made sure not to laugh. He threw himself on me again and caught my hair under his elbow. I let out a cry. He took it for a sign of impatience and headed directly for the target. My hair was still pinned. I was worried he'd scalp me. He finished and rolled off me. I patted my hair back into place. I had just had the second man of my life.

He put an arm around me and whispered, "I love you."

"I love you, too," I whispered back.

I asked myself when he was going to leave. Then the phone rang. It was Sulfia. I had to answer. Otherwise she'd call the police according to my instructions. But it hadn't been more than half an hour. She couldn't even read a clock correctly. I told her everything was fine, and told my guest that my daughter was on her way over to see me.

He began to collect his things, he straightened his wedding ring, and approached me with his eyes gleaming and his arms held wide.

"When will we see each other again?" he asked.

I shrugged my shoulders. He asked for my phone number. I could hardly say I had no phone since he had just heard me talking in the foyer. I rattled off a random series of numbers, which he wrote on his hand with a pen. Next to it he drew a rose, something I found charming.

Once he had finally left, I took a shower. It was strange to smell of a man. I scrubbed myself. I sprayed myself too generously with perfume I'd bought three months before at a bazaar. Now I smelled like a girl who worked as a cashier. I got back in the shower and washed off the scent.

I was making tea when Klavdia came home. She was breathing heavily. In the last few years she had added to her already excessive weight by gaining at least thirty more pounds. She plopped onto a stool, pulled my plate of cookies to her, and began to stuff them into her mouth one after another. I watched her, happy not to be in her skin.

"If you smack your lips like Klavdia while eating, then one day you will look like Klavdia," I told Aminat sometimes.

"You're so strange," said Klavdia, looking me up and down. I was worried she'd smell the man on me and, just to be sure, went and took a bath.

I was used to male attention. Men had always turned to watch me go by. They held their umbrellas for me and let me slip into line in front of them. That was earlier. What happened now bordered on magic.

I was constantly stopped and asked for my number. Several times men spontaneously handed me bouquets of flowers on the street. I ate pastries at cafés more often than I had ever before in my entire life. I could leave my wallet at home with confidence. Strange men paid for me at cafés, on the bus, and in grocery stores, saying it would be their pleasure.

I couldn't have them all. That just wouldn't work. I didn't want to have them all anyway. But even among those I wanted in theory, I couldn't have them all. I still had to work, eat, sleep, and call Aminat on the phone to go over homework.

I had a scheme to make it easier to choose. I immediately eliminated men who smelled, who had acne, or who had a cold. Good manners were important, and so were clean fingernails. And I always sent men to the bathroom to wash their hands before they could get in bed with me. After all, they would be touching intimate parts of my body. Talking too much was a negative, as was a sullen look.

Male beauty made me weak. I was an aesthete. A wedding ring was always good. Someone like that wouldn't be always pestering me. Nice clothes—yes. That was impressive because it was so rare. Same with owning a car—I began to automatically eliminate men who rode the bus. With one exception: those who looked as though they were riding the bus because their car was in the shop.

I must say that I rarely made mistakes. I had a good eye for men with enough sense to be tender and decisive in the right moments, and who were man enough to understand when I no longer wanted to see them. On occasion one would ambush me at a bus stop or in front of my office to ask why I no longer wanted to meet him. Every once in a while one cried, too. Two took sleeping pills but were saved. Flowers often appeared on my doorstep or in my mailbox. Hardly any calls, though: I let everyone know I didn't appreciate it when my phone was monopolized.

In my spare room, sumptuous bars of chocolate piled up along with shrink-wrapped bottles of perfume, a few books, costly bottles of liquor in gift boxes, cast-iron sculptures, vases, imported nylons, a Russian-Polish dictionary (you never knew what you might need), and a little oil painting of an orange on a wooden table (one of the men had a studio).

Of course, it wasn't possible to hide all of this from the ever-watchful Klavdia. Too often she was sitting in her dirty bathrobe sipping tea in the kitchen as I was tasting a new acquaintance's lips for the first time and reaching as I did for the key to my room. That's why, right from the start, I didn't try to keep her out of the stuff. I gave her the perfumes I didn't like or had multiple bottles of. I gave her most of the chocolate (I had to watch my figure), a pair of nylons, some foreign buttons with animated film characters on them, and a cassette by a woman who shared her name with the mother of God.

Klavdia changed, too. She got a perm and polished her nails with the nail polish I gave her from among the ones I'd received. But she began to be nasty to me, and I realized what she needed.

I wasn't greedy. Klavdia could have my discarded men. The next time I broke it off with one for good, Klavdia took over, looked after him with tea and chocolates from among the gifts of his predecessors, and let him cry in her lap. This took the bite out of her nastiness and allowed us to put up with each other again.

It just wasn't possible without me

One Sunday, a lover had just gotten up and dressed himself to go pick up his wife and mother-in-law at the airport. While I lay in bed playing with my new ring, I realized what I had been forgetting the whole time.

I kissed my lover and pushed him toward the door: "You'll be late!" I said, though in reality it was I who was in a rush.

I put on a pair of Indian jeans and a sky-blue sweater that I had knitted myself. I zipped up my boots and put my hair up in a bun with knitting needles.

Klavdia stuck her head out the door of her room, looking satisfied; she'd had a man the day before.

"What are you wearing?" she said. "Has all that sperm gone to your head? Have you forgotten how old you are?"

"In the West," I said, smoothing out my sweater, "everyone dresses like this."

At work I often leafed through the pages of a sewing magazine one of my co-workers borrowed from her neighbor and brought with her to the office. I couldn't take it home with me and make copies of the patterns. But I took note of the things that appealed to me.

I took a private taxi to Aminat and Sulfia's place. Although I had bought new clothes, mostly from private collections rather than from shops, I still had more money than ever. Sometimes I found large banknotes in my coat pockets.

I hadn't seen Aminat in four weeks because I'd been so busy. I had just called her from time to time. Now I was suddenly anxious: how was she doing without me?

Sulfia was sitting in the living room, sewing. She was putting cuffs and a collar on Aminat's school uniform.

The school clothes were brown but had cuffs and collar made out of white lace. The clothes didn't need to be washed very often because they didn't show dirt—and besides, it took them ages to dry. But the cuffs were constantly dirty. All the mothers took the cuffs and collar off each weekend, washed them, ironed them, and reattached them.

I had done this for Aminat, too, so she wouldn't look messy. Later I had shown Sulfia how you reattached the ends, and I had also gotten hold of a second set of cuffs and a spare collar. That way she could exchange them without having to wash them immediately.

Now I saw Sulfia trying to sew them on. She held a large needle in her hand, and her fingertips were covered with red pinpricks. As I walked in, she stuck herself once again and shoved her finger into her mouth. She was so clumsy. She held a cuff with her thumb and pressed it onto the needle. She stuck herself again. She was a nurse, or a half-nurse, I thought to myself—is this how she tried to stitch up her patients?

She looked up from her sewing, let Aminat's dress fall, stood up, came over to me, and without warning draped herself around my neck. I patted her bony back. I put my arms around her not because I wanted to but out of a sense of duty.

"Where's Aminat?" I asked.

She looked at me.

"Aminat," I repeated.

"Aminat?"

"Aminat. The girl, Aminat. My granddaughter, your daughter."

Sulfia looked at me silently. \

"AMINAT!" I roared.

I spent the next hour running through the building. I managed to get out of Sulfia that Aminat had been there at noon. What had happened after that, she didn't know. I rang the neighbor's doorbell.

From almost a dozen mouths on four different floors I heard that nobody had seen her that day, and that, changing the subject, it would be nice if she wouldn't stomp and scream so loudly. The walls were thin, and the floors, too. I promised to tame Aminat. Three times I was asked to make sure Aminat stopped putting stray cats and their newborn litters behind the dumpster. One neighbor said he had found the animals and thrown the kittens into the dumpster and chased off the mother cat. I promised everything to everyone and ran on, until I heard Aminat's voice calling from above.

I went back up to the apartment, angry and panting heavily. Aminat was standing in the door smiling. She had a gap in her teeth. Her hair, which had already grown back somewhat, was standing up; she had dirty fingernails. She wore a nightgown she'd long since outgrown, along with tights that had a hole in the knee. She was a neglected child once again. I looked at her and sighed. My men would have to wait for me a bit until this child had grown up. It just wasn't possible without me. I had to invest every second in this child or else everything would fall to pieces.

"Where were you?" I asked, my voice shaking with rage.

"In the wardrobe," said Aminat. "I often hide in there, ha ha. And mama looks for me."

I reached out and smacked her in the face.

"Whore," I said. "Evil, evil child. Show me your notebooks."

Aminat silently brought me her schoolwork. I looked through everything, reading every page. I was amazed. The notebooks were clean. No smudges, no stray marks, precise and orderly handwriting, straight lines.

I looked at her journal. The grades were flawless, all her homework had been completed, and there were just a few things here and there in red: "Was fresh to the teacher," "Ruined the other children's appetite."

I closed the journal.

"You've done well at that, at least."

I pulled out my wallet, found a one-ruble banknote, and gave it to her. It was a lot of money. She wasn't sure whether to take it. Apparently no one had ever given her money; it must be a mistake.

"It's for you," I said. "You earned it."

I had an idea. I called Aminat over to me, gave her a pen and piece of paper, and asked her, "What do you want most in the world?"

"A father and a cat," said Aminat without hesitation.

"Then listen up," I said. "If, first, you take care not to look so messy, and, second, keep doing so well in school, and, third, you do the washing up every other night, switching off with your mother, and, fourth, you vacuum every Saturday, and, fifth, lay your clothes out so they are easy for your mother to wash, and, sixth, remind her when it's time to buy food . . . Have you got all that? Good. If you do all that for three months, you can have a cat."

Aminat listened without blinking. She held the pen firmly in her fist.

"Go on now, write it down. Do I need to repeat it?"

Aminat scratched her neck with the pen, then began to write. A few minutes later she showed me a numbered list. The last line read: "If I do this, I get a CAT."

I took the pen and signed my name beneath it.

My private life I put on ice. We women always have more important things to worry about. After work, I went to Sulfia's. I opened the door with my own key and went through the rooms peering into the corners. It was as if a confirmed bachelor had suddenly gotten married. Dirty laundry no longer lay around, the floor was clean, and the piles of empty milk and kefir containers had disappeared.

Finally there was a housewife in this apartment, a head of the family, a proxy for me, all rolled into one person: my eight-year-old granddaughter Aminat.

When she was at home she was always busy doing some kind of work, warbling the theme songs from movies as she worked. You barely had to instruct her because she had learned so many things on her own. She collected the empty plastic bags, rinsed them out in the sink, and hung them to dry on the heaters as if she'd done it her whole life. She never threw out any food. When a sausage in the refrigerator started to turn green, she cut off the bad spots, boiled the sausage, and then pan-fried it briefly. I couldn't have done it more expertly myself.

It was clear. Children need responsibility. Maybe I had gone about things wrong with Sulfia; because of her shortcomings I had done much too much for her. Aminat greeted every visit with a loud command: "Take your boots off, I just mopped!"

Even her voice changed, and she often held herself a certain way in order to speak. She reminded me uncomfortably of someone I knew. But I couldn't think who it might be. I asked Sulfia.

"She's imitating you," said Sulfia.

I thought of my childhood. I had always been hungry, had only one dress and one pair of tights, and four of us lived in a single room. And those were the best parts of it. In comparison, Aminat was spoiled.

I met my end of the bargain shortly before three months had passed.

Aminat had not once spoken of it. Three months was a long time—it represented many hours with the vacuum and countless cleaned plates. But Aminat didn't whine or ask about it. Later, stuck to the inside of a cabinet door, I discovered a piece of paper on which she had been crossing off the days.

On a Saturday seven days before the end of her obligations, I picked Aminat up. I had on a somewhat older jacket that I usually wore only when I went to my garden out in the country. Sulfia was peeling potatoes. Aminat's mother had followed her example. She too had picked up some skills that would make survival easier.

I told Aminat to dress herself warmly but not in her good clothes. A surprise awaited her. I was secretive. Aminat grew very quiet as we got off the bus near the bird market. She had never been to the bird market, and if I had told her where we were heading she would have been disappointed because she might have taken the name literally.

There were birds for sale here, of course—canaries, parakeets, parrots, ravens, and chickens, birds bred and birds caught, in all sizes and colors. Chirps and tweets from thousands of throats hung in the air, mixed with the barks and whines of other animals that for a few rubles would change hands today.

"Oh!" was all Aminat said, and her eyes became big and round. "Oh! Oh!"

The birds, flapping around in cages far too small for them, chirped frantically. Puppies and piglets were sold out of the trunks of cars. Falsified certifications of origin were shuffled here and there.

Aminat watched a little girl walk off with a hamster in a plastic bag. The little animal flailed in agony in the shredded paper lining the bag. It would suffocate by the time she made it to the trolley, I guessed. At the latest. But I didn't say anything. People need to make their own mistakes. It was enough that I helped guide my own family.

"Can I as well?" breathed Aminat.

"What?"

"Get a hamster like that."

"I thought you wanted a cat?"

She smiled tentatively, one side of her mouth curling upward. She didn't trust me. We walked along the rows. There were loads of cats: little fur balls purring in baskets, boxes, and on spread-out blankets.

"Pick one out," I said.

Aminat took me by the hand. The backs of her hands were raw and cracked, which happened when she walked around in freezing temperatures without gloves or when she didn't dry her hands sufficiently. I would have to rub glycerin into her skin that night so her skin would get soft again.

"I want that one!" said Aminat, pointing to a gray kitten sitting in the palm of a bearded man who reeked of alcohol. It was certainly the smallest and most nondescript cat that would be sold here today.

"Pick out another one," I said. "That one's too small—it'll die immediately."

"No, I want that one," said Aminat and asked the man, "How much is this cat?"

The bearded man moved his giant hand and squinted at Aminat. The kitten fell to the ground and he picked it up again.

"This is a pure-blooded Chinese shorthair," he said passionately. "It's a special cat. It's ten rubles."

"What?" I said, annoyed. "Let's go, Aminat."

"I want this one," she said stubbornly.

I walked on but she just stood there. The bearded oaf stretched out his hand to her. Aminat stroked the tiny kitten with one finger as the man talked persuasively.

"You should be ashamed," I said indignantly.

"A better cat you will not find," said the man conspiratorially in Aminat's ear. He had leaned way down to her. I could tell Aminat was doing her best not to show her disgust at the smell of his breath.

"You're not getting this one, Aminat," I said from a few steps away.

"Then I don't want one at all," she said.

"But look at all the beautiful cats here."

"I want this one."

"We can try to find one like it," I said. I made clear my strong opposition, but she just shook her head.

"This one."

"Then we'll go home," I said and took her hand.

She immediately tore her hand away.

We headed for the exit. I was upset with myself. I was here to indulge Aminat, and that had backfired badly. I should have known. Trying to fulfill a child's dreams was treacherous business. Instead of love and gratitude I had earned only resentment. Aminat was about to cry.

"Stop!" we heard from behind. "Wait, Tartar woman!"

The bearded liar was running after us in his giant rubber boots.

"Don't pay attention to him," I ordered.

Aminat dug in her heels and waited until he caught up to us.

"Here," he said, placing the gray fur ball in Aminat's hands. "You should have it. For free."

Then he trudged back to his car and Aminat, her eyes lit up, turned her triumphant gaze to me.

"Aren't I lucky, grandma? Don't I have the most incredible luck?"

I said nothing. It had been a bad idea to take her to the bird market and let her choose. Aminat began to shower the little cat with kisses and terms of endearment. Before I could react, she had surely infected herself with all the diseases this runt had in its miserable body.

"Keep it away from your face!" I cried. "Cats are dangerous. You can get blotches over your entire body from them, and intestinal worms."

Aminat was no longer listening to me.

Rosenbaum

For the first few weeks I waited for the little cat to die. I'd been through this kind of thing before: if I didn't happen to like someone, then sometimes that person just up and died. But the cat didn't die. It just got very sick—no wonder, since it had been separated from its mother too early. The cat came down with sticky eyes and diarrhea, and Sulfia called me in a panic.

In the background I could hear Aminat sobbing. At first I thought the problem had taken care of itself, but I had underestimated this cat's will to live. I told Sulfia that she had to take care of at least a few things on her own. Sulfia agreed with me, apologized, and hung up.

I later found out that she went to a veterinarian and got a prescription for medicines and a special food mixture. It cost a fortune. This cat was tough. First it managed to get up from its deathbed, and eventually it returned to full health. Aminat named the cat Little Peter, but I always called it Parasite.

The cat had its pluses. For some incomprehensible reason, Aminat assumed Parasite belonged to me. All I had to do was threaten to take it away from her and Aminat did anything I wanted. Among those things was to stop taking leftover sausage to the stray cats.

I had heard that cats brought luck to a home. And sure enough, Sulfia met another man just one month later. This man also had been one of her patients. One day I found him in Sulfia's kitchen. I had managed to get hold of two pounds of oranges for Aminat—after waiting in line for hours—and I was worried this man was immediately going to eat them all up. I had the impression that with Sulfia that when she fell for a man, he could have anything from her. But not Aminat's oranges!

This man wasn't bad. He was cleanly dressed, and his shirt had a dignified pattern. He was, however, a Jew. I could always recognize a Jew. When he saw me, he stood up and kissed my hand. He seemed chivalrous. He told me his name—Michail. I asked about his last name. And sure enough—his name was Rosenbaum.

I found this alarming, but not catastrophic. Jews were Jews. You had to watch out for them, but wasn't that true of everybody? I was sure that it had never occurred to Sulfia that he was a Jew. She smiled at him shyly, like a little girl, and he smiled back. He must have noticed what a great apartment Sulfia had. Jews were practical.

"Where do you live?" I asked.

He lived near the main station, which wasn't exactly around the corner. Did he work someplace near here, I wondered—was he trying to use this acquaintance to shorten his commute? If you were unlucky and had to get to the far side of the city every morning for work, you might wait for an hour for a bus that was then too full to squeeze your way onto when it finally arrived.

"And do you live alone?" I asked.

"With my parents," he said in a friendly tone.

"And what do you do for work, if I may ask?"

He was an engineer.

"That's original," I said.

He was also into sports. In winter he skied and in summer he climbed mountains. I was astounded that Jews did such things. I had always thought them to be too sensible. He'd sustained a compound fracture on one climb. Sulfia had nursed him back to health. Admittedly, he did have a limp, but there was nothing she could have done about that. He was bald and nearly forty years old. That was good. It was probably best for Sulfia not to be with a man any other woman might want.

I said a friendly goodbye. Out in the hallway I found Parasite chewing on one of my boots and shoved the beast aside. Once I got home, I rang Sulfia. The Jew had already left, which spoke well of him. A man who wanted to stay too long was suspicious. I told Sulfia he had nice teeth. Sulfia didn't understand what I was really trying to tell her: that I thought the Jew was alright and that I wished her luck with him.

Of course, I didn't mean that she should get pregnant straight away. But Sulfia was still haunted by Sergej and remembered what might happen if she ignored my advice. In any event, she was soon pregnant with a tiny Jew. I wouldn't have expected such virility from Rosenbaum.

Sulfia was happy. Aminat as well. Her deepest wishes were being fulfilled. First she got a cat, and now a baby sibling would soon follow. She began to sort her toys so the new baby would have things to play with.

There was just one problem: Rosenbaum was in no hurry to marry despite the fact that my daughter was carrying his Jewish baby beneath her Tartar heart. I sat Sulfia down for a talk and found out he hadn't even proposed to her. Worse still, his parents didn't know that she even existed.

"His parents are old, and his mother has heart problems," said Sulfia. She was already in her fourth month.

"He needs to tell his parents and marry you," I insisted. "Immediately. Otherwise he'll weasel his way out of it."

"He wouldn't do that," said Sulfia dreamily.

"Then he should marry you."

"He will. Later."

"With some things, you shouldn't wait too long."

It was clear that I'd have to look after everything once again.

"Give me his address," I said.

"What for?"

"Just give me his address."

"Please don't, mother."

"I'm not going to do anything. I just need the address."

"No," said Sulfia.

"Don't tell me you don't have his address!"

She said nothing. I had hit the bull's-eye again.

I found the address in the phone book.

As always, I prepared myself systematically. I didn't want to attack them, I wanted to give them a chance to treat my pregnant daughter right. They should see me as a sort of dove—an emissary of peace.

I took two bars of chocolate with me from Sulfia's supply— I wanted to be friendly but also humble. I rang the bell by a wood-paneled door (just the kind of door I had always wanted) and waited.

It took a few minutes before the door was opened. First I saw a dark shadow in the peephole—someone looked at me for a long time.

The door opened slowly, with the chain still on. I saw a nose and the lens of a pair of glasses, then the whole woman—small, gray-haired, intellectual.

"Hello," I said. "I'm Rosalinda Achmetowna and I'd like to speak to you about your son. About Michail," I added, so she knew I wasn't just bluffing, that I really knew him.

The eyes behind the glasses took on a look of concern. "Has something happened?"

"Depends on how you look at it," I said.

She took off the chain and let me in.

Rosenbaum's mother was round and tense. Her entire being gave off a sense of distrust. Nonetheless, she gave me a pair of slippers to slip over the skin-colored nylons on my delicate feet and led me into the kitchen, where she sat down and folded her hands in her lap.

She blinked, agitated. I wondered what she was expecting. The situation was clear: Rosenbaum was a Jewish mama's boy. Here in this place, lined with carpets and filled with heavy furniture, he had grown up like a frail flower in a greenhouse.

"It's about my daughter Sulfia," I said. "She's a very sweet girl."

Rosenbaum's mother blinked repeatedly.

"We're unbelievably excited about the baby," I said.

She opened her mouth and froze, a dumbfounded look on her face.

"It's so nice to have a chance to meet you," I said. "I'm sure our families will get along swimmingly."

She clutched at her chest.

"We're Tartars," I said. "And you're . . . well, anyway, my husband says all people are the same. The only important thing is that they have a sense of decency."

Rosenbaum's mother started to keel over.

Rosenbaum was upset with me because his mother had had a heart attack. He put the blame on me. I put it right back on him. He shouldn't try to make me responsible for his failure to tell his parents about Sulfia and about his imminent fatherhood.

One thing that spoke well of him: once Rosenbaum's mother had been released from the hospital he immediately arranged a get-together. He wanted his parents to invite us over. I wanted it the other way around. I wanted to show that Sulfia had a good family and that she would be a good mother. I knew Jews were very critical. That was something we had in common with them.

The Rosenbaums accepted my invitation. What else could they do? With this occasion in mind, I phoned the teacher of Russian and literature and asked to speak to my husband. I always called him "my husband" so the ownership of the title remained clear, this despite the fact that "my husband" sounded increasingly like "my problem."

He got on the phone and said, "Rosie, how nice to hear your voice."

I got right to the point.

I said, "Kalganow, your daughter is getting married."

He said nothing.

"Sulfia," I said, helping him along. "She found a man."

I told him what I wanted. The parents of the groom were coming to see us, to have dinner with us, and I wanted them to have a good impression of the family—first and foremost of the bride's parents.

"That's me and you," I clarified. "Do you understand?"

"But . . . " he said and fell silent again.

I sighed. Then I started to explain everything again from the beginning. I told him this had nothing to do with him coming back to me. It was just to create a good image. The Jews needed to have the impression that our family was whole. Kalganow breathed heavily into the phone. He'd been in better shape when he was with me.

"What is it?" I asked, annoyed. "Will you come or not? It's for your daughter's sake."

"For Sulfia," he said.

"Have you any other daughters?" I asked and hung up.

He would come. Of that I was sure.

112 · ALINA BRONSKY

Gefilte fish

I told Sulfia what she should wear. I didn't want to leave anything to chance this time. Even Sulfia seemed to understand this.

I had a feeling that the situation this time worked in our favor. Sulfia's ugliness and shyness would make her the perfect bride in the eyes of the Rosenbaums. She was modest and a nurse to boot. After all, the Jews knew what it was all about. Now all that was left to do was to cover up her shortcomings as a housewife.

First, I wanted to tell them that the meal I served them had been cooked entirely by Sulfia. I rummaged through cookbooks and asked co-workers and thought long and hard. I decided to make gefilte fish and *vorschmack*, and for dessert *tzimmes*. I'd be making all of these things for the first time in my life, which excited me. The *vorschmack* turned out to be the same as an appetizer I'd made every New Year's Eve for years. I put chunks of brined herring, moistened white bread, onion, and a large apple through a meat grinder and grated hard-boiled egg yolks with vinegar.

The gefilte fish turned out to be a sort of cold fishcake that took hours of my time only to taste like nothing at all. I didn't think the effort was worth it. The grated mixture of horseradish and red beets made up for that a bit, and I ate a large amount of it on white bread to make sure I had gotten it just right. As for the *tzimmes*, I decided not to hold myself responsible for the flavor. Braised carrots with raisins and dried plums, served with balls of cream of wheat—if that was what the Jews ate, there was no magic I could perform to improve things.

Sulfia dressed herself properly for once. That is, not particularly attractively, but at least appropriately for the occasion. Her knee-length gray dress looked cheap, but at least it was clean. She had pulled her hair into a ponytail like a schoolgirl.

It was obvious that a daughter-in-law like this wouldn't spend all the money on clothes.

Aminat had to be there, though I'd rather have been rid of her. I had worked so hard with her and had made a lot of progress, but she was still so unpredictable. But the Jews should see the whole family. Aminat was also the best evidence that Sulfia was capable of producing a pretty and healthy child.

I took Aminat aside and insisted to her that Sulfia would become sick if she, Aminat, acted out of line. Other than losing her cat Parasite, that was the only thing Aminat really feared.

An hour before our guests arrived, Kalganow rang the door-bell. He had on a gray suit that we had bought together once. Lint and threads hung from the arms, so I took a brush and cleaned it up. I retied his tie, too—at least Kalganow hadn't forgotten it. I had called him three times to remind him.

"Sit down somewhere and wait for the guests to get here," I said. "Don't make a mess or get yourself dirty."

"Yes, Rosie," he answered.

And then they arrived—the Rosenbaums, in their brown clothes made out of high-quality material. They brought Aminat a piece of halva and were all quite shy. Rosenbaum wasn't a big man, but his parents were tiny.

Sulfia hid herself behind my back. I grabbed her and shoved her in front of me. Then I pulled Aminat aside by her pigtail. She shouldn't steer all the attention to herself. Sulfia was the one who was supposed to be getting married.

Her conduct was exemplary. She faced Rosenbaum's parents, nearly as short as they were, very bashful, and smiled at the floor as red splotches spread across her face. I thought to myself: if I had such a mama's boy as Rosenbaum, I'd be quite pleased with a daughter-in-law like Sulfia. And indeed Rosenbaum's parents seemed to look on her favorably.

I sat Aminat next to me so I could monitor her at all times.

Sulfia I sat between the two old Rosenbaums. The young Rosenbaum sat beside me.

I instructed Kalganow to sit at the head of the table and, given the opportunity, to talk about his work—but not about anything else.

I had made just one mistake: I had forgotten to tell him that Sulfia was pregnant. And so it came to pass that we were in the middle of a perfectly smooth conversation about how children were the joy in life, and Rosenbaum's parents, like Kalganow, were poking at their fish with preoccupied looks on their faces, when Kalganow, pulling a bone from his mouth, cried, "But of course, we've got one already, and that's more than enough!"

Sulfia turned a shade of pink. I tried to kick Kalganow under the table. Then Rosenbaum's father wiped his lips with a napkin and started to make strange noises. I looked at his small mouth and tried to figure out what the sounds meant. Only gradually was I able to figure out he was giggling. Yes, giggling like some demented fool. God, he wasn't going to keel over, was he? Just because his son had impregnated a not-so-young Tartar girl? He pointed with his finger at the fish left on his plate and laughed himself senseless. I had just explained that Sulfia made these strange fishcakes once a week. (Somehow I'd be able to get her to master it by the time of the wedding, I thought. If I really wanted to, I could teach even a guinea pig to cook.) Then I said that all people were friends, something like what Kalganow had always told me at the beginning of our marriage. Then old giggling Rosenbaum lost his balance and his gray-haired head fell onto his plate.

His wife looked at him sternly and he straightened himself up again and kissed her on the temple. Then he reached across the table, took my hand, and kissed it. I wasn't sure for a second how to take this. His wife looked on rigidly, but not upset. Apparently he did this kind of thing often.

I found him gallant. My husband had never been so gallant. He, Kalganow, was now leaning slightly to the side. No, it couldn't be true. He was about to fall asleep at the table. How could he? What had the teacher of Russian and literature let him become? He was on the verge of falling out of his chair snoring, and nobody but me had noticed. Unfortunately I couldn't reach him to nudge him discreetly.

Something had to be done to distract the guests before he disgraced us all. I couldn't think of anything except setting the tablecloth on fire. I had a pack of matches in the pocket of my skirt; I always needed them for the gas stove. I decided to sacrifice my beautiful tablecloth to this higher cause. And as the flames began to dance up the cloth and everyone screamed and jumped up, nobody noticed how hard I yanked on Kalganow's ear in order to wake him.

The young Rosenbaum brought a bucket of water and dumped it on the dirty plates. Soon the fire was out. Kalganow looked around with an irritated look on his face, as if he no longer knew where he was. Dinner was over.

Rosenbaum went out laughing. His wife hissed and cursed at him—I could hear her from the staircase. Apparently the Jews lived just like normal people.

Rosenbaum and Sulfia wed on a bleak, cold winter day. The wedding was modest. It snowed nonstop, and as the bridal couple left City Hall, giant snowflakes stuck unmelted in Sulfia's black hair. Neither family had invited many guests. Rosenbaum's side thought big weddings were bourgeois. In reality they were just cheap, but I acted as if I took their reasoning at face value. I had decided it was wiser not to insult them before Sulfia had the ring on her finger. And anyway, as far as I was concerned it made sense—no reason to draw undue attention from potentially jealous people to the fact that Sulfia had once again somehow ended up with a good man.

She wore the bridal dress that Rosenbaum's mother had worn to her own wedding. They were both scrawny women, but that cream-colored dress could make a princess out of anyone. Even out of Sulfia. Her black hair was pinned up, the train reached to the ground, and her eyes glowed so with happiness that it was tempting to take her for pretty. She was now Sulfia Rosenbaum. I'd have to get used to that.

For the photos, Rosenbaum's father stood behind Sulfia and giggled the whole time. Rosenbaum's mother stood next to him holding her husband's arm and trying to keep him under control. I was grateful to Kalganow for leaving his teacher at home. The Rosenbaums didn't need to know the family wasn't whole until after the wedding.

Rosenbaum didn't move in immediately with Sulfia and Aminat. I was prepared to give him some time. Not too much, of course. By the time of the birth of the new baby he should have gotten used to being Sulfia's husband. Little by little, the newlyweds developed a certain rhythm. Rosenbaum began to stay with Sulfia and Aminat over the weekend, then also during the week. He brought things from home when he had a chance, homemade cookies, a piece of a roast, meatballs, or a jar of marinated tomatoes. He didn't boss Aminat around and he washed his own dirty dishes. He took his laundry home to mother Rosenbaum. It wasn't a situation meant for the long term, but it was perfect for Sulfia.

The end of the world

One night I was awakened by a bang. I quickly fell back to sleep. In the morning I pulled aside the heavy curtain on the window and was shocked. A huge black column of smoke curled up into the sky on the horizon. The main train station was in that area. Sulfia and Aminat lived in another direction, but I called them anyway. Aminat answered.

"Why aren't you at school?" I asked.

"Mama's crying," said Aminat. "Because of the explosion."

"She's not allowed to cry," I said.

I called my office and said I couldn't come in because of the explosion. They apparently knew more than I did because they didn't ask any questions. Out on the sidewalk, broken glass crunched beneath my boots. I raised my arm and a little orange Moskwitsch pulled over immediately. At the steering wheel sat a cheerful bearded man. I gave him Sulfia's address and cursed about the shards of glass that had ruined the soles of my shoes.

"Is your window cracked, too, lady?" the driver asked me.

I wiped my hand across the upholstery.

"This is unacceptable—it's a pigsty," I said.

"I asked whether your window was cracked."

"Why?"

"Because in our building a lot of windows are blown out."

"Did someone break them?"

"No—were you drunk last night? A tanker blew up at the main station."

By the time I got to Sulfia's, I knew everything. At the station, a rail car filled with something flammable went off the rails and slammed into another. There was a detonation that almost leveled some buildings in the area around the station and damaged a lot of others.

An emergency doctor was already there. Sulfia lay in bed pressing one hand to her belly and the other to her face. Tears dripped through her fingers.

"Michail's buried," Sulfia gasped when I pushed past the white lab coats to ask what was wrong with her this time.

"Aha," I said. "Don't get upset, daughter."

But Sulfia didn't listen to me, and became terribly agitated.

Her body shook with fits of crying. I could understand a little of this; she had just married, so this was a pity.

"Did he die immediately?" I asked.

She screamed at me: "Dead?! What are you saying? Why would you?"

"He isn't even dead?" I asked.

"Listen, lady, please wait outside the door," said the emergency doctor as Sulfia reared up like a lunatic.

A few minutes later she was carried past me on a stretcher. She reached for my hand.

"Mother, please promise me . . . "

"What?"

"That you'll take care of them."

"Of whom?" That I would take care of Aminat and that damn Parasite went without saying.

"Of Michail, mother, and father," whispered Sulfia.

"Mother and father?"

The medic wanted to get past me. I pulled my hand away from Sulfia and quickly wiped her cheeks dry.

"Have a nice time in the hospital, daughter," I said.

"Will you promise me that? That you won't leave them in a lurch?"

"My god, Sulfia, don't we have enough worries of our own?"

"Please!"

Against my will I nodded yes, and then remained in the apartment with a weeping Aminat and an intimidated Parasite, who now climbed out of the shoe rack where she had been hiding from all the strangers.

I was too honest and too good-natured. I kept my word once again. I began to make calls. Yes, the floor above the Rosenbaums' apartment had collapsed, as had some of their own walls. Mother and son Rosenbaum were basically uninjured. But a piece of the falling wall had put a dent in the old man's skull. He was now in the hospital, at Sulfia's surgery station. Everyone apparently crossed paths there. Except now Sulfia, who was in a gynecological unit.

A little while later the two healthy Rosenbaums stood in front of the door. The old woman was hysterical.

"Don't be so sad, my dear," I said as I let them into the apartment along with a heavy bundle that they were carrying like war refugees.

"My house was destroyed," his mother cried loudly, pulling at her hair, which was also a mess.

"But you're still whole," I said.

"My husband is badly injured," she sobbed.

"Men are tough," I assured her.

The woman was totally worked up. She certainly was a sensitive type—mustn't forget that my very first meeting with her had ended with an ambulance coming. At least now she was still standing. Though she looked like a homeless person; where were her poise and style? The young Rosenbaum stood behind her, looking around helplessly.

"Where's Sulfia?" he asked.

I explained that she was in danger of losing the baby because she had been so worried about him.

Rosenbaum sat down on a kitchen stool and covered his face with his hands. His mother broke into even louder shrieks of anguish.

"Oh, no!" she cried. "Not that, too! It's the end of the world!"

It took everything I had just to tolerate her, and on top of it all, Aminat was not handling the situation well. She always became strange when anything was wrong with Sulfia.

"Please be considerate of the child," I said sharply.

"This world is not good for children, no, it's not good for children," yammered the old Rosenbaum woman.

"CUP OF TEA?" I asked in a thunderous voice.

"Yes, mother, pull yourself together," said Rosenbaum, finally taking his hands away from his face.

"Our house was destroyed!" screeched his mother.

She went on about how she had awoken in the middle of the night and felt as though the end of the world was imminent. How the walls collapsed on her, how the ceiling crashed down and shelves fell over, how she crawled through the rubble to get into the next room to save her child.

"That child there?" I asked, pointing to Rosenbaum, who was helping himself to a poppyseed cookie from a jar.

"I don't have any others," she wailed.

"Calm down," I said. "My child just left for the hospital with sirens blaring and lights flashing while your child sits here happily munching on poppyseed cookies."

Rosenbaum's mother choked back her sobs.

"But where are we supposed to live?" she asked somewhat more sedately.

"Here," I said with a sigh. I knew this was what Sulfia had in mind.

The old woman looked around intently. The craziness in her eyes slowly faded.

"It is a pretty big apartment," she said matter-of-factly.

The moment I officially offered Sulfia's apartment as a refuge, the old woman managed to get over her shock and began to settle in. First she unpacked the bundle she had brought. Inside were some rags which apparently had once been her clothes and which she had heroically rescued as the world ended. Then she splashed around in the bathtub for a long time, probably using up all the shampoo Sergej had brought back from East Germany. There was very little left and I'd been saving it for Aminat. Rosenbaum's mother finally emerged wearing Sulfia's bathrobe. She had wet hair and rosy cheeks, fresh as a bride, and asked hurriedly: "So where am I sleeping?"

Rosenbaum himself had sat the entire time in the kitchen and stared at the wall. It must have been his way of worrying about Sulfia and the baby. I made sure his mother didn't try to install herself in Sulfia's nice bedroom. I figured it would be Sulfia's wish to have Rosenbaum himself sleep in the bedroom—after all, he was her husband and the father of the unborn child.

To his mother I said pleasantly but firmly: "In the living room."

Yes, she was disappointed. Clearly she had bet on Aminat's room. Though I was no Jew, I would have done the same. I was happy I'd been able to arrange everything without Sulfia. She would have given mother Rosenbaum Aminat's room or perhaps even her own.

We set up the sleep sofa together. I showed Rosenbaum how comfortable she'd be.

"It's upsetting to lose your home," said mother Rosenbaum while I put sheets on the couch, laid down a pillow, and spread out the comforter.

I asked the young Rosenbaum to look after Aminat. As long as he was here, he shouldn't sit around doing nothing.

Then I went to see the two patients. But first I walked all around town looking for vitamins. Normally this would have made as much sense as looking for a piece of gold in a compost heap. But I begged God for help and got it. By the end I was bathed in sweat, but I had procured a mesh bag full of oranges, two pounds of grapes, and a couple of newspapers.

For Sulfia I took underwear, two ironed nightgowns, a bathrobe, and a toothbrush. For old man Rosenbaum I had packed the old tracksuit Sergej had left behind when he moved out. Old Rosenbaum would have to roll up the sleeves and pant legs. The old Rosenbaum woman was in no shape to look after her husband, so I'd have to do everything, as usual.

First I visited Sulfia, who lay in a ten-bed room. When she caught sight of me she bravely tried to smile. She was attached to an IV drip and her eyes were red from crying. I unpacked my little presents and cleaned up her nightstand. The fruit came from the south and, naturally, was full of germs. I took the fruit to the sink and washed it carefully under running water, then went to the nurses to ask for boiling water to pour over the fruit. Predictably, they didn't want to give it to me, saying this wasn't a restaurant. But I reminded them that Sulfia was a colleague of theirs and that God saw everything. I got my water and was able to sterilize the fruit.

I put everything on the nightstand and shoved a grape between Sulfia's lips. I peeled an orange, segmented it and skinned it, and pulled off the white threads. I put the segments into Sulfia's mouth one after another.

"Chew it thoroughly," I said. Her eyes were tired and orange juice ran down her chin. I wiped the dribbles away with my handkerchief.

"I'll come again tomorrow," I said.

I left to find old Rosenbaum in the surgical clinic. Nobody would let me in to see him. He was still unresponsive; the dent in his head was apparently quite deep. I gave the nurses a few oranges to make sure they took good care of old Rosenbaum. Then I went home.

We came up with a system. It turned out that Rosenbaum could cook many different varieties of porridge. Not just oatmeal but also millet and buckwheat gruels, and on weekends he'd make sweet cream of wheat or rice pudding. In addition, he ironed Aminat's school uniform. His mother spent most of her time in front of the television, all the while talking about how television made people stupid. I cursed Sulfia when I figured out that she had given all her grapes away to the other patients in her room. Sulfia and Rosenbaum were sent home from the hospital at almost the same time.

This meant things were about to get very tight in the apartment.

The Rosenbaums showed no sign of looking for another place to live. I asked young Rosenbaum whether they had any other relatives or friends. He shook his head sadly.

Sulfia arrived home pale almost to the point of transparency. She moved with small, soft steps, always holding her belly as if she were afraid the baby might fall out. I told her she should eat more oranges. I looked for oranges to buy before and after work and during lunch. It got to the point where I was hardly ever at work anymore.

Then I received unexpected support in the form of Rosenbaum's mother. Whenever I wasn't around, she assumed my role and followed Sulfia around with pieces of orange, her slippers, and a blanket, and urged her to lie down, not to bend over, not to lift anything heavier than a toothbrush, and not to stand near the drafty window. Three times a day the old woman insisted Sulfia get in bed and wrap herself in blankets so she could open all the windows to make sure there was fresh air in the apartment.

Rosenbaum's father, on the other hand, should have stayed in the hospital for a year, I thought. He still wasn't himself. He wore bandages on his head that made him look like a mummy. He never giggled anymore. He spent all day sitting at the window in the spot where Sulfia wasn't allowed to sit because of the draft. He just stared vacantly. Sometimes he said things I couldn't understand; I assumed it was Yiddish. Then the old woman would always say, "Shhh, father, it was just a bad dream," even though he wasn't sleeping at all, but rather wide awake, sitting upright on a chair.

Once in a while Sulfia changed his bandages and stroked his hand. She spoke tenderly to him and he'd occasionally snicker like in the old days. In those moments the old woman would say, "My angel, don't worry about the old one. Look after yourself. There's no helping him now."

I agreed completely.

But Sulfia was obstinate. One day she just walked out. I was out again at the time. With tears in her eyes, the old woman told me how she had tried to keep Sulfia from leaving the apartment and had finally given up—"I couldn't wrestle with her physically—what if something were to happen?"

Sulfia returned soon after and she had a radio with her. It remained her secret where she had gotten it, but it didn't work anyway. She put it down on the windowsill in front of old Rosenbaum and gave him a screwdriver. His eyes lit up.

The old woman and I later rued the day we'd allowed Sulfia to bring that radio home. Because old Rosenbaum took the screwdriver in his hand and began to fiddle with it. After an hour, the windowsill was overflowing with countless little parts, screws, wires, and circuit boards. And whenever old lady Rosenbaum got near the mess with a cleaning rag, old Rosenbaum shrieked and waved his arms. He came off a bit like a hen protecting its eggs.

"Let him be," Sulfia begged from the bedroom.

"Out of the question," called the old woman and tried to approach him from the other side. Old Rosenbaum shoved her away with his fist.

"Now he's getting violent, too," said the old Rosenbaum woman tearfully. "Lie back down!" she said to Sulfia, who appeared with her bulging belly in the doorway.

"Let him be," begged Sulfia. "For my sake."

She put a hand on her belly.

The old woman found herself in a quandary. It was clear that Sulfia had declared old Rosenbaum's tinkering her own personal matter. Any attempt to clear away his mess would from now on be seen as a kick to Sulfia's belly. The Rosenbaum woman understood this. The hand in which she was holding the cleaning rag fell to her side and she looked at her husband with hatred.

"But why, little Sonja?" asked the Rosenbaum woman. "Look what a mess he's making. That's not good for the baby, either."

The matter seemed settled once and for all. Old lady Rosen-

THE HOTTEST DISHES · 125

baum could wipe up somewhere else with her rag and old man Rosenbaum could cover the living room with bits and pieces of the radio. But two days later all the parts had disappeared. I thought at first that the old woman had ignored Sulfia's orders and thrown everything out. Instead, all the parts were back inside the housing of the device. Rosenbaum had reassembled the radio. When he plugged it in it began to emit crackly voices speaking in English. Sulfia clutched her hands together and kissed the old man on his bald head. Later the same day she brought him another old radio and the whole process started over again.

Not my baby

Rosenbaum and Sulfia's daughter was born at exactly the same time that I succeeded in prying free a new apartment for the old Rosenbaum couple. To do so I had pounded down the doors of many different government agencies, shoved the paperwork concerning old Rosenbaum's head injury in front of countless officials, handed out pounds and pounds of chocolates from Sulfia's stockpile, and finally called Kalganow and demanded that as chairman of the union he fulfill his fatherly and grand-fatherly duties. From all of that emerged a one-bedroom apartment which had nothing of the old grandeur of the Rosenbaums' previous apartment, but which could be occupied immediately. Other victims of the explosion had to wait much longer for new accommodations. But they didn't have Rosalinda on their side.

It wasn't very big, but I considered that a plus: if things ever took a turn for the worse, Rosenbaum would think twice before beating a path for his parents' place. I knew that a lot of young fathers had such thoughts when a newborn arrived. I was only too happy to help the Rosenbaums pack their things back into sacks and boxes.

*

The new baby was undoubtedly a Rosenbaum. It was even bald like the father. It was a heavy girl with a big head. They named her Jelena. Lena. This child wasn't mine. It belonged to everyone. It was very ugly.

"I hope she improves quickly," I said the first time I saw her.

Everyone agreed except Aminat, who screamed at me angrily, "How can you say something so mean about my sister?"

Aminat of all people had immediately taken the new baby into her heart.

Sulfia and Rosenbaum wanted to put the crib in their bedroom, where it belonged. But Aminat insisted that her sister sleep in her room at night. Everyone was opposed, myself most of all: if anyone needed their sleep, it was nine-year-old Aminat. But first Sulfia and then Rosenbaum gave in. The crib was carried into Aminat's room.

Now my daughter Sulfia had a complete family. She had a husband who cooked a different porridge every morning and in-laws she worshipped. She had a big, exceptional daughter and a little ugly one, though the latter did come with a real father. She even had a cat.

I didn't take care of little Lena. I already had a granddaughter, and for the Rosenbaums Lena was their first.

They were odd. They came by constantly and rocked the bald-headed, goggle-eyed child. They made sure the refrigerator and soup pots were always full. The old Rosenbaum woman washed Lena's diapers and the young Rosenbaum ironed them on both sides.

Old Rosenbaum slowly became a bit more clear-headed. Sulfia put Lena in Aminat's old yellow stroller, covered her with a pillow, and old Rosenbaum pushed her through the park. If it had been my child, I would never have let her out with a brain-damaged old man. Sulfia seemed to share this thought at least at some level, because when old Rosenbaum was out in the park with Lena, she often stood at the window and watched. There was a good view of the park from the ninth-floor window.

Unlike Aminat, Lena was perpetually sick. She had bronchitis and diarrhea and allergies to everything under the sun.

Must have been the Rosenbaum genes.

I had often noticed that things I wished for frequently came true. A sign that God was with me. Occasionally He overshot the target, but that was only because I'd failed to formulate my wish precisely enough.

It came to pass, for instance, that a great many Jews were returning to their historical homeland during these years. Everyone knew somebody who wanted to emigrate to Israel. Even the Rosenbaum family, to whom my daughter now belonged, began to prepare to flee our country.

I found out one evening when I came by to check on Aminat's homework and fingernails. Sulfia sat in the kitchen crying, and Rosenbaum paced back and forth in the kitchen waving his hands as if swatting a swarm of mosquitoes. Aminat was playing in her room with little sniffling Lena.

"What's going on?" I asked.

They were going to emigrate in three months.

"It's not so bad," I told Sulfia. "It's nice and warm there."

I was assuming that Aminat would stay with me. What would she do all alone among all those Jews? I'd heard that in Israel there were sandstorms and that they didn't even have a proper alphabet.

"We will come visit," I said.

"Who is 'we'?" asked Sulfia, training her bunny-rabbit eyes on me.

"Aminat and I."

"Ah," said Rosenbaum.

Sulfia covered her face with her hands and groaned.

*

I was prepared to let Sulfia move far away with her new Jewish family. But Aminat emigrating was out of the question. Aminat was my child. I was happy that Sulfia had Lena now. Aminat was older, prettier, healthier. Aminat would be fine without Sulfia—she had me.

The situation was clear. I figured I could now move into Sulfia's apartment. Three rooms for me and Aminat, with no roommate and no cleaning schedule for common areas. It was a pleasing prospect. I just had to be careful not to let Klavdia get her hands on my two bedrooms. I was sure she wouldn't tell the housing authority I wasn't living in the communal apartment anymore. Because then they would reallocate the rooms in a blink of an eye, and the new neighbors would never be as nice, as friendly, and as helpful as I was.

Sulfia looked worse and worse (if that was even possible). I told her she needed to eat more vitamins. She'd need them in Israel. Books—all labeled *ulpan*—lay strewn about their apartment along with brochures such as "Welcome, New Citizen." Once I caught Aminat with one of the books in her hand. I went to take it away from her and said, "You don't need that."

She clutched the book and wouldn't let go as I tugged on it from the other side.

"Papa says I should read it," she said.

Suddenly she was calling Rosenbaum "papa." It was like earlier, when I had to stop her from calling every male stranger on the street "papa."

"You don't need it," I repeated, and succeeded in ripping the book away from her. As I did, the cover made an unpleasant sound. I placed the book as high on the shelf as possible so she couldn't reach it.

I went to Rosenbaum, who was reheating noodles from the previous night in a frying pan, and asked, "Have you told Aminat yet?"

"What?"

He looked at me through his thick glasses with a friendly look on his face.

"About Israel."

"Of course."

"So why should she read those crazy books then?"

"Because it's good preparation."

"For staying here?"

"No," he said in a friendly tone. "For emigrating."

"Aminat's not emigrating," I shot back. "Did you not understand that? Aminat's staying here, with me."

He shook the pan back and forth and busily stirred the noodles. Before he answered me, he reduced the gas flame and turned his face, red from the heat, toward me.

"Aminat is coming with us. That was clear from the start."

"But Sulfia . . . " I gasped. It felt as though someone had slammed my head against the wall. "But Sulfia!"

"For Sulfia," said Rosenbaum, dividing up the noodles onto four plates, "it was never a question. Believe me."

Poor sow

Something had gone wrong in my life. I should never have allowed Sulfia to take up with a Jew. This was the consequence. Now my own daughter was bound to a Jewish family by an ugly, chubby-faced baby. And they wanted to leave; they always wanted to leave, and I had nothing against it. But what gave them the right to destroy me? What did they imagine would happen? What was I supposed to do without Aminat? Here in this city, or on earth at all? If Aminat disappeared from my life, she would take all color and sound with her. And then there was no point to anything anymore.

Rosenbaum whirled around Sulfia's apartment now, putting things in boxes and hanging lists on the wall that he was constantly adding to or crossing things off of: "meet one last time with . . . " or "desperately need to get . . . " or "ask whether they want to have: what/who . . . " or "documents." He was very friendly to me, and behind the thick glasses the look in his eyes was so sympathetic as to be insulting.

I went to Sulfia's clinic so I could talk to her undisturbed.

I waited for her in front of the entrance, as I had so many times before. Poor sick people stood around, leaned against the wall, bandages on their heads, legs, or arms, cigarettes in their hands. I didn't even feel sorry for them anymore—because now I had it far worse than they did. They might be injured, but nobody had reached into their living bodies and ripped the very heart from their chests.

Sulfia emerged and walked right past me. She hadn't seen me. Then she turned around, looked at me, surprised, and walked back.

"Mother, what are you doing here, for God's sake?"

"I have to talk to you," I rasped.

"Then come to our place."

"No. I want to talk to you alone. Without him."

"Without whom?"

"Without him. You need to come to my place."

We took the trolley. Sulfia said nothing. She held her purse tightly in her lap. She finally had a nice handbag like a real woman. Brown leather with a gold closure.

"Nice handbag," I said, though the time for pleasantries was long past.

Sulfia opened the bag, took out her wallet, a folded cloth handkerchief, and her date book, and handed it to me. The bag was empty; I looked inside to make sure. Then I handed it back to her. I couldn't be bought off so cheaply.

I had difficulty unlocking the door. Every movement made

a dull echo in my soul. I looked my loneliness in the face and
it grimaced nastily back at me.

Without Aminat I would be alone and my life would have
no meaning. I explained this to Sulfia.

"Why do you want to kill me?" I asked her.

"We could try to take you with us," said Sulfia, avoiding
looking me in the eyes.

I'm not a piece of luggage, I wanted to shout, but said nothing. I was less than a piece of luggage. Unlike all their stuff,
they didn't actually want me with them.

"What would I do among all those Jews?" I asked. "And
what will my little girl do?"

"Aminat is *my* little girl, mother," said Sulfia.

I didn't know what else I could do at this point.

"Without Aminat I'll wither away," I said. "Please leave
Aminat here. I'll look after her well. I beg you. You're my only
daughter."

Sulfia stood slowly and straightened out her dress.

"I'm very sorry, mother. Truly. Very."

I didn't say anything more. I helped them pack. I went over
and helped Aminat pick out the toys and books she wanted to
take. I didn't want to make her sad too far in advance.

Aminat was in good spirits. She quizzed me about Israel.
That's when I realized she thought I'd be coming soon after
them. Sulfia had been clever. Aminat would happily go with
them, she'd wait for me—and she'd forget me.

One evening I knocked on Klavdia's door. She was now
broader than she was tall. Since the stream of men through my
door had stopped, she was both frustrated and resigned. She
was surprised at the way I looked. I had changed since I found
out I would be losing Aminat. I'd become a poor sow.

But I had a plan, and Klavdia would help me with it.

I told her that Sulfia wanted to take a huge stockpile of

sleeping pills with her to Israel because they were so expensive there.

"Does she want to resell them there?" asked Klavdia, businesslike.

"Of course. How many can you get hold of?" I asked.

Two days later I had fourteen packages of some pill. I didn't know anything about this kind of thing—I'd never taken any medications in my whole life. Klavdia still had moxie. When she sensed there was a chance to make some money at something, she didn't hesitate. She sympathized with me—less because of the imminent parting and more because from now on my daughter and granddaughter would be living among Jews. Klavdia was at odds with herself. On the one hand, she thought that any Jew who left the country was a good Jew. On the other, she begrudged them their sunny foreign destination. Klavdia thought the Mongolian steppes would be a much better place for them all to go.

My farewell

The Rosenbaums threw a big goodbye party on their last day. They wanted to party until their departure flight. The suitcases and boxes were packed, some sent ahead. The apartment was nearly empty. There was just a large table in the middle, and on it all the salads and cakes the guests had brought. Afterward, one of Rosenbaum's co-workers who owned a car was supposed to take the family to the airport. Their luggage would be transported in a separate car. No one said it outright, but the duty to clean up after the party fell to me. I didn't say anything—cleaning up wasn't going be a problem for me.

Aminat sang and danced and threw around strange words she'd picked up in her *ulpan* books. I sat silently on a chair and watched how Sulfia was hugged by countless people I'd never before seen in my life, how old Rosenbaum spent half the night drying his tears with Sulfia's handkerchief, how promises were exchanged never to forget one another. I was probably the only one who knew at that moment that such promises are never kept.

Shortly after midnight I stood up. Tired Aminat had curled up on a mattress in the room she had shared with her sister. She held little sleeping Lena in her arms. I leaned down and kissed Aminat on her sweaty forehead.

Nobody noticed as I slipped out of the apartment. I hailed a taxi on the street and rode home. I gave the driver a big banknote and he obviously thought I was drunk. I told him always to be nice to other people. Now he thought I was insane.

At home I grabbed the sleeping pill packets, a glass, and a bottle of milk and went to my room. I undressed, threw on my bathrobe, and went to the bathroom. I washed myself thoroughly and then made myself up. I couldn't have done it any more meticulously if it had been for my own wedding. Of course, marriage could be tried more than once, death usually not.

I liked what I saw in the mirror. My cheeks were pale with powder, and together with my black eyes and red lipstick, I looked beautiful and eternally young. Just a shame no one would think to take a picture of me in the coffin.

I sat down on the bed and began to open the packets and squeeze the pills from the blister packs. They fell onto the bedcovers and I shoveled them into a pile with my hands. I threw them in my mouth ten at a time, chewed them up, and washed them down with half a glass of milk. I hadn't noticed any effects beyond an unusually strong heartbeat.

I realized I hadn't left a farewell note. But it wasn't necessary. I wouldn't be found until after Aminat and Sulfia had already arrived in Tel Aviv. Sulfia would probably have to fly back to take care of the funeral. Oh well, she'd just have to get through it.

Now I felt strange. I couldn't tell whether I had a stomachache or I was dizzy. I heard my pulse racing in my temples and pressed my head in my hands. At the same time I could tell I was about to throw up. That couldn't happen. I shoveled some of the remaining tablets into the empty glass, poured in a little milk, and mixed it up with a spoon. The tablets didn't dissolve, so I tried to break them up and realized my fingers were no longer responding. I was probably half dead. I poured the pill porridge into my mouth, filled the glass with milk, drank it down, and lay down quickly under the blankets. I folded my hands and closed my eyes. My second to last thought was of Aminat and my last of God.

Just us

When I reopened my aching eyes, I saw Sulfia, who, with her eyes averted, was measuring my blood pressure. I closed my eyes again and tried to think.

I remembered the goodbye party, Aminat's sweaty forehead, her cheek pressed to the mattress, and her arm holding little Lena in her sleep. That was my misfortune: I was about to lose Aminat to the land of the Jews just because Sulfia had married a Rosenbaum. It was light outside, and Sulfia, who should have long since transferred to an airplane in Moscow bound for Tel Aviv, stood before me in the flesh, packing up her blood pressure cuff. I must have missed something.

Sulfia stood up and went to the window. I opened my eyes a bit and looked at her skinny back. On the windowsill were two large bags, and Sulfia rummaged around in one of them now.

I felt my body under the covers. I had on a different nightgown. Someone had changed me. I touched my hair to check on the state of it. I wet my fingers with saliva and felt my eyelashes. Someone had changed me and washed my face.

I didn't realize right away that Sulfia had turned back around and was looking at me. It was too late to close my eyes again. I looked back at her silently.

"How do you feel?" she asked without smiling.

"What are you doing here?" I asked. Speaking proved difficult. My throat was raw and dry.

Sulfia didn't answer.

"Where's Aminat?" I wheezed.

Sulfia left and returned with a half-filled glass of water. She put her hand under my back and pulled me upright. She held the glass to my lips. I took a sip of water. The cold moisture hurt my throat.

"Where's Aminat?"

Sulfia put the glass down on the windowsill.

"At school."

"And the Rosenbaums?"

Sulfia turned to face the window, with her back to me.

"In Tel Aviv."

"And you? When are you flying there?"

"I'm not."

"And Lena?"

"What about Lena?"

"Where is she?"

Sulfia turned and looked at me with dull eyes.

"Lena is in Tel Aviv. Sleep now, mother."

It was just us again: Aminat, Sulfia, and me, with no men, no new children, in two huge apartments, one of which was unfurnished. That's why Aminat and Sulfia had moved in here, into the room where the two of them had lived just after Aminat's birth.

"She's afraid that you'll do something to yourself again," Klavdia told me in the kitchen. But that was nonsense. Why would I do something to myself now that my darling was with me again?

Sulfia never talked about that night, the one during which she had decided not to get on the plane. She must have changed her mind in the space of a few hours. I never found out what made her come after me, or what happened when she did. She had obviously saved me without the help of a medic, because otherwise I'd have awoken not in my own home but locked in a psychiatric ward as suicidal. I could tell Klavdia knew more than she let on, and I suspected something was wrong with her tablets—they were too cheap and apparently didn't have enough active ingredient.

My throat burned for a long time, and my stomach was shredded and raw, as if I'd puked up rocks. I didn't complain. I lay in bed, hands folded over the covers, and Sulfia stayed with me. Sometimes I had the feeling that the blankets were too warm. I didn't have to say anything. Sulfia could tell from the look on my face. She shook the blankets out and turned them over. She was my daughter and I'd spent a lifetime taking care of her. Now it was her turn to do something for me.

While Sulfia shook out the blankets, wiped my face with a moist towel, gave me things to drink, injected me with this and that, and monitored my blood pressure, Aminat fumed in the next room. Through the wall I could hear her stomping her feet and jumping up and down, slamming herself against the wall, and throwing things around. It was as if she'd gone mad. Sometimes she screamed, and then Sulfia would leave and go into the next room. I heard her dry whispers. Aminat would quiet down.

While I was sick, Aminat didn't come into my room a single time. At first I was glad. I was too weak, and I wouldn't have known what to say to her. Then I began to miss her. I asked Sulfia about her. Sulfia said I was still too weak and Aminat too ill-behaved. I understood what she meant. Aminat wouldn't be able to control herself around me; she'd scream and rant and say things to me that she'd bitterly regret some-time after my death, which had been delayed for now.

If I hadn't been found in time, she would have shed a few tears in Tel Aviv and perhaps called out my name in the night until the memories of me eventually faded. I would have become just a photo on her wall.

Now everything would be different. The Rosenbaums would be bathing in the Dead Sea alone.

Sulfia went back to work at the surgical clinic, Aminat went back to school, and I had sufficiently recovered to take a few strolls around the block, though I did stop frequently to catch my breath. Sulfia was transformed into an old woman in a matter of a few days. It mustn't last, I thought to myself—with such an embittered expression on her face she'd never get another man.

Aminat had changed, too. She had stopped throwing fits. She became an oddly quiet child, never said a word too many, and came straight home from school and did her homework. When she was finished, she would lie on the bed with her face to the wall.

"What's her problem?" I asked Sulfia. "Promise her we'll take a beach holiday soon. Rosenbaum should send you money. Surely he's rich by now."

Sulfia looked at me and said, "What are you talking about the beach for? She misses her sister."

Of course. Now I saw it, too. Aminat was longing for that chubby-faced baby with the messy fluff on her head. She had stashed photos in her books and notebooks: Lena on a rocking horse, Lena with an apple, Lena on her potty. She never mentioned her sister, but photos slipped out all over the place, and Aminat quickly gathered them up and tucked them back into her things.

Sulfia never mentioned Lena either. When in the evening

she went into the room she was sharing with Aminat I heard only silence. They didn't speak to each other. I had the feeling they were both refusing to speak about the same thing.

Meanwhile the phone continued to ring at our place. Aminat would run to the foyer and grab for the phone. Initially Rosenbaum called often. He reported that they had settled in well, said how hot it was, explained that they were living in an empty apartment—just the four of them—and then that they'd gotten some secondhand furniture from the neighbors. How they were attending language classes, how he sorted fruit at a stand early in the morning because there was no other work, how his mother was in poor health but his father was thriving.

"Let me talk to Lena," Aminat pleaded, and then I heard her shout, "Lena, it's your big sister Aminat!" and then whisper things into the phone that only Lena was supposed to hear. "Now you tell me something," she demanded, and was quiet for a little while.

Lena couldn't talk at all yet. At two, she was a little overdue. Rosenbaum probably took the phone away from Lena quickly because it was expensive to call. Aminat went to her room and closed the door. The silence pressed against the walls.

One day a letter of several pages arrived from Rosenbaum, which, according to the postmark, had been in transit for two months. On the stamps were contorted letters, and the address sounded like something from another world. In the envelope were photos: Lena at the beach, in front of a stone wall, and eating an ice cream.

"She's gotten so big!" said Aminat, though Lena looked exactly the same as she had before her departure. She was wearing strange things. A t-shirt with a cartoon mouse on it, a sunhat, and wet shorts. There was a deserted sandy beach in the background.

THE HOTTEST DISHES · 139

Aminat spent hours looking at the photos, unlike Sulfia, who took only a fleeting look at them and then looked away.

"Look, mama," said Aminat.

"Yes, yes, sweetie," said Sulfia.

"You have to see this!"

"I already have, sweetie."

Sulfia didn't read Rosenbaum's long letter, either. Aminat really wanted to know what it said, but she couldn't decipher the erratic handwriting. So I read it to her. For the most part Rosenbaum just enumerated all the products available in the stores and their prices, but he also wrote that Lena's first word was in Hebrew and that they couldn't wait to welcome the missing members of the family so they'd be whole again. At that point I stopped and peered over the edge of the letter at Aminat, who was looking at me through narrowed eyes.

I folded the letter. Aminat ripped it out of my hand and went to her room.

Sulfia, you need a foreigner

Times were getting tougher.

Sulfia moved through the day like a ghost and Aminat began to adopt the same facial expression as her mother: the corners of her mouth hung down and her eyes stared off into space. I noticed that neither of them had any respect for me anymore, either. Sulfia and Aminat looked politely in my direction when I offered my thoughts on the weather or the ruble's nosedive, but their faces betrayed the fact that they couldn't wait for me to finally stop talking.

Times had changed outside, too. The shelves in the grocery stores were empty. It was a struggle to get enough to eat. Before I went shopping, I first returned all the empty milk and kefir bottles, thoroughly rinsed, for the deposits, carefully counting the coins I got back. With that money I bought bread and potatoes. Fortunately I had my garden outside the city, which got us through these times. My cucumbers and tomatoes grew in a greenhouse. The bus ride to the garden took nearly two hours. I would have preferred to call Kalganow so he could drive us there in his car and, more importantly, drive us back with our boxes of vegetables and baskets of fruit. I took Aminat with me, and she wandered silently between the plant beds and picked chives and stuffed them in her mouth by the bushel. She needed vitamins.

We didn't let anything go to waste. Sulfia spent hours on a ladder, a bucket hanging from a rope around her neck, picking sea buckthorn berries for marmalade. It was hard work, and I was happy Sulfia didn't complain, even when thorny branches cut her hands and juice from burst berries ran into the cuts and burned. For nights on end I stood in the kitchen sterilizing the canning jars filled with tomatoes, peppers, cucumbers, and mushrooms, with marmalade and compote, and dreamed occasionally of having a freezer.

Politics didn't interest me. I stopped reading the papers, too, because there were things in there that further depressed me. I didn't need bad news from the paper. I could see everything with my own eyes. While the economy imploded, I made sure my family didn't go hungry. The rows of canning jars stacked neatly in the bedroom and covered with old wool blankets served as a daily reminder that without me, life would be impossible. But things still got more and more difficult. It was a stroke of luck when you could buy sugar, for instance, and I needed it for the marmalades and for my tea fungus.

We had long since gotten used to food rationing. It was nothing new for someone from the housing authority to sit in the staircase and have all the residents line up to get coupons that entitled them to purchase a certain amount of sausage or sugar. The difficulty was actually using the coupons. As soon as I heard there was sugar for sale someplace, I immediately dropped what I was doing at work and went straight there. I always had Sulfia's, Aminat's, and my coupons with me just in case. I traded sausage coupons with my coworkers for sugar coupons. I had decided the vitamins in my marmalade were better than the mix of gristle, skin, and paper they called sausage, and which took a lot of luck to get hold of anyway.

At some point I had to concede that I would no longer be able to service the tea fungus's enormous appetite for sugar. I took it to my garden and threw it on the compost pile, though it hurt me to my soul.

If there was one thing I would really like to have had during this time, it was a cow. Milk had become a rarity. Near our building was a pavilion with an automated milk dispenser, where people took milk cans and empty three-liter bottles to fill. Long lines formed in front of the pavilion, and murmurs would race through the line when the dispenser had run out. Of course, in front of most of the milk dispensaries hung signs that read "No Milk Today." I couldn't understand why milk would suddenly become so scarce. Where were all the dairy farmers? Had the endless grasslands of our country been abandoned?

The same mystery surrounded eggs. It had been a long time since I had eaten an egg. A woman who lived upstairs kept a live chicken in her kitchen. Once in a while she took it out and let it pick through the flowerbeds outside. I was wildly envious.

Aminat's school building was too small to hold all the students, and there were too few teachers. Her class now had the afternoon shift: her school day began at two. She came home after dark. Mornings she hung around by herself. When I finished work early enough, I would pick her up from school in the evening. A lot of girls went missing in broad daylight during those years only to be found raped and murdered in the basements of random buildings.

Letters from Tel Aviv became shorter and less frequent. Eventually all that came were postcards for birthdays. Every card said basically the same thing, with only slight variations: "We send best wishes, optimism, and sunshine." Lena had long hair in the photos. International calls, which were recognizable by the different ringtone, became very seldom and very short, and the conversation was always the same. We didn't have anything more to say to each other.

"Sulfia," I said one morning, "you need a man."

She was stirring a spoonful of coffee powder into her cup. The canister was nearly empty; in two days we'd have no more coffee, with little chance of getting more for a long time to come. I didn't think I had said anything special. But Sulfia, calm, ugly, bitter-looking Sulfia, threw her cup to the floor and began to scream.

She screamed that I should never again interfere in her life, a life I had already destroyed, this time forever, broken her heart, robbed her of her dear little daughter, taken away her family, shattered her future, and chained her and poor Aminat to me.

It was clear that Sulfia was on the verge of a nervous breakdown. Which is why I didn't let her words bother me. In her moments of madness she sometimes said hurtful things. But I didn't hold a grudge.

"Sulfia," I said tenderly, "it's for Aminat's sake, don't you see? She has no future in this country. It will eat her up and won't even spit out the bones. You need to find a foreigner, Sulfia."

Sulfia sat down on the floor right next to the puddle of coffee and the shards of the broken cup and broke down in tears.

She had just signed some divorce papers. Rosenbaum had asked her in a very amiable way to take this step. Based on her behavior, he had concluded that she never really intended to join him; he had given up hope and fallen in love with another émigré in Tel Aviv.

Sulfia signed everything and gave the papers to a man who had introduced himself as an emissary and lawyer for the Rosenbaum family. He spoke good Russian, but with a velvety accent. He seemed pleasantly surprised that everything had been so easily resolved. When he left, he kissed both me and Sulfia on the hand and said Rosenbaum intended never again to set foot on Russian soil.

I looked him up and down, from his bald head to his expensively shod feet, and let him leave. He wore a showy, unmistakably new wedding ring.

The comotose German

I wouldn't be easily defeated. I prayed to God for another chance for Sulfia. Aminat needed to grow up someplace where milk was available for purchase everyday, not just on lucky days. And it shouldn't be someplace hot and full of Jews. It should be someplace like, perhaps, Europe.

God answered my prayers more quickly than I had expected. In fact, that same day a foreigner was brought into Sulfia's nursing station. A fantastic foreigner: early forties, clean, in a coma— and German.

I heard about him when Sulfia and Aminat were arguing about foreign languages in the kitchen. Aminat would soon be entering the fifth grade and had to decide between English and German. Aminat said there was no reason to learn German because nobody spoke it. Sulfia contradicted her: just three days ago a man had been admitted who would speak German as soon as he regained consciousness. I perked up my ears.

"Does he have a wedding ring?" I asked immediately.

Sulfia shook her head. The German had been found unconscious on the street, apparently beaten and robbed, she said. He didn't have a briefcase with him, but fortunately he did have a passport. It was possible he'd had a wedding ring and it had been stolen.

"No, no," I said. "Wedding rings don't come off so easily. They would have to have cut off his finger."

Sulfia rubbed the sleep from her eyes.

"What's his name?" I asked.

"Dieter Rossman."

"What a nice name!" I said. "And you're taking care of him? Has he said anything to you yet?"

"I already said he was unconscious, mother."

"Sulfia," I said, "this is your last chance."

This comatose German revitalized our family. We had something to talk about. Every day I asked Sulfia how he was. At first she brushed me aside, annoyed, but eventually she began to talk about him. She always worried about her patients. Dieter appeared to be all alone in our city. Nobody had turned up looking for him. It wasn't even clear whether he had been staying at a hotel or in someone's home, or what he had been doing here.

"You have to be there when he wakes up," I insisted.

"Oh, mother," said Sulfia. But this exact approach had already yielded two husbands.

"How does it work," I asked, "when somebody like that wakes up from a coma—can they speak right away?"

"It varies a lot, mother. But for the most part, no."

"And can you tell right away whether or not the person can remember things from before the accident?"

"Only gradually, mother. It takes time when someone is so badly injured."

"And if you were to tell him that you were his Russian fiancée, would he believe you?"

"Please don't talk such nonsense, mother," said Sulfia. She had no respect for me anymore.

She was also always busy. We had grown accustomed to the fact that hot water came out of the tap only occasionally and that otherwise we had to heat it on the stove. I thought nothing could shock us anymore. And then came the first winter in ages when the water was shut off completely, time and time again, for days on end, and I felt the pain of life without men. I was still weak, and for the most part Sulfia had to go to the water station a kilometer away and carry home two full buckets, taking small steps so as not to spill a drop. Once home she spent a long time rubbing her hands and the small of her back.

When I told her she should wear her hair up at work but let a few playful strands trail down her forehead, or when I offered to do her hair for her, or suggested she wear a nice skirt under her nurse's apron, Sulfia just rolled her eyes.

One overcast evening the doorbell rang. Sulfia had the late shift and Aminat was still at school. Through the peephole I saw a round, clownishly distorted face and an oversized bald pate. I threw open the door and found my husband Kalganow, who had left me a long time ago for a teacher of Russian and literature. His body was hunched to one side, the result of his holding a huge suitcase in his hand.

"Forgive me, Rosie," he said.

I stepped aside to let him into the apartment. I was too shocked to do anything else. And he looked sort of pitiful. He walked in, put his bag down on the floor, closed the door, and turned to me.

"My love, I'm back now," he said, and, to my horror, wrapped me in his arms.

It took my breath away. He smelled like an unwashed, sick old man. I wasn't used to it anymore.

I pushed him away.

"Tea?" I asked.

I hadn't had any visitors in a long time and I wanted to know what had gotten into Kalganow.

He sat down at the kitchen table as naturally as if this were still his home.

"I'm happy to be served by you, Rosie," he said.

"It's not easy out there these days," I said, so he wouldn't get the idea that I was going to put a plate of food in front of him.

"Particularly for a single woman," said Kalganow meaningfully, taking my hand and putting it to his lips.

"What's gotten into you?"

Kalganow's brow furrowed.

"It was a huge mistake, Rosie. But you were always so strong. I never thought that you'd suffer so badly."

"What?" I asked.

"Please, don't ever do it again, my beautiful wife," said Kalganow, getting off the chair, scooting toward me on his knees, and placing his head in my lap.

I jumped up in surprise and caught his jaw with my knee. He groaned and wrapped both his arms around my legs. I found the feeling of his hands on my skin uncomfortable. As far as I was concerned, he'd lost the right to grope me. I put my hands on the table and carefully moved my legs. He just held on to me more tightly.

"Kalganow, sit back down," I demanded. "I want to look you in the face."

He sat back down on his chair and looked at me sadly.

"Why didn't you tell me?" he asked.

"What on earth are you talking about?"

"The fact that without me, you lost the will to live."

"Without you . . . ," I repeated. "The will to live?"

Now he put on his trustworthy face.

"I know everything, Rosie. Our daughter told me everything."

"Our daughter."

"Sulfia."

"Who else."

Kalganow took a sip of his tea and pulled the sugar bowl toward himself.

"A little bitter," he said as he shoveled four spoons of sugar into his cup. I began to shake inside—this was the last of our sugar, and I used it to sweeten Aminat's oatmeal.

"You know, through it all, I never forgot you."

"Clearly," I said.

"I did what I could," said Kalganow. "I know how proud you are, so I did it secretly."

I wanted to ask what he meant, but then I remembered the banknotes I'd find in my pockets. He had a key the whole time and had come and gone and filled my shelves and drawers without me ever noticing. To thank him now, however, seemed a bit much.

"You were never alone," said Kalganow. "As long as I live, I'll be with you. And afterward, too."

I looked at him silently.

"Now we'll stay together forever, Rosie," said Kalganow.

His hand started to wander across the table toward mine. Sulfia had set a trap for me.

That night I took a bottle of vodka and knocked on Klavdia's door. Klavdia was lying in bed watching a concert on the screen of her tiny black-and-white television set, but with the sound turned off. I closed the door behind me and leaned backward against it. Meanwhile Kalganow was talking to Aminat about her grades. She answered civilly but curtly—she didn't really know who he was anymore.

"What is it?" asked Klavdia. I hoisted the bottle. Klavdia's eyes began to gleam.

"Hang on, hang on," she said. "Just a second. Don't go anywhere."

She took two empty glasses from the windowsill and put them down on the little table next to the bed. I poured, we clinked our glasses without a word. She drained half of hers. I took a sip. That was enough to start my tears flowing.

"He waaaants me baaaaack," I sobbed as Klavdia refilled her glass.

"Yikes," she said. "What on earth's gotten into him?"

"He thinks I can't live without him."

"Pig," said Klavdia.

I told her about my dilemma—that I didn't know whether to take Kalganow back or leave him outside the door, because it probably wouldn't be bad to have a man in the house in such tough times. But that the idea of lying next to him in bed seemed unbearable.

Klavdia nodded sympathetically, without taking her eyes off the television screen.

"I just can't!" I howled.

Klavdia said, "Then kick him out!"

"But he always slipped money to me, and we need to count our pennies."

"Then let him stay."

"Keep the bottle," I said and left the room.

I went to the phone, opened a drawer, and found the piece of paper with the telephone number of the teacher of Russian and literature, written down years ago and rarely touched since. It was late, but nobody was ever considerate of me, either. I dialed the number and it was answered immediately. She had been sitting by the phone waiting.

"This is Rosalinda Achmetowna," I said courteously. "Please excuse me for disturbing you so late, but my husband is suddenly back here. Did you possibly have an argument?"

She said nothing.

"Can you hear me?" I asked. "Could you possibly pick him up? I would like to go to bed. Take a taxi. He'll give you the money back."

She hung up. I waited ten minutes and went into my bedroom. Kalganow was sitting on the edge of the bed in his underwear and an undershirt as if he'd never left.

"Your teacher called," I said. "She can't fall asleep without you. She's picking you up."

"What?" he asked.

"Get dressed. Don't keep her waiting."

"What?" he asked again.

When she rang the door, I'd just convinced him to get dressed. I gave him his heavy suitcase and sent him out into the foyer. He opened the apartment door, and I heard the clap of a smack in the face and Kalganow moaned sorrowfully. The door clicked shut. I went into the foyer and locked it.

The next morning I woke up well rested. I went into the kitchen and found Sulfia sitting at the table with her head resting on her hands, which were folded on the tabletop. Sometimes she was so tired after work that she fell asleep sitting up.

I touched her shoulder. She lifted her head and looked at me. Her hands shook, her lips were swollen and bitten, and her eyes had a maniacal glint.

"Dieter came out of the coma," said Sulfia.

It turned out that Dieter Rossman had blue eyes and spoke a little Russian. He didn't remember the accident, but he did know who he was and what unusual concern had brought him to our cold city.

"You have to talk to him a lot," I insisted. "You have to

become his one and only while he's lying in bed and you're caring for him."

"Oh, mother," said Sulfia.

But she finally listened to me. Before work she made up her eyes and lips and let me put waves in her black hair with the curling iron. It gave her hair a bit more body. I tried quickly to remember as much as I could of the German vocabulary I'd learned in school and taught it to Sulfia. "Good day," "How are you," "Hands up," "My name is Sulfia, and what is yours," and "It's a pleasure to meet you."

Unfortunately I didn't know how to ask, "Are you married or engaged?" But Sulfia said Dieter knew how to say all the important things in Russian anyway.

"It doesn't matter," I said. "If you make an effort to speak his language, you'll immediately have a key to his heart."

"Oh, mother," said Sulfia, though she wasn't as stubborn as usual.

"Germany is a good country," I told her. "I've heard they wash the streets with shampoo there."

I tried to understand what Dieter was doing in our city. He was the only foreigner I'd ever heard of here. Sulfia said he was some sort of journalist and was writing some sort of book.

"A book about what?" I asked.

I'd heard about foreign journalists before, but nothing good. They illegally gained access to our orphanages and prisons and wrote about sex trafficking and HIV infections.

Dieter wrote about food, said Sulfia.

"What about food?" I asked.

"About our national cuisine," said Sulfia. He had already traveled around the Caucuses and wanted to go to the villages of the Ural Mountains to track down more recipes from our multiethnic country.

"Recipes?" I said, confused.

We'd all had the same recipes here for a long time: noodles

with butter, sausage with boiled potatoes, oatmeal with old marmalade, tea with rock-hard cookies. Those were the only foodstuffs you could get hold of without connections.

"What would a man want with recipes?" I asked Sulfia. "Is he gay?"

"He's writing a book," she repeated.

"Have you told him yet that you're Tartar?"

She shook her head.

"Oh, boy, are you stupid, Sulfia. Tell him he should visit us. Explain to him that I'll tell him all about Tartar cuisine—tell him I'll give him old, secret Tartar recipes passed down from generation to generation."

"Then what?"

"Sulfia," I said, "just do it."

A foreign idiot

It took a few months before Dieter was sufficiently recuperated to accept my friendly offer.

During that time, I felt as if I had gotten to know him quite well. Sulfia seemed to have established a good rapport with him. Sometimes I wondered why her coworkers didn't fight her over such patients. Then I realized—Sulfia's men had faults. You could tell at first glance that Sergej was a skirt chaser and Michail a Jew. I knew too little about Dieter. He was a foreigner, yes, but whether he was much of a catch wasn't clear at first glance. He apparently had no relationships and little money— otherwise he wouldn't have spent several months in Sulfia's care in a ten-bed hospital room without receiving a single visit. It was fitting that Sulfia's foreigner wasn't the luxury model. But Dieter Rossman was certainly better than nothing.

He had blue eyes, a snub nose, and a small mouth. His face

reminded me of a pig. He was wearing a leather jacket, and beneath that a coarsely knit sweater he'd probably bought at a bazaar from some old lady.

He looked pale and malnourished, but still had a big stomach. When I went to give him slippers, he lifted a foot to show me his thick woolen socks that matched the sweater. If he hadn't been a foreigner and our situation so dire, I would have decided at that moment that Sulfia could just as well grow old in peace without a man.

Dieter had a look that must have attracted small-time criminals on the street. His smile said, "I'm new here and don't have the slightest clue. Please take all my money and punch me in the head."

I invited him to the table with a smile so sugary sweet that the corners of my mouth hurt.

It wasn't so easy in these meager times to put something on the table. I got hold of some old beef that had been several times deep-frozen and thawed, but I was missing butter, eggs, and sour cream. I tried to make up for that with carrots, potatoes, and sour pickles from my garden. We sat down at the table and I was already sorry about the effort and the money I'd sunk into this.

Dieter sat across from Aminat and looked at her intently.

"Is this also your daughter?" he asked me in his funny Russian.

"*No, that is her daughter,*" I said, pointing to Sulfia.

My German was improving with every sentence.

"*How are you?*" I asked. "*Does your head still hurt?*"

I filled Dieter's bowl with a kvass soup into which I'd cut vegetables. It was actually a summer dish, but at least I had the ingredients. Dieter took his napkin, unfolded it, and spread it across his lap.

"Don't stare," I said quietly to Aminat.

"She looks like you," said Dieter to me.

"Who?" I asked.

"She," Dieter said, pointing his spoon at Aminat.

"That's right," I said proudly.

Dieter ate oddly. He skewered pieces of vegetable with his fork, guided them into his mouth, and closed his eyes. As he chewed his eyeballs moved beneath his closed eyelids. We were all a bit embarrassed. Sulfia and I averted our eyes at the same time. Aminat snorted. I kicked her under the table. Dieter swallowed and opened his eyes. He picked up his wine glass, raised it to his mouth, and sniffed at it extensively.

"The wine's not gone off," I said hurriedly. Sulfia had received it as a gift, but naturally I didn't say that.

Dieter moved his eyebrows, which crawled around his pig face like two fat caterpillars, and took a sip. It looked disgusting: instead of swallowing, he slurped the wine from one cheek to the other as if he were rinsing his mouth to dull a toothache. The only thing left was for him to start gargling it.

"I've heard that you collect recipes," I said, so he would stop eating. I was practically nauseous. It was easier for Sulfia. As a nurse, she was used to much worse.

Dieter finally swallowed the wine.

"Oh yes, oh yes," he said with his childlike delivery.

"And what do you do with them?"

He took a corner of the napkin in his lap and dabbed at the grease on his lips.

"I'm writing a book," he said.

"What about, if I may ask?"

"About recipes, just recipes," said Dieter. "Old, original recipes."

"And who will make the recipes—your wife?" I asked unhopefully.

"I am a person who is not with a woman married," is how Dieter formulated his answer in his funny Russian.

"Then your mother?"

"God forbid."

I was getting a headache. Dieter smiled broadly.
"I cook," he said. "I, I, I."
"Oh," I said.
A foreign idiot. As if we didn't have enough of our own.

I could hardly wait for him to leave. He stubbornly remained seated, however. He probably felt comfortable here. Because he ate in such tiny bites and chewed for such a long time, it took forever for us to work from one course to the next. I waited for him to ask questions about the dishes, but he didn't. He ate my born-out-of-necessity delicacies as if they were the-day-before-yesterday's mashed potatoes. I was a bit relieved, though, that I didn't have to provide him with commentary and answers. I had tried to remember the dishes Kalganow's country relatives prepared, but they certainly weren't the types of things that would interest the German. And in order to get the right ingredients for them I would have to have been a magician. I had decided that in a pinch I would just lie and make up recipes and say they had been passed down from generation to generation. But I was also happy to be able to put that off.

Between the main dish and the dessert, Dieter suddenly asked Aminat to show him her room. I pinched her under the table. They withdrew together and I cleared the dirty plates with Sulfia and put out the clean ones. We put a new tablecloth out. I pulled out the dessert of my own invention—a sort of cold cake made out of ground-up butter cookies, margarine, and apples.

Then I went to Aminat's room, stood behind the partially closed door, and eavesdropped. Dieter was playing with Aminat's things. He had taken a little stool, covered it like a table, and placed three of her old puppets and a teddy bear around it. Aminat hadn't played with dolls in a long time, but she played along so as not to offend the guest.

"And what should they eat now?" asked Aminat. I could hear how annoyed she was in the tone of her voice. But she fought bravely to improve our living conditions.

"*Kystybyi*," said Dieter. "Do you like it?"

"I don't know it," said Aminat.

"*Kullama?*"

"Don't know it."

"*Talkysh-kaleve?*"

"What are you talking about?"

Aminat didn't know anything about Tartar cuisine, and I had failed to prime her for the unusual questions. She had become a Soviet girl, just as Kalganow always wanted. She had no idea what the words were and didn't hide her ignorance.

"Will you give me a kiss?" asked Dieter.

"Only if you marry my mama," said Aminat.

I didn't tell Sulfia about the conversation I'd overheard. I had to think it over first. Of course, now I knew I could reach my goal much more quickly than I had planned, and that it didn't matter whether Sulfia wore short skirts or fishnet stockings. I kept my knowledge to myself—I wanted to wait until we had red passports in our hands.

Sulfia had watched Dieter sorrowfully after he stuck his wool-stockinged feet in his shoes and laboriously tied the laces. He formed loops with each set of laces and wrapped them around each other in an odd, very foreign fashion.

Aminat, Sulfia, and I stood in a row in front of him, watched, and waited until he was finished. This didn't disturb him. He pulled on a finished knot and undid the entire structure. Aminat sighed and shifted her weight from one foot to the other. Sulfia moved her fingers. She was barely able to keep herself from kneeling in front of Dieter and doing the task for him.

As the door closed behind him, I looked around. Aminat's face was contorted, as it always was when she had to keep herself under control. She had really worked wonders as far as her composure. Sulfia looked sad and wistful. I cast a sideways glance at my face in the mirror. It had a look of grim determination.

"And now?" asked Sulfia, heading into the kitchen with her head hanging. I followed her. She turned on the water but nothing came out. We were prepared and had a supply in buckets and in the bathtub. I poured some into our largest pot and put it on the stove in order to heat it to use to wash the dishes.

"We'll see him again soon," I said.

"You think so?"

She looked at me as if once again she believed I knew everything in the world. Unlike Aminat, she was apparently reaching an age at which she finally valued maternal wisdom.

"He'll be back very soon, my daughter," I said. "Didn't you notice—he practically devoured you with his eyes. There are no women like you in Germany."

"But he barely looked at me," Sulfia countered tentatively.

"Out of shyness," I said. "Chin up, daughter. If we all play our cards right, we'll soon be in Germany."

For a better life

Sulfia believed me. She was stupid and wanted to stay that way. She believed in good, and with a whole lot of imagination she was able to interpret Dieter's regular visits as interest in her, Sulfia—as gratitude for her care, as fondness for the entire family, as interest in my marmalade. His interest in my marmalade was genuine, that much was true. In Germany, said Dieter, marmalade was made quickly, with gelling sugar— sugar mixed with pectin—and ended up an acidic, jellyfish-like blob. Me, on the other hand, I peeled apples and cut them in pieces, poured sugar syrup over them and let the mixture soak, cooked that, let it cool again for hours, and then heated and cooled it two more times. The apple pieces took on a translucent beauty, the sun shone through them, and they left the taste of summer in your mouth.

We ate marmalade with tea because we didn't have any other sweets. After a conversation about the art of cooking Dieter stood up and went, as if coincidentally, to Aminat's room. He said he could speak Russian particularly well with a child, that he learned things in a completely different way, especially from Aminat. And that she had a pretty voice and he liked to listen to her, but she stopped singing as soon as she noticed. Only someone as blind as Sulfia could fail to see how much Aminat hated his visits.

I had spoken to Aminat about how tough things had gotten. I told her that we all had to clench our teeth and be friendly to people we didn't particularly like because it might lead to a better life for us.

Aminat listened to me without looking at me. We had yet to patch up our relationship and get close again. But I could count on her understanding. Every once in a while when I was out and about with Aminat, I would take a detour through the gypsy enclave, a few streets of squalor in the middle of our city. Dirty black-haired children played there; in winter they wore layers of wool shawls over their hole-riddled jackets. They screamed hoarsely in an indecipherable language and threw stones at passersby. I knew that for some incomprehensible reason Aminat thought these gypsy children were Tartars and all somehow related to us. This helped my argument. If Aminat conducted herself well, we would end up in Germany; if not, I assured her, we'd end up in the gypsy ghetto.

Aminat smiled for the first and only time in Dieter's presence when he announced he would be flying home in three days' time.

"Already?" I asked, wavering between relief and disappointment.

We waited, expecting him to say something more. Nothing happened. He shook each of our hands, as if we were an official delegation. I looked at his outstretched arm, pulled him by his hand to me, and kissed him three times on the cheek. It would have been better if Aminat had done it. But I was afraid she might also then throw up on him.

When Dieter was gone, Aminat ran up and down the hallway singing: "The foreign asshole is gone, hurray! Finally the foreign asshole is gone, hurray!"

Sulfia went without a word into her room and lay down in bed.

"He'll be back soon," I said persuasively, though I had doubts.

Life had too often kicked me in the backside—I was no longer sure of anything.

All three or none

Two weeks later the phone rang, giving us all a start. We hadn't heard anything from Israel for a long time, and the ringtone signaled an international call. Sulfia whisked the phone to her ear.

As the voice in the phone quacked away, telltale redness spread across Sulfia's face. She listened with a furrowed brow; she didn't understanding anything and the red blotches spread as she strained to try. I took the phone from her hand.

It was Dieter, though I barely recognized him. First of all, he was talking very fast and squeaky. Second, it wasn't clear what language he was using.

Then suddenly I understood a word, one single word, but at least it was an important one: "invitation."

"Invitation, yes," I said. "For three: Rosalinda, Sulfia, Aminat."

The phone went deathly quiet.

"All three or none," I relayed to the suddenly mute Dieter.

After I had hung up, I turned to Sulfia, who was pressing the palms of her hands against her heated cheeks.

"You see?" I said. "He invited us to Germany."

Sulfia's eyes got really big.

"When?"

"Soon," I said, though I wasn't feeling particularly cheerful.

We had a long road ahead of us, and the prospect felt like a gallstone.

In order to stoke Dieter's fire I needed a nice photo of Aminat. I rang the doorbell of a neighbor I'd heard made his living selling photos of women. I had to ring for a long time. He had on only underwear when he opened the door.

"Whatcha want?" he asked looking me over with his open eye. The other was still closed.

"Photos," I said.

He led me into the foyer and disappeared behind one of the many doors. I looked around. The walls were white, presumably. But they were covered floor to ceiling—practically wallpapered—with black-and-white shots of naked women.

"Did you take these all yourself?" I asked when he reemerged.

He had an open container of milk in his hand and a white trickle was running down his chin. I looked at him and gulped. I would like to have asked him where he was able to get the milk.

When he told me what he charged for photos, I asked him to quit joking—this was a serious matter.

"Then do it yourself," said the neighbor.

I slammed the door as I walked out.

I could do almost anything. Except take photographs. I didn't even own a camera. I had a vague memory of how years before Kalganow would hole up in the bathroom with a red light and dunk photo paper in little tubs and the contours of faces would slowly take shape on the paper. But I didn't trust Kalganow to take a nice photo.

I went to a photo studio on the corner and studied the pictures in the window. All the men looked like mass murderers and all the children seemed to have their eyes crossed. And Aminat wasn't even photogenic.

Back home I opened my wardrobe. I owned two fur coats, an old one and a newer one that one of my admirers had given me, back when I still had some. I tried the coat on one last time. I hadn't worn it recently. Hold-ups took place in broad daylight these days; only someone with a death wish would dare to wear something of such value on the street.

I stroked the fur. It was cool and feathery, and caressed my hands, which were cracked and rough from doing lots of dishes. I folded the fur coat and pushed it into a black duffel bag.

The whole way to the consignment shop my heart beat nervously. I put great effort into trying to look scruffy so no robber would think I had such a treasure hidden in my bag. When I arrived, I breathed a sigh of relief. The saleswoman refused to take me and my coat into the back room, so I spread it out in the shop itself and said I'd like to have my money immediately rather than wait until someone bought the fur to get my share. It was obvious that the coat wouldn't be hanging in the shop for long anyway.

The saleswoman looked at my magnificent piece with a look of slight disgust. I wasn't going to be fooled by that. I waited as the woman felt the fur with her fingers, turned it over, and pulled on individual hairs. She was still scowling skeptically, and then she said a sum that was half of what I had figured the worst-case scenario might be.

"No," I said. I knew these lazy tricks. "Either you ask your manager or I'll take it to another shop."

The saleswoman shrugged her shoulders, disappeared into the back, and returned with another woman who looked exactly the same, right down to her hairdo. The second woman didn't even look at me. She immediately started to poke at the fur with her thumb and forefinger. I had the feeling she might hurt my fur. This second woman said an even lower number.

"Wait just a minute," I said. "Your co-worker . . . "

The look from her cool, nearly colorless eyes silenced me. I suddenly understood: every word was going to cost me five rubles.

"You can have it," I said, watching as she carried my coat into the back and returned with a pile of tattered banknotes. My life had just become one prized possession poorer.

A good girl

Aminat was grimly silent as I washed her hair with the last of the foreign shampoo, dried it with a blow-dryer, and put waves in it with the curling iron. I refrained from using starched bows or other vulgar trinkets, but I did insist Aminat put on the dress I had made her for the New Year's holiday two years prior. I had wanted Aminat to play the snow princess in the annual school show. It was a major role, one every normal girl wanted. I had given the teachers money and chocolate and made this dress, a pale blue dream made of silk and lace that nonetheless remained unworn: Aminat refused to put on the dress or take the role. After days of fighting, I was forced to write off the gifts as useless investments.

Now Aminat was quiet and obedient like a good little girl. The dress was too small. I fluffed the collar and sleeves and

draped Aminat's black hair—now wavy after much labor—
over her shoulders. She looked small and fragile, younger than
she actually was, except that the look on her face spoiled it.

"You have to try to look more friendly," I said once she had
taken her place on a tall stool in the apartment of our neighbor.

The photographer stood at the window, smoked, and
flicked the ash onto the heads of passersby below. He said
there was no point in picking up the camera as long as Aminat
insisted on looking like a crocodile.

"I hate kids," he said, and I couldn't resist twisting a lock
of Aminat's hair around my finger and yanking it.

"That's what you do to my nerves all the time," I hissed as
tears welled up in Aminat's eyes from pain and rage.

At that moment, the neighbor turned around, shouted at
me to step aside, and held the camera to his face.

He clicked away for an hour, changing the film multiple
times, adjusting the lens, trying shots from the front and the
side. I kept running in to poke Aminat in her back with my
forefinger to make her sit up straight or to tousle her hair.
When it was over, Aminat climbed off the stool and scratched
her head. There were beads of sweat on her forehead. Her hair
was stuck together. And she looked light-headed from the
much-too-small dress.

I didn't have high hopes when the neighbor knocked on
our door and grumpily told me the photos were ready. I went
along with him trying to inwardly steel myself to fight over the
money. When I caught my first glance at the rectangular photos spread out on his kitchen table, I thought they were shots
of someone else. These pictures showed an angel, still very
young, with a bottomless sadness in her dark black eyes, with
her hair ruffled by a light summer breeze. It wasn't until I bent
down closer to the table to have a closer look at the angel's
divine dress that I realized the shots were of Aminat.

I picked up a photo. It was like magic. Aminat's otherwise defiant, angular face shone with melancholy. It hit you right in the heart, reminded you of the beauty of creation, and made you want to do something good right on the spot. Without hesitation, I pulled out the envelope with the money I'd gotten for my fur coat and slid it across the table.

"You are a true artist," I said. "Thank you."

I told Aminat she should draw a picture for Dieter. She brought me a white piece of paper with a naked tree in the middle. I shouted at her to put more effort into it. Then I had an idea: I looked through our old encyclopedia and found the picture of a Tartar woman in traditional costume. I placed the heavy book, open to that page, in front of Aminat.

"Who goes around looking like that?" asked Aminat.

"Your ancestors," I said.

Aminat leaned down over the open pages and traced her finger on the colorful figures, the lopsided hats, the corded clothing. The encyclopedia had pictures of all the countless ethnic groups of the Soviet Union in their traditional garb.

"Are those real people?" she asked.

"Draw yourself in that outfit," I said.

Against all odds, Aminat had fun with this task. She drew careful outlines of the traditional clothes and filled them in with colored markers. Over the collar she drew a red-cheeked face with dark slits for eyes and black hair pulled into two wreathed braids.

"Write your name underneath," I said. "And on top write 'for Dieter.' Wait, write in German—I'll show you how."

I put the drawing into an envelope along with one single photo. I hadn't shown the photos to anyone. I'd hidden them in my wardrobe beneath a pile of laundry. I understood: the pictures were like a drug and needed to be carefully administered in doses.

I wrote Dieter's address on the envelope and took it to the post office.

It took two weeks. Then the phone rang. My envelope had arrived. Dieter sounded very bashful. He asked me to pass along his thanks to Aminat for the picture she'd drawn. I promised to do so. I waited for him to say something about the photo, but Dieter didn't mention it. So he had understood everything correctly.

"Invitation," I repeated in my fluid school German. "Invitation for three."

A month later a stranger called and said Dieter had given him a package to bring to us. I picked it up. It was a beautiful plastic bag printed with a picture of bright red strawberries. Back home I called Aminat and Sulfia into the kitchen and turned the bag upside down above the table. A large brown envelope fell out in which we found the invitations. In addition, three chocolate bars, a packet of hazelnuts, a pack of peppermint gum, and two little tubes filled with crumbly, fruity-smelling tablets (we turned them all around until we were finally able to decipher the word "vitamins" on the side), a tin of milk powder, and a large white packet decorated with pink cherry blossoms and a smiling woman's face. The German words "sanitary napkins" on it made me think that it might be for dressing wounds.

"Look, how nice of the foreigner even to include medical supplies," I said to Sulfia.

The two of them were so busy looking through the various things that they didn't notice the most important thing: a small white paper envelope full of Deutschmark notes.

"Think about what you want to bring," I said. "We're flying to Germany."

It took months and a lot of money and aggravation before we had everything sorted. I went to Moscow, twenty-seven hours by train, and stood in line at the German embassy until I was ready to drop. By the time I had the visas and plane tickets I had assembled the necessary certifications: that none of us was insane, none had a contagious disease, none had served time in prison. I went from one government office to the next, always with a stockpile of little gifts in my bag.

The last of our money I spent on souvenirs. I called friends and acquaintances and collected things that, as best I could tell, would please people in Germany: painted wooden spoons in all different sizes, cast-iron statuettes, pins with cartoon characters on them.

We packed two big suitcases and tied them up with laundry line so they wouldn't come open. It had been fifteen years since they had last been used. We had taken them to the Black Sea that time.

I was excited and very tired. Kalganow drove us to the airport. I looked out the window of the car at the rain and had no desire ever to return.

Deeply saddened, Kalganow carried our bags. Sulfia wanted to help him, but I held her back.

"We'll bring you back something," I said to cheer him up.

"Not necessary, Rosie," he said.

He kissed me, bowed to Aminat, and hugged a sobbing Sulfia. She was getting on my nerves, and I said someone like her should only be allowed to travel as far as the other side of town.

I felt empty and exhausted and tried to cheer myself up by envisioning the winter boots I'd buy first thing in Germany.

The country that had never conquered us

Sulfia and Aminat had never flown before, and my only experience had been thirty years prior. We were as excited as children, at least Sulfia and I were. Everything seemed magical, especially the stewardesses and the seat belts.

"Look, look!" Sulfia kept saying.

She pointed out the window, though the view was always the same: clouds, white like cotton candy. Aminat sat silently staring straight ahead. Her cat Parasite had taken the chaos of the packing process as an opportunity to slip out of the apartment, and at the time of our departure had yet to turn up again. Apparently the animal was more intelligent than I gave it credit for.

We landed in Moscow. We had to wait a day and a half for the connecting flight.

I had heard about a new restaurant that had opened on Moscow's Gorki Street. Apparently people stood in long lines to get into it. We took the Metro there and it was true: when you were at the front of the line you couldn't even see the back. Of course, we got in line. I took turns with Sulfia—one of us waited while the other rested her legs on a park bench in the sun. After three and a half hours we reached the front. We studied the huge colorful photos of the food on the wall and then read out the names of the things we wanted, names we had never heard before. We ordered thinly sliced, crispy, light potatoes, meat in an unbelievably soft roll, and hot dough pockets filled with apples and berries. Everything was daintily wrapped in paper boxes and placed in a paper bag.

"This is a very good restaurant," I said to Sulfia.

We stood around a tall table and unpacked our food. Before long, all the little boxes were empty. I put two into my bag—they looked very practical. As we left the restaurant we had to pass a woman who said, "Thank you for your visit, we look forward to seeing you again soon!"

Sulfia was so confused she cowered against the wall. Not even I could come up with a good answer.

Once we were a few meters beyond the door, I turned around and looked at the long line of people waiting to get into this temple of culinary pleasure. I had a feeling we had just tasted the West.

We flew from Moscow to Frankfurt. It was no longer as exciting. Aminat looked quietly out the window. She was tired. We had spent a lot of time walking around Moscow, and she had kept having pain in her stomach.

The air in Frankfurt was warmer than at home. I changed the time on my watch.

"Now we'll live according to German time," I said.

Our bags hadn't been stolen while in transit. At the passport control, my heart beat so wildly that I was afraid it might pop out of my chest. I was worried something would be wrong with our passports or visas.

A young man in a sharp uniform opened my passport. His hands were clean and groomed like a woman's. He looked at the hologram in the visa, quickly paged through the passport, looked at my photo and at me. I felt my smile freeze. He winked, closed the passport, and handed it back to me. I grabbed it, took Sulfia by the elbow (her passport had been of much less interest to the immigration official), and took Aminat with my free hand. We walked a few more meters and were finally officially in Germany.

I could hardly believe it: we were abroad, all three of us— and not just anyplace abroad, but in Germany. The country that had never conquered us. I was proud of myself. Aminat was only twelve and had already crossed an international border, something I had only read about in books before.

Everything was very clean. Our shoes reflected on the flooring.

We walked with our bags to Dieter.

At first I hadn't recognized him. Sulfia saw him first and pointed with her finger—a gesture I'd managed to curtail in Aminat.

His face had gotten rounder. His hair was short, and his pink scalp showed through it. His stomach hung over his belt.

"*Guten Tag!*" cried Sulfia, running ahead and wrapping her arms around his neck.

Aminat and I watched as he patted her back and then tried to shake her off.

It didn't occur to him to help us carry the bags. He walked alongside us and pointed the way with hand motions. Between indicating directions he tried to take Aminat by the hand, which Aminat deftly managed to avoid.

Germany seemed green and not very densely populated. We drove for a long time in the car. We left the fast roads, drove on smaller, narrower roads, drove past hills and forests.

"Here we are," said Dieter as we stopped in front of a multistory gray building.

Apparently he didn't own the entire building, just the apartment on the top floor. I looked around as soon as we entered. The first thing I noticed were the angular walls. They looked as if they might fall on your head at any time. I put down the suitcase and went on into the apartment. It was difficult to tell where one room ended and the next began. There were no doors.

I went through an arch and found myself in the kitchen. The whole place was stark and bare. No carpets, not much furniture. It looked as if someone had just moved in and their boxes had yet to be unpacked. I asked myself how someone could live here. But everything was very clean. Dieter showed us a room with a table with a real computer on it, a couch, and, next to that, an air mattress.

We understood we were to sleep here.

"Two people," said Dieter. "And Aminat—here."

He pointed with his hand to the living room.

"What's he saying?" asked Aminat nervously.

Nobody answered her.

He needed a woman

"Your first meal in the West should be a hamburger," said Dieter.

We sat down at the table—white plates, gray utensils, floral paper napkins—and found ourselves looking at a plate of large meatballs, and another with rolls cut in half and slices of tomato and pickle and pieces of lettuce leaf. There was also a bottle of something we'd gotten acquainted with the day before at McDonald's: ketchup. It looked as if Dieter hadn't quite finished preparing the meal. He obviously needed a woman.

I watched as Dieter picked up a roll, opened it, laid a meatball down on it, squirted on some ketchup, piled on some of the raw vegetables, and closed the roll again. And to think this person had once had the nerve to turn his nose up at my cooking! He raised this monstrosity to his mouth, which he then opened wide enough to show his gold fillings, and took a bite. The lettuce crunched between his teeth and tomato juice sprayed out onto our faces.

I exchanged looks with Sulfia, then nodded to Aminat. We each picked up a roll. We tried to mimic Dieter, using our hands to pick things up from the plates, stacking the vegetables, squirting the ketchup. Aminat couldn't open her mouth wide enough to take a bite, so she opened her roll again.

After a length of time that seemed appropriate, we said, "Thanks." All of us still had food left on our plates—we'd eaten only the rolls because we weren't too hungry.

Dieter began to clear the plates. I nodded to Sulfia. She jumped up to help him. It irritated Dieter. Sulfia put on the kitchen apron to wash up the utensils. She'd acted too quickly. Dieter tried to take the apron. They bumped into each other. Finally Sulfia sat back down and Dieter brought out a huge platter, the sight of which finally put a smile on Aminat's face.

On the platter were more sweets than Aminat had seen in her entire life. Little chocolate bars wrapped in colorful paper, squares and circles wrapped in gold foil, little boxes one of which Aminat immediately opened—out fell colorful tablets also made of chocolate—long sticks filled with sweet cream, chocolate-covered nuts and raisins, even apples covered in chocolate, along with cookies, with and without chocolate covering, strange jellied things, hard candies, waffle cones . . .

Aminat behaved terribly. But she must also have been really hungry after that inedible meal. She tore into the sweets with both hands. We sat there like statues while she stuffed her mouth full, crazily, as if she were afraid she might not get to try all of them if she didn't do it then and there, all at once.

"Slowly, slowly," I whispered.

But Aminat wasn't listening to me.

"Does it taste good?" asked Dieter in Russian.

She looked at him with her mouth full and her chin smeared and nodded grudgingly.

I told Dieter that Aminat wouldn't sleep on the couch in the living room at first, but with me in the little room with the computer. Sulfia would sleep in the living room. I made it clear that he was no longer the man of the house. Deciding where everyone would sleep was my duty.

Aminat collapsed onto the air mattress. She was too tired even to brush her teeth. With Sulfia's help I undressed her and put the covers over her as Dieter stood in the doorway and watched.

Unlike Aminat, I had trouble falling asleep. And just as I was finally dozing off I heard an awful noise. Aminat was kneeling on the mattress throwing up. Vomit spewed everywhere—so much I could hardly believe it. While I was still trying to figure out whether I was in the middle of a nightmare, Sulfia peeked into the room and reacted like a bolt of lightning. She quickly emptied a suitcase and held it beneath Aminat's head.

After a moment it was all over. Aminat rolled onto the mattress and fell back to sleep. She moaned softly. Sulfia and I looked at each other and then surveyed the situation. It was a disaster.

"Close the door," I said, and we got to work.

Of course, we wouldn't be able to completely hide this unpleasant episode from Dieter. The smell was too bad, even though we had immediately opened the window. We mopped up the vomit with Sulfia's gray t-shirts because we didn't know where Dieter stored his rags. Several times I slinked down the hall to the bathroom, once to get a roll of toilet paper to wipe the floor and walls, then back to flush the used paper. Just then Dieter came out of his room.

"Aminat—sick," I explained in German, flushing the toilet again. Dieter came closer and peered at the swirl of dirty toilet paper scraps in the toilet bowl. The water level remained high and then began to rise.

"Clogged!" cried Dieter in a high, feeble voice.

This German word I did not know, but from his tone it couldn't have been good.

Luckily I didn't understand whatever else he said. He gave me and Sulfia a brightly colored plastic bucket and a strange fluffy thing, both of which looked more like toys than cleaning devices, and we scrubbed the carpet again, this time with foamy, scented water. Unfortunately you could still see the stains, and the stubborn smell now had a hint of lemon and vinegar.

Aminat woke up late. She was hungry. I sent her to take a shower and to brush her teeth so at least she would smell good, and I forbade her to eat sweets.

Once Dieter had recovered from this incident, he outlined his plans for us: towns we were to visit, castles, palaces, and a zoo. I brought along a plastic bag with us in the car and pleaded with God to leave the contents of Aminat's stomach where they belonged. I had a feeling Dieter couldn't cope with another assault on his property.

I had to carefully consider who was wearing what and when, because we had very few clothes with us. I had packed a red dress, and I put that on along with a pair of golden pumps. Instead of a handbag, I took the plastic bag with strawberries on it. Sulfia wore a pair of formless jeans and a t-shirt. Later I realized that Sulfia had hit the bull's-eye as far as German women's style—flat shoes, no makeup, no skirts.

Dieter drove us to Frankfurt, where we strolled along cobblestone streets and the riverbank. On every street corner were stands selling sausages, ice cream, and crepes. I would have liked to try them, but I had no money. I had just two ten mark notes left, which I left in our suitcase because they seemed safer there. We were crazy with hunger.

Finally I said to Dieter that children need to eat frequently or else they won't grow. He bought a slice of pizza for Aminat and later an ice cream cone. At least there were a few people in Germany who cared whether Aminat was hungry or not.

Nice to Sulfia

We went to several towns. The cobblestones in one of them ruined my high heels, though in which town exactly I couldn't say. I had blisters on my feet. At some point I'd seen enough castles. I wanted to go shopping and told Dieter. I could tell immediately that he didn't like the idea. I said perhaps we could get a few things for Aminat. I could see the battle raging in his head. No doubt, we wouldn't get anything for free here.

Later we sat on the couch in his living room and said nothing. Dieter looked at his fingernails. Sulfia shuffled through the postcards he had so generously bought for her. Aminat blinked at the light and yawned. Then I felt her head on my shoulder and the warmth of her breath on my neck. She slept.

I leaned Aminat onto the sofa back. Then I stood up and left the room. When I returned, Dieter was sitting in my place. Aminat's head rested on his shoulder. I said nothing and settled into a low-slung chair across the room from him. Sulfia looked up from her postcards and smiled.

"Sulfia," I said, "bring me a glass of water."

When she was out of earshot, I stood up, leaned over the peacefully breathing Aminat, and whispered in Dieter's ear, "It would be nice if she could stay here."

He flinched.

"If her mother married a German, Aminat could stay in Germany," I said.

Then I sat down again. Sulfia returned with a glass of water. I put it on the low table in front of me. I wasn't thirsty, and I was suddenly very tired. I got up and went to bed, leaving the three of them there.

The next morning I had a migraine. It was a new plague. I couldn't even get up. When I finally opened my aching eyes, Aminat was already awake. She was lying on the mattress, staring into space. She was like her mother in this regard. I had to tell her it didn't work that way. In Germany you couldn't just lazily sit around. Here you got nothing for free and nothing done for you.

But today I couldn't say a thing, because not only every spoken word but even every thought resulted in pain in my inflamed brain. I begged God to have someone draw the curtains for me.

Aminat looked at me. I tried not to think about the fact that I had missed the moment when Aminat stopped loving me.

It was as if I were disabled. The only one who paid any attention to my situation was Sulfia. She sat down next to me and put her cool hand on my forehead. Then she brought me a tablet and pulled the curtains closed.

God had taken up the matter for me. I had already prepared everything. In any case, things played out the way I had planned. A little later in the day, Sulfia sat down on the edge of my bed and removed the washcloth she had earlier wet, placed in the freezer, and put on my forehead. By now it had been warmed by my skin. She held it in her hand and wiped my face with it. That annoyed me.

"I have to tell you something," she said gravely and softly. I could barely hear her.

"Speak louder," I said. "I can't understand you."

She raised her voice, but only for a second. She said that Dieter had offered to keep Aminat here. She could go to school here and he would look after her. And for some reason she thought this was a very generous offer.

Indignantly I pulled myself upright, threw the blanket to the side, and stood up. The pain throbbed in my temples, but I ignored it. I got dressed and knocked on Dieter's bedroom door.

It was the first time I'd been into his room. He locked it whenever he left us alone in the apartment.

I looked around curiously.

A huge bed stood in the room. In the corner was an ironing board with a shirt on it. On the walls hung photos of slant-eyed children playing in front of the huts of some village. I quickly spotted what I was looking for: Aminat's angelic photo was sitting on the nightstand. When Dieter laid with his head on his pillow, he could look into Aminat's eyes.

Dieter protested, but I had already learned to understand only what I wanted to.

"Aminat stays if Sulfia and I stay," I said in my German. "Otherwise not. Otherwise Aminat immediately home with me. And then with another man to Germany."

I sat down on his bed and crossed one leg over the other. I had nice legs, but Dieter wasn't interested in my legs.

"Nice to Sulfia," I said. "You nice to Sulfia. Only way."

I leaned back. Dieter looked away disgustedly.

"Aminat, Sulfia, Rosalinda," I said. "Only together."

Dieter had decided and as a result became a slightly more pleasant companion. Most likely he was so impressed with his own audacity that nothing mattered to him. For a few days he even forgot his stinginess. He went shopping with Aminat and Sulfia and came home with a stack of white Mickey Mouse t-shirts, jeans, and snow-white tennis shoes that you could only wear here in Germany, where the streets were always freshly cleaned.

Sulfia beamed with joy. She was experiencing happy days. I cannot even imagine how moronic someone would have to be to take Dieter's meager attention for genuine affection. Anything strange Sulfia wrote off to cultural differences or Dieter's reserved nature. And she did earn a few ounces of his sympathy because of the fact that she never wanted anything for herself when they went on shopping tours. Absolutely nothing. Even when it was just the two of us.

I let Dieter give me 150 Deutschmarks (I thought any amount he paid for our little girl was too little) and led Sulfia through shoe stores and the perfume sections of department stores. But she had no interest. She didn't even share my excitement at the striking variety and beauty of all the wares. She smiled when I took pictures of the shelves stacked with yoghurt containers in the supermarket with Dieter's camera. I wanted to show Klavdia. But Sulfia wouldn't try anything on. The only thing we bought for her were five pairs of white underpants.

I avoided asking myself what Sulfia thought of it all. Dieter had asked her to marry him. He had kissed her on the cheek. Sulfia thought he was romantic. She liked him and was happy.

She never asked herself what a man like Dieter could see in a woman like her.

It was Sulfia who flew home to settle a few affairs. It was clear to me that you couldn't leave Aminat alone at Dieter's. Of course he was a coward, but I never trusted anyone.

We returned two of the airplane tickets. I could hardly believe my good fortune. This was exactly what I had wished for—that I wouldn't use the return tickets. Sulfia flew back alone. I gave her specific instructions: what she should say to whom, what she needed to take care of, what documents she would need to produce. Dieter and Sulfia had already been to City Hall and gotten a list of the papers that were necessary for marriage. Apparently marriage was a civil ceremony in Germany. Fine, that didn't scare me. Later, when Sulfia returned, I could go home and take care of the remaining concerns.

We didn't tell Aminat that she wasn't ever going back to Russia. We just told her she would be staying a bit longer. To go to school, to buy a few more nice things, to learn a bit of German. I didn't ask her what she thought.

I was very proud of myself. Aminat was in Germany. I was by her side.

And Sulfia was about the marry for the third time.

You should be happy

So there we were in Germany, in Dieter's three-room apartment. I had gotten a temporary residence permit. The first thing I did was take away all of Aminat's Russian books so that from now on she would read only German. Second, I told Dieter he needed to enroll her in school. A child belonged in school. I had already noticed that Dieter liked to do things the way they were supposed to be done. He strayed too far from the correct path in some areas to risk not toeing the line in others.

Gradually I came to better understand where exactly we were. Dieter lived in a suburb of a city that wasn't very big or very nice. A bus went into the city once an hour—punctual to the minute. A schedule hung at the bus stop. The Germans had such things well organized.

The ride into town cost three marks and 40 pfennigs. Much too expensive, Dieter told me. Especially if you considered the cost of a round trip. Once in a while he drove himself into town in his car, and he would take me and Aminat.

During the second week after Sulfia had left, Aminat started going to school. She had to take the bus into town and switch to a tram.

We bought notebooks and pens, and Dieter pulled a gray backpack out of the attic. This was what children here took to school, he explained. We flipped through the glossy pages of the notebook and smelled the new rubber erasers, which looked like strawberries.

"Be happy," I said to Aminat.

Aminat looked past me.

Sometimes I picked Aminat up from school in order to see how she was settling in. I found the school easily because shouting children were streaming out of it. Let it be stated that German children were very loud. I first realized that on the tram. Their shouting reverberated through the entire trolley car. At first I thought they were about to have a fistfight. But they were laughing. I also saw that most of the children were dressed very messily. I always made sure that Aminat left the house with her hair braided and in freshly ironed pants and a freshly ironed sweater. That way she would stand out.

It was easy to recognize Aminat in the flood of children

spilling out of the school. She was the only one with nicely pressed clothes but also the only one who was always alone. And she moved at a different pace from the other children. Her face warned everyone not to talk to her.

I asked myself what else she could possibly want. She was already in Germany. She had new pens and t-shirts. She was driven to school almost every morning in a car. And still she looked like that.

I took her aside and told her that it just wasn't acceptable. Dieter had not yet married Sulfia. They had been to City Hall, but only to pick up the list of necessary documents. He could easily get out of it still since he wasn't bound except by his word, which for men carried no weight at all. If Aminat kept up this behavior, Dieter would probably send us back and go look somewhere else for a sweet, affectionate little girl.

I explained all of this to Aminat one night in our shared room. I slept on the couch and she continued to sleep on the air mattress. I had offered to let her sleep next to me, but she didn't want to. She didn't want to be anywhere near me. And naturally, she wanted to be anywhere near Dieter even less. But she also made an effort—perhaps because I told her that without Dieter her mother wouldn't be allowed back into Germany. And then Sulfia would never get well, I said. Shortly before our departure we had found out that she was sick. Her body was destroying her organs from within. That's why she was often tired and had to take medicine. I told Aminat that Sulfia's health depended entirely on her.

I didn't allow Aminat to write to her friends back home. Who knew, maybe we would have to go back. The friends shouldn't find out that we had been in rich Germany. Calling was out of the question because it was so expensive.

Aminat wrote letters to Sulfia. I read them before I put them in the envelope. Aminat wrote many letters, but they all began with the same words: "Dear Mama, how are you? I'm fine." I collected them and sent a few at a time in one envelope in order to save on postage.

Dieter said he wasn't in a position to support us. He didn't go to work. He just wrote on his computer and pored over books. He had written a few himself, too. I had found a few on the shelves with his name on the spine. Probably nobody wanted to buy them.

I should do something, too, Dieter said. I would love to, I answered. I'd done highly skilled work my entire life. Dieter should support his new family—meaning Aminat and Sulfia. I could get by without him somehow. Surely there were teachers' colleges here, too.

When I said this to Dieter, he laughed hard. In fact, he laughed so hard I thought he was having some sort of nervous breakdown. I'd already noticed he had a few nervous tics. Now he said, "But you can't speak any German."

Of course I could speak German. I tried to explain this to Dieter in his own language, but he didn't want to understand, the same way I often didn't want to understand him. He explained something about my having a residency permit without a work permit and then he said he had a great idea for me.

Two days later I had a job.

Dieter gave me a piece of paper with an address on it, a map of the city, and money for bus fare. I left two hours before the actual appointment. I never showed up late, at least not to an important job. And this was going to be my first job in Germany. I dressed myself well, in a trim pair of slacks, a cream-colored blouse, fishnet stockings, and a new pair of summer heels. I put my hair up and accentuated my facial features with powder, rouge, and eye shadow.

It was smart on my part to leave early. I had a little difficulty with the address. I asked several people on the street. What they said was difficult to understand. They spoke far too fast and indistinctly. I showed them my map and they traced their finger up and down and along the streets and dug their nail in where my target was supposed to be. But they didn't look me in the eye.

Eventually I found myself in front of a fence with a little gate. I compared the name on the bell to the one on my piece of paper—Schmidtbauer. Odd name, though a lot of people in Germany had names like that. The lawn in front of the building was well manicured, each blade of grass the same length as the rest. The Germans had their lawns under control.

Farther back were a brightly colored plastic slide and a sandbox with pails and shovels. It was a kindergarten. Good. I wasn't a kindergarten teacher, but I did have a degree in education.

A woman appeared at the door. My first thought was that I hoped she wasn't going to be my boss, for it had practically become the norm for supervisors to be younger than their workers. The woman let me into the building. She had short hair and dark rings under her eyes. I could also see the straps of her bra in the neck opening of her shirt, which seemed a little sloppy. She waved me into a large room with a white couch and several chairs. A conference room? She motioned to a chair and I sat down.

Next I understood her to be asking whether I would like something to drink.

"Coffee," I said. "With milk and sugar."

The woman brought me a coffee with a white foam crown. I tried it. She had forgotten the sugar.

"Sugar," I said again.

"Oh, forgive me," she said. She stood up and brought me a metal jar and a spoon.

It was quiet. The children must already have been picked up. It was clear to me that this couldn't be a normal kindergarten. It was obviously very exclusive—which, I knew as an educator, usually meant problematic children.

I tried to understand what the woman said to me. She made a gesture with her hand—an invitation to follow her. I stood up elegantly. Not everyone had the ability to gracefully extricate oneself from a soft chair. But I did.

I followed the woman, who showed me the rooms and made circular motions with her hands. She was a little agitated. In the kitchen she opened the microwave and again made a circular motion. Then we went on and she showed me the toilet and even the toilet brush. We went up a marble staircase and I was stunned: the room she showed me was definitely a bedroom. Did she think I wanted to move in?

Then she pulled open another door, flipped on the light switch, and stepped to the side. I looked in with curiosity.

It was a very small room filled with shelves. On the shelves sat bottles and tubes. I had seen such things in the supermarket: they were cleaning materials.

The woman made another gesture, another invitation.

Then she walked away. I stood there staring at all the colorful bottles. I'd never seen such a sumptuous supply of chemical cleaning aids. The woman returned and handed me a pair of rubber gloves. In her other hand was a pair of orange slippers. She put them down at my feet and left me alone.

There had obviously been some sort of misunderstanding. I considered my next move. Then I took off my shoes and put my feet into the slippers. I left my fishnet stockings on—you never knew who had worn the shoes before, and the last thing I needed was German foot fungus on my toes. I put my shoes in an empty spot on a shelf in the cleaning pantry.

I put on the gloves and looked down at myself. I wasn't very appropriately dressed, but I was capable of working without getting myself dirty. I filled a bucket with water, poured in some light blue liquid, and began to mop the floor.

I mopped for several hours. There were a lot of floors in this building. But they were already quite clean. I soon got bored. So I abandoned the floor and went looking for dirt elsewhere. I looked under the kitchen table and found some crumbs. I took care of them immediately. I checked the stove. It consisted of a single smooth surface, but there were lots of stains on it. I had just taken a sponge out of the bucket when the woman suddenly walked up behind me and started gesticulating wildly.

"Ceramic cooking surface! Don't scratch! Ceramic! Don't scratch!" she said.

I shrugged my shoulders and devoted myself instead to the floor.

Now she stayed near me. When I went into the bedroom she brought me a vacuum cleaner. I plugged it in and began to vacuum beneath the bed. Now I understood: this was *her* bed. I just didn't understand why she had lured me here. I would never have tolerated any strangers in my bedroom, even if I were too lazy to clean it up myself.

The vacuum hose crackled—it had picked up some dirt. I went around the woman with it and vacuumed in the corners. I looked up at the ceiling and saw a few spider webs. I vacuumed those up. I lost track of time and stopped only when she tapped me on the shoulder from behind and said, "Enough! Enough!"

Apparently she said everything twice. It didn't bother me if it helped her.

I nodded, stripped off the rubber gloves, and hung them over the rim of the bucket. I put my nice shoes back on, went into the bathroom that I'd just cleaned, and freshened up. When I emerged the woman was standing there with an envelope.

"Thanks a lot! Thanks a lot!" she said.

I took the envelope, nodded, and put it in my pocket. Then I went to the door. The woman stopped me.

"Next Tuesday? Next Tuesday?" she asked.

I looked over my shoulder at her.

"Okay. Okay," I said.

Out on the street I opened the envelope and looked inside. There were three ten mark notes. Ten marks for an hour's work. I began to calculate. Eighty marks for an eight-hour workday. 560 marks per week—it was a start.

I took the bus home. I paid for my own ticket. I felt like a queen.

Dieter said my new profession was called "cleaning lady." I thought it sounded rather regal. Dieter said he'd make sure I got more jobs. I nodded majestically.

He said I should keep my mouth shut since I wasn't paying any taxes. I didn't know who I would have told anyway. I didn't know anyone here.

As was the case with everything I had ever turned my hand to, I shone at this new enterprise, too.

Naturally, I could clean. Of course, I'd never been paid for it before. It was clear to me, however, that it took talent to clean. And I certainly had it.

You only had to see how I worked. When I entered a house I was happy if it was dirty. And soon I went into a lot of houses. The first woman who had asked me to clean her house quickly gave my number to all of her friends who were likewise incapable of tidying up on their own. I soon had a map in my head. I was able to orient myself by my own set of landmarks: over there is the toilet that smells so bad, and there is the kitchen where I had to wash red splashes off the wall.

I felt as if all these apartments and houses belonged to me. They waited for me to arrive and make them clean. I was pleased to find spiderwebs, breadcrumbs, and streaks on the mirror. I brought proper work clothes: rubber gloves, rubber shoes, and a nicely fitted blue coverall that one of the apartment owners gave me in order to shield a pair of stretch pants I had on one day.

I felt a bit sorry for the people whose places I cleaned. They were like children—unable to look after themselves. Without me they'd have been forced to bathe in a tub of standing water because the drain was clogged with hair.

I began to expand the scope of my skills. I didn't just clean brilliantly but also very quickly. That way I had time for a few extras. Instead of just wiping the refrigerator clean, I also sorted out the food inside. Things that were about to go off I pulled to the front. Moldy or rotten things I threw out. When I found an open bottle of wine in the refrigerator I poured it out.

Sometimes I took a few things home, especially if I had the feeling that they were still good but wouldn't be eaten there anyway. I took apples from the fruit drawer, baggies of trail mix when their expiration dates were approaching, even vitamin pills.

That was something I loved about Germany: you could buy so many vitamins and even minerals. I found a lot of them in kitchen and bathroom cabinets. I sometimes refilled the little plastic tubes I always had with me. And if I found aspirin, suppositories for an upset stomach, or other useful things, I took a few of those, too. I assembled a little home pharmacy that way, and it made me feel more comfortable.

Not quite Germany

Aminat kept asking about Sulfia. She was already in Germany, with me by her side; she was going to school and did her homework with the help of a dictionary; she even got a little allowance from me—one mark per week. And despite all of that, she asked about Sulfia. Whether she would return.

Where else would she go, I replied.

We couldn't talk on the phone much—it was too expensive for Sulfia, and Dieter got nervous whenever we dialed an international number on his phone. I pressured him by saying I'd take Aminat home if something didn't suit us, though I had my doubts as to how effective this argument still was.

Aminat had become disagreeable. She had gained weight. Never before had a woman in our family been fat, and it outraged me that she might be the first. She just plunged into sweets. No wonder she also had pimples. Every morning when I looked at her, I thought, Oh my God, there are even more.

Naturally I fought these developments. I still believed that somewhere deep inside her was her old beauty—the beauty she had inherited from me. I just needed to exhume it from beneath layers of fat and pimples.

I waged a constant battle against Aminat's pimples. Twice a week I made her a steam bath. I boiled water with dried chamomile leaves and made Aminat hold her face over the pot. Afterward I popped all her pimples and disinfected them with Dieter's aftershave.

Any sweets I found I threw in the garbage. I eliminated her one-mark allowance so she couldn't buy any on her own. The only thing I was unable to stop was Dieter bringing her sweets. It was the only tender connection between the two of them. The otherwise petulant, incorruptible Aminat simply could not resist sweets.

My worry that Dieter would send us back home as a result of Aminat's altered appearance came to nothing. He circled her the way a child does a dog on a leash, torn between the desire to get up the nerve to pet it and the fear of getting bitten. Because I was so busy with my cleaning work, I began to note capabilities in Dieter that had earlier escaped my notice: he was indeed able to keep the refrigerator stocked by himself, as well as to ensure a child had regular meals and clean laundry.

At first I took care of our laundry myself when I had time.

I washed everything by hand in the sink and hung it to dry in the bathtub. Dieter explained how much more water I used by washing everything by hand. I let him show me where the laundry basket was and how the washing machine worked. There were a lot of buttons, but I wasn't stupid. Our dirty underwear, however, I continued to keep in a plastic bag in our room and wash by hand.

One thing was clear: Dieter's apartment was not quite Germany. No, suddenly I found his place a bit shabby. I'd seen a lot of other places by this point. And Dieter himself also no longer fit my image of a German. Now that I had a basis for comparison, I realized that some German men wore much more expensive shoes.

Aminat was no longer the granddaughter I had pictured, either.

I didn't like the local children at all. At first glance, most of them were very poorly dressed. Then I started to look more closely. My perspective changed. There came a day when I found myself looking at a German girl on the tram—not a Turk, a real German girl—and realized I no longer thought the look was sloppy. I could have looked at her all day. The girl seemed so relaxed, so totally different from Aminat, who always had a stiff look on her face and hunched her shoulders awkwardly around her neck.

At first I thought Aminat could never become German. She always had a look on her face as if she didn't understand anything. But that was deceptive on her part.

Once I came home and heard her shouting angrily. I was worried she would do something to Dieter, and ran to her room. Fortunately he wasn't injured. His frightened muttering continued like a second track beneath Aminat's shouts. I stood outside the door and listened. I understood only a few words. I couldn't catch what they were saying. Aminat cursed in

German, in long, complicated sentences. She didn't just speak better than I did, she spoke worlds better. She spoke like German children. I hadn't noticed.

As I entered, they both stopped. Aminat turned her back to me and started hammering on Dieter's computer keyboard.

"What's going on?" I asked.

"Nothing," said Aminat.

"Everything's fine," said Dieter.

"When's Sulfia coming back?" Aminat asked. Me. In German!

"In four days," I said. That meant that a week later I would be flying to Russia. Dieter had paid for my flight in exchange for me taking care of some of the household tasks. I also bought my own clothes. I had found a few shops where I was able to shop cheaply. They sold used clothing by the kilo and it cost practically nothing. And if you looked long enough you could find nice stuff. At first I'd been disgusted, but eventually I started going almost every day to see whether anything nice had come in.

A lot of women in Germany didn't pay much attention to their appearance, so it was easy for me to outdo them. Point to any random woman on the street and I was better dressed, better made-up, and I had a more enticing figure—which I showed off better than most young girls did here in Germany.

"You'll finally be gone," said Aminat. In German. To me.

But Sulfia didn't come. Two days prior to her planned arrival, she called. I had suspected she might have problems. She couldn't assemble documents as brilliantly as I could. She let herself be too easily intimidated or gotten rid of. I had sent twenty bars of chocolate back with her—milk chocolate with hazelnuts—so she could give them to the various officials at the right moment. But Sulfia found that embarrassing. That's why, when I heard Sulfia's voice on the phone, I thought she was calling to prepare me for all the work I had ahead of me back in Russia. But it was something else. Sulfia said Kalganow had suffered a stroke the day before.

"So?" I cried, and quickly tried to remember how Russian inheritance law worked. We were still not divorced, Kalganow and I.

"He's not doing so well," said Sulfia.

"What do you mean—he's alive? If he's not dead yet, won't he survive now?" I asked.

"It's possible," said Sulfia, the professional.

What I heard next I could hardly believe. Sulfia was calling to say she wouldn't be coming to Germany because she intended to take care of her father. The conditions in the hospitals had become so horrible that you couldn't leave a living relative in one—as a healthcare worker she knew this, she said.

"What?" I screamed. "Are you completely crazy? He walked out on me and on you, too! You cannot be serious."

Sulfia was stupid, and there was nothing I could do about it. It was beyond my powers to fly home, grab her by the hair, and drag her to the airport. It meant I would have to remain in Germany after all.

I couldn't leave Aminat alone with Dieter. If she were to stab him over something she didn't like, even if it were an accident, we could forget about marriage and citizenship.

A second Sulfia

Dieter wasn't too upset that Sulfia didn't come back. I could see that. Presumably he regretted the fact that I was still there. In the next few weeks I talked a lot on the phone with Sulfia. I still needed to find someone to sublet Sulfia and Aminat's old apartment. I counseled Sulfia over the phone—she needed to make sure that the new tenant knew she couldn't smoke in the apartment, couldn't drink, and couldn't throw parties with more than ten people. Sulfia repaid me with reports on Kalganow's health. He was still in bed, drooling and staring into space.

"And the teacher?" I asked.

"She's taken it hard," said Sulfia.

I almost forgot that Sulfia was herself also sick. She didn't like to talk about her own health. She always just said everything was fine.

Aminat was angry—at me. She seemed to think that I controlled everything in the world. Which wasn't entirely wrong. She said to me, "It's your fault mama isn't coming!"

I told her what the real story was: Sulfia didn't want to come because Kalganow was sick.

"Like you that time?" Aminat asked hatefully.

I thought she had long since forgotten the whole Israel episode. In the meantime we had all learned that Israel was a dangerous place. Buses constantly blew up there. Germany was much safer—and the climate here wasn't so harsh, either.

The most important thing was that Aminat did her homework. I had made clear that she had to do well in school. She needed to get good grades, study medicine, become a doctor, and make lots of money. I alternated the end goal: either "make lots of money" or "discover a treatment that will heal Sulfia."

Aminat sat reading books in her room a lot because she didn't have any friends. I picked up on this at some point—it wasn't normal for a girl to sit in her room all the time and never get a phone call or have a visitor. She needed friends, particularly as she was letting her looks go. She would end up turning into a second Sulfia otherwise. I told Dieter that she needed some girlfriends.

I realized as I did that I actually liked him a little bit. Maybe for his loyalty to Aminat. There were many things about me that annoyed him, but he always reacted patiently to Aminat.

He had yelled at me once when I was cooking spaghetti and broke the dry strands so they would fit into the pot. When Aminat did the same thing (and she was often hungry in the evening and crept into the kitchen to make herself noodles that she gulped down with ketchup and grated cheese), Dieter never said a word—not even that she shouldn't eat so much. Even when she left the water running while she brushed her teeth rather than filling a cup and turning off the faucet, he kept his composure. He was different with me.

Still, he was horribly cheap. He saved on light, water, paper, heat, and even supermarket bags—despite the fact that they were free. He put his garbage in shopping bags and avoided paying for nice, practical garbage bags. As soon as I left a room, he actually ran in after me to make sure I had turned off the lights. When it began to get slightly dark outside, he lowered the shades. That way the apartment wouldn't lose heat, he explained, and the neighbors wouldn't be able to see inside the lit apartment.

Dieter didn't bring a woman home a single time. He was never gone long enough to be meeting a woman somewhere else, either. He never called anybody. He had only us. He and I were bound by the fact that we both loved the same girl, one who had lately become repellent.

Dieter said it was normal. Aminat was approaching puberty. I found even the word "puberty" obscene. Dieter said it happened to every girl. I tried to remember what it had been like for Sulfia, or even for myself, and concluded that neither of us had gone through anything like this. First you were a child, then at some point you were an adult. There was no reason to get fat, ugly, or belligerent.

On the positive side, said Dieter, Aminat was intelligent. I just looked at him silently. Fine, if that was his opinion, he was entitled to it. But it didn't make things any better. Only an attractive woman could allow herself to show any intelligence if she ever hoped to get a man. Dieter said things were different in Germany, but I didn't believe him.

On the street, Aminat was often taken for a Turk. I couldn't understand it. I liked little Turkish girls with their pretty dresses and the colorful clips in their hair. The older ones were no longer pretty or well dressed, though you couldn't see them beneath their shrouds anyway. And Turkish was somewhat similar to Tartar. But I was still happy that Aminat kept her distance from the Turks. From everyone else as well, unfortunately.

Once she came home and asked what a Tartar was. She had to write an essay on the topic.

"Who asked you to do that?" I wondered.

"The teacher," said Aminat.

Everyone in class had to write an essay about the place their family was from. I considered this a stupid assignment—why should the children busy themselves with things that had no relevance in their lives anymore?

"Write that you're a descendent of Genghis Khan," I said to encourage Aminat.

"Who?" asked Aminat.

I tried to explain things to her. Unfortunately I realized I didn't remember much. It was probably Kalganow's influence. He never wanted anything to do with such things, and now Aminat was paying the price. I didn't know much about my family because my parents had died so early and then my brother did, too. I had never even seen my grandmother Aminat from the mountains. We had never discussed Tartar traditions in the orphanage or in school. I always had something better to do. I spoke perfect Russian and worked hard. I had always lived among Russians, and Aminat's questions annoyed me now.

She looked at me through squinted eyes and then went to Dieter. He pulled out some books and thick notebooks full of scribbled notes. I shrugged my shoulders and cleaned the stove as a diversion.

That evening after Aminat had gone to bed, I went and got her folders out of her backpack and read through what she had written. There were five pages.

I did not understand a single word.

Now, one insight followed another. I spoke better and better German because I got to know so many people. I cleaned so many people's places that I hardly had time to clean up at home. So at home Dieter cleaned. He said he couldn't afford me. It was a joke.

I observed the women whose beds I aired and whose toilets I scrubbed, and naturally I observed their men as well. In fact I knew a lot about these people: who was diabetic, who had something on their thyroid gland, who was cheating, and which of them took pills.

Some houses appealed to me so much that I looked at the women who lived there and wondered whether Sulfia could take the place of one of them. Unfortunately even German women looked better than Sulfia.

I liked German men. They were tall and fair, and often outdoors. All of them except Dieter. I didn't like Turks. They reminded me of Kalganow. I liked Poles even less—for the same reason. But I liked to look at German men. Though since the experience with Dieter, I also knew the dangers of building up expectations just because something is unfamiliar.

Once I was cleaning a kitchen and my employer, a driving instructor with spiky blond hair, came in. I realized only when he gave my backside a pat. I had dealt mostly with his wife, who was currently pregnant. She was in the hospital just then because she had nearly miscarried, and he stood in front of me and smiled.

I looked him up and down. He had a whiff of beer about

him, which doesn't necessarily detract from a man, I find. I wagged my finger at him playfully and then turned my back to him again. I felt his breath on my ear as his hand slid into my blouse.

I hadn't had a man in a long time, and this one here was very red-blooded and ready to go. Perhaps too much so, in fact. I felt sorry for his wife—as a change of pace this sort of man could be nice, but on a regular basis he would really rub someone raw. I was worried about the bottom seam of my silk dress. I had my coverall in the laundry, so I was cleaning in that silk dress, flesh-tone nylons, and pumps. He obviously didn't understand how the nylons worked. I will have to just throw them out, I thought the whole time.

When I turned around again, he left the kitchen.

I went into the bathroom and got myself back together. I threw my nylons and underwear in the trashcan under the sink, removed the plastic bag, and knotted it so I could get rid of it on the way home. I used the bidet that I had just polished—I didn't like the idea of smelling like the man. I had another pair of nylons in my bag but no spare underwear, so I stayed as I was. I dried the hemline of my dress with a washcloth. Then I went back into the kitchen and continued where I had left off.

Later, when I finished the job, I hung up the apron in the kitchen pantry and looked around. I had always found the money in an envelope with my name on it sitting on the table, but today the woman was in the hospital and there was no envelope.

"Hello!" I called through the house. "Sir?"

I found him in the bedroom. He was lying on the bed I had just made with his shoes on, reading the paper. His entire face expressed disapproval at the fact that I had not just vanished into thin air.

"What?" he asked.

"I need my money," I said.

I leaned against the doorframe and watched as he picked himself up, looked for his wallet, and finally found it in the pocket of the coat he had thrown on the floor.

"How much is it again?" he asked without looking at me.

"Four hundred marks," I said calmly.

He dropped the wallet, but caught it in the air. I knew the house belonged to his wife, because I had cleaned their den and their desk and tidied their papers.

He found a twenty-mark note and gave it to me.

"Five hundred," I said.

We looked each other in the eyes. I never looked away first. He handed me four one-hundred mark notes. I waited. He gave me a fifty and three tens. I waited. He started to rummage through the coins in his wallet. Once he had gathered up all the change, he put it in my hand and dashed out of the room.

That, I thought, should take care of that.

Iron maiden

Aminat and Sulfia wrote letters to each other. Sulfia kept them pretty short. She began them always with the same words: "My beloved little daughter, dear mother, and Dieter." Then she reported on Kalganow: "Better and better." She said she thought about us often and felt bad that we were alone in a foreign land. I lingered on the sections where she talked about grocery prices and skimmed the rest.

Aminat's letters, on the other hand, I read far more closely.

It was handy that she had to give me her letters—I reigned sovereign over our supply of envelopes and stamps. That way I always knew what Aminat wrote. Most of it was uninteresting. She wrote about her school, her class schedule, the individual subjects, and the material being taught in each. I looked for places where she alluded to me or Dieter: "Grandma works a lot and is often gone. We're doing well. Kisses, your daughter Aminat."

One day Aminat stayed home and said she wasn't feeling well. I had no time because I had to get to a job. I felt her forehead, which was cool, and decided she couldn't be too sick. I told Dieter he should make her a chamomile tea, and then I left.

When I came home that evening, Aminat was lying in bed again. Dieter said she had been quiet all day long. She had gotten out of bed once in a while, then she would go back and lie down. She didn't drink her tea. She did, however, write another letter to Sulfia, a short one ending with the words, "I'll write again when my stomach doesn't hurt so horribly."

I went into the room and looked at Aminat. She was curled up on her side and still awake, despite the fact that it was late. When I felt her forehead, it was still cool and moist.

"Are you feeling better?" I asked.

"I don't know," said Aminat.

I told her she needed to sleep. In order to get healthy, you need to sleep a lot.

In the morning, Aminat couldn't stand up. I told Dieter she would spend another day in bed. While I was in the shower, Dieter called an ambulance. When I emerged from the bathroom, dressed, with my hair nicely done, an emergency doctor was pressing with his hand around Aminat's torso. Her legs shot into the air and she screamed. I figured out that the German word everyone was saying, *Blinddarmentzündung*, was just banal appendicitis. Now Aminat had a fever. I still intended to work. It wasn't as if I could operate on Aminat myself.

"I'll go," said Dieter, whose hands were trembling.

"Calm down, calm down," I said. "This is Germany. Nothing bad happens to people here."

Dieter looked at me as if I were crazy. He often looked at me that way.

After work, I went straight to the children's hospital. I asked for Aminat Kalganova. Nobody recognized the name. I wrote it down. I held my stomach, to show what was wrong with her. A nurse told me Aminat was in the gynecological ward.

"What?" I asked.

She wrote something on a piece of paper, the name of the ward and another name, probably the name of the doctor.

I hurried along the corridors with the piece of paper. My heart pounded in my ears. I was unbelievably upset. I could put two and two together. I could tell how red in the face I was and thought I might pass out from a sudden attack of high blood pressure. I yanked open a glass door and went down the hall. Dieter was sitting in a recessed seating area beside a fish tank, looking at colorful recipes in a magazine.

"You pig!" I screamed, before I ripped the magazine out of his hands, rolled it up, and batted his face with it. I didn't know how to say much more than that in German, so I switched to my native tongue.

"How dare you . . . she's only fourteen . . . that wasn't the deal! I trusted you. And you still haven't married Sulfia!"

Dieter shielded his face with his hands. But I tossed the magazine aside and looked around for something harder. The aquarium was too big, as was the pot with the yucca plant in it. I reached into the pot and grabbed a handful of potting soil and threw it in Dieter's face.

I stopped only when I heard footsteps in the hall. Dieter had also managed to grab my wrists. Switching back to German, I screamed: "Let me go, you child-fucker." He let my wrists go and held my mouth shut. Just then two nurses appeared and said that if we didn't immediately leave the building, they would call the police.

Outside I sat down next to Dieter on a bench in the shadows. I lit a cigarette. When I got upset I liked to smoke, but only very rarely because I didn't want to lose the freshness of my face.

Dieter wasn't to blame. Aminat wasn't pregnant. She was a virgin. In fact, that was the problem—she was an iron maiden, a little medical wonder. She had reached an age at which she had been overcome by the plague of all women. But Aminat was impermeable and had to be de-virginized on an operating table with a scalpel. The doctor said a half liter of blood sloshed onto his pants when he did it. That was what they had taken for appendicitis prior to the first operation: the hardened stomach, the pain, and the infected fluid in the abdominal cavity. Now they had opened the sluice of Aminat's central canal and cleaned her abdomen from inside.

I had known for a while that something wasn't right with Aminat. I hadn't hit upon an explanation like this, however. Who would think of something like that? A scalpel was far preferable to Dieter in my mind, and certainly cleaner.

I liked the doctor who operated on Aminat. He wore jeans and a white smock and had gray hair and a boyish grin. When he came in to see his patient, he joked with everyone.

Aminat did not joke around. She lay there with a look on her face like a soon-to-be mass murderer. I was a little ashamed of her for being so antisocial. Sure, the surroundings were probably a bit much for a young girl. I remembered Aminat's conception—in a dream—and I asked myself how it all fit together. I asked the gray-haired doctor whether she would still be able to have children.

"As many as she wants," he said.

"I'm going to throw up," said Aminat.

Out in the hallway I took the doctor by the sleeve of his smock and told him how Aminat had come into the world. The doctor listened with a furrowed brow. It was the first time I'd ever let a stranger burrow so deeply into our family history.

The doctor said, "Don't worry, she is healthy."

Then he added that I should wait for him, he wanted to give me something. I waited in the hall while he left and returned.

Bowing formally he handed me a brochure for an organization called the Family Education Center.

I didn't say anything to Sulfia about Aminat having an operation. Aminat agreed that it would just have unnecessarily alarmed her mother. Sulfia was doing poorly enough without bad news from Germany. Kalganow's teacher called me and said desperately that I needed to get hold of some medicine for Sulfia. The medicine she usually took had suddenly stopped being produced. We needed to get it for her in Germany. She read me the name of the medicine.

I took the matter seriously. I called them back and Sulfia answered. She sounded feeble and didn't want to talk about medicine. She said it was true about the medicine but that there was a substitute; she was taking that now and, as a result, everything was fine. That I shouldn't think twice about it, that I had enough troubles of my own to worry about.

A young woman

I noticed that by German standards, I was a fairly young woman. It was as if I had stopped aging. Of course, I hadn't forgotten my real age. In Russia I knew I was young but that other women my age no longer were. Here I realized that the women my age really were young, even if they looked worse than me.

Even some women much older than me were still young. I stared at the first real old lady I saw—one with violet-colored hair—after she passed me on her bicycle. I took a picture of the second one. The third time I saw an older woman on a bike, it made me think. Then I bought myself a secondhand bicycle from a newspaper ad.

I sat for the first time ever on a bike. It wasn't easy. But if these grannies could do it, I wanted to be able to do it as well.

At first I tried to ride by myself. The bike fell over. I remembered how children learned to ride a bike. They always had an adult who pushed them.

I made Dieter do it. He didn't have anything else to do. Evenings we went to an empty supermarket parking lot, I stepped on the pedals, and Dieter steadied my bike. At first it took a lot of effort on his part. I screamed at him when the bike began to tip to one side or the other. We practiced for a few weeks and I could have sworn that Dieter's skin took on a healthier hue during that time.

I managed pretty quickly to keep my balance. After a few weeks I could ride a couple meters without being braced. I released Dieter from his obligation. He had already begun to intimate that I was too heavy and that he had a weak back. After that I practiced by myself again. I rode in circles in the parking lot and soon also on the sidewalk.

I always rode on the sidewalk regardless of how crowded it was. I just didn't trust car drivers.

Next, I learned to drive a car.

I already knew a man who ran a driving school, whose wife had in the meantime given birth to the baby and whose face I never glimpsed once she was back home. The woman wore a sour-smelling burp cloth on her shoulder as a constant accessory. Milk apparently didn't agree with her baby, and the entire house was covered with stains now.

I went to driving school at night. For a working woman like myself, it was very practical that the school was open at night. There were a lot of women in Germany who did not work, and the world revolved around them. In any event, at the school I saw the man whose wife paid me to clean. He was filling out some piece of paper on a table. He looked at me and said, "Ah! What now?"

"I want to learn to drive," I said.

"Ever tried before?" he asked.

"No," I said.

He pulled out a registration form and began to fill it out. I moved closer to him and bent down.

"At a steep discount," I said conspiratorially in his hairy ear. We looked each other in the eyes. I was sure that he wouldn't kill me. In Germany you ended up in jail for that kind of thing. He shoved a piece of paper at me to sign and then gave me a couple brochures. I was to begin the classroom portion of the training in two days.

Soon I was sitting on a plastic chair along with ten seventeen-year-olds, all of us listening to the rules governing right of way. The owner of the driving school stood in front of a chalkboard, moved around magnets of various colors, and scrawled arrows around them. I preferred to look over the rules in my book afterward because I wasn't sure he was explaining them correctly.

I passed the theory test with only a few errors (Aminat had quizzed me beforehand), and then I had my first hour of practice behind the wheel.

My instructor was a little old uncle-type with big ears and sad eyes behind thick glasses. I sat down at the wheel and he sat next to me. He showed me the mirrors and the pedals and the blinkers. I wanted to start driving and turned the key in the ignition. The car jumped. The instructor pulled out the key, put it in his pocket, and started again from the beginning. But I was the customer here and this was Germany.

"I'm here to drive," I said.

The instructor told me that older women in particular had a lot of problems mastering driving. Even those who were capable of grasping the process intellectually tended to be too fearful at the wheel. They couldn't drive because they got hung up on feelings. That's why an older woman had to go over the procedures several times and practice a lot in parking lots before she had sufficiently steeled her nerves to venture into real traffic on even the least busy roads.

"Give me the key, you know-it-all," I said, pointing to the pocket where he had stashed the key.

Then we had a brief skirmish. He was not the quickest. I got the key, put it in the ignition, stepped on the pedal, and yanked the gearshift. The car must have been in need of repairs, because it moved in a series of jumps before coughing and stalling.

I kept trying, elbowing the instructor as he tried again to take the key. He muttered and cursed in his soft voice.

"Pssst, grandpa," I said, "why don't you tell me how this works instead."

He wiped his forehead with a cloth handkerchief. His knees seemed to be cramping. He had pedals on his side, too, which he had been standing on the whole time—that must have been the reason I couldn't get anywhere.

He was amazed when I was able to steer the car across the parking lot. I caressed the steering wheel, stepped more confi-dently on the pedals, and started to develop a feel for the brakes and gas with my own body. I drove. I drove from the parking lot out onto the street. It was loud and lots of cars honked. The instructor beside me kept flinching and grabbing the wheel. I decided to let him if it made him feel better. The important thing was that I was driving.

I learned quickly. I had nerves of steel. Unfortunately I failed the practical portion of the driving test twice. But that was understandable: even in Germany there were mafias, and the driving testers must have wanted money; I had failed to understand. I registered for the test again, paid the requisite fee, and soon had a driver's license in my hands. Later, how-ever, when I looked at my receipt, I realized that I hadn't paid anything beyond the standard test fee.

All the money I earned I put in envelopes and stashed them in my stacks of underwear. When I had a chance, I would count it, but for the most part I just kept an accounting ledger in my head. I earned so much because I was so good. I needed only say the word and my employers raised my rate by a couple marks per hour. And I didn't spend much.

For haircuts I didn't go to a salon because the prices were horrendous. One of my employers hired a hairdresser to come to her house and cut the entire family's hair. I was permitted to join them. I had excellent hair, good genes, no gray. My nails I had done the same way at the home of another employer. I couldn't do much with my fingernails because I needed them for work. But my toenails were perfect. Filed beautifully and polished cherry red. I had really nice feet, narrow, not too big and not too small, very well groomed, perfect to cuddle.

Dieter didn't want to let me get behind the wheel of his car. But I had come to realize it was old and ugly—I'd seen a lot of others by now. So I started to take it without a word. He was home most of the time, and when I needed the car I would just take the keys out of the drawer and drive off.

I picked up Sulfia from the airport in Dieter's car. It was the first time I had driven such a long way. Strictly speaking, it was also the first time I'd been on the autobahn by myself. I was bursting with pride and excitement. I took a few wrong turns, but I still managed to get there on time.

I hadn't missed Sulfia because I'd been so busy. It was nonetheless good that she was here. Sulfia had yearned to see us. I couldn't go see her because I didn't want to leave Aminat alone with Dieter, and I couldn't take her with me because I didn't want to interrupt the acculturation process, in which she lagged so far behind me. Now Sulfia stood before me with a suitcase that I had gotten for her when she planned to emigrate long ago. It had wheels but she could barely pull it along. Her face was puffy, her skin doughy, and she had deep shadows beneath her eyes. I looked at her and felt nothing but deep hatred for Kalganow.

The third husband

Sulfia planned to stay two weeks. She said any longer was impossible—she couldn't leave Kalganow and his teacher of Russian and literature in a lurch. She had all the necessary paperwork for the marriage with her, though. She threw her arms around Dieter's neck, stroked his cheek, and said how much she had missed him. Aminat likewise threw her arms around Sulfia's neck and hung on her for a while, until I reprimanded her. Even a blind man could have seen how tired Sulfia was. She could barely keep herself upright.

I had cooked a chicken, potatoes, and vegetables and made a salad to go along with the meal. And for dessert I baked a torte. Sulfia didn't eat much. She smiled the entire time, but I found her smile deplorable.

I wanted Sulfia first to marry and then to recuperate a little. She hadn't had a vacation in so long. I gave her all my vitamins. Sulfia said thank you to everything. But she was listless. Even her own wedding didn't interest her much. She lay down often. And then out of nowhere she told me she didn't want to marry Dieter because she couldn't be a good wife.

"You're crazy," I said. "You are the best wife ever."

She squinted.

The appointment at City Hall was two days before her return flight.

Beforehand I had rummaged around a little in Sulfia's suitcase. It was very messily packed. I took everything out, washed it all, ironed it, and folded it. By chance I had also found a cosmetic bag in which Sulfia kept all her medicines. There must have been a pound of one particular concoction, and a few others besides. I wrote down the names on the packages. That way I could take the names to one of my clients, a specialist in internal medicine, and show him what Sulfia was taking.

My employer, quite a good looking man with a goatee that made him look younger than his fifty-five years (I had cleaned up his home office many times and knew his birth date), shook his head and said that putting her on these medicines was negligent. The original drug, the one no longer manufactured in Russia, couldn't be replaced with these. No wonder Sulfia was so listless.

"I need the correct medicine!" I said. "Is it available in Germany?"

Everything was available in Germany. My client wrote out a prescription for a one-year supply. I took his hand and kissed it. I was so happy that my work put me in touch with people like this.

Then he said it would be a good idea for Sulfia to have a thorough examination. I asked whether he could do it. He asked about her health insurance. I asked whether she might be able to come by his office. We could figure out the payment later; he should have a look at her. The man stroked his goatee. The kiss on the hand was perhaps a little too hasty. I prayed to God for help. It worked: the man gave me his business card and said I should make an appointment at his office.

The year's supply of medicine cost more than the driving school and plane ticket combined. The pharmacy had to order it specially. I was very happy my job had allowed me to make so much money. I emptied all my envelopes. It didn't matter. I could make more, because unlike Sulfia, I was healthy.

"You shouldn't have done it, mother," said Sulfia. But she immediately started taking the tablets and said they made her feel better.

What she didn't want to do was to go to the doctor. She said that she didn't have the time and that her travel insurance would cover only emergencies.

"Look at yourself—you're a walking emergency," I said.

But she was as stubborn as ten mules. I just couldn't convince her to go to the doctor. I should have done it, but it was beyond me.

It was hard enough to get her to marry. For that I used Aminat. She needed to stay in Germany, and everything had its price.

I wanted to go shopping with Sulfia for the wedding. But she said she couldn't manage it. She lay on the couch breathing heavily. I looked at her and wondered how she had managed back at home to take care of someone bedridden. I had a strong desire to fly to Russia and put a pillow over Kalganow's face because barring that, I thought, Sulfia would never be at peace.

I went to a secondhand boutique and bought a cream-colored silk dress for Sulfia. It was a valuable, finely tailored piece of clothing. I didn't buy anything new for myself. I planned to wear a striking red dress that showed off my legs.

The ceremony was set for ten in the morning. We got up at seven. I combed Sulfia's hair and put it up, put makeup on her sallow skin and a little rouge on her cheeks. She looked a bit more alive that way. I touched up her eyelashes.

"You look pretty, mama," said Aminat.

Sulfia smiled.

Dieter put on a gray suit that he'd probably inherited from his grandfather. We went by foot to City Hall in the little village where Dieter lived, thus forcing us to live there as well. It was a small wedding. Just the four of us. It took ten minutes.

Afterward we went to an ice cream parlor. Aminat had a huge sundae with strawberries; the rest of us had coffee.

I was proud of myself. My daughter Sulfia, once the ugliest girl on the block, had her third husband.

Two days later I took Sulfia, the wife of a German, to the airport in Dieter's car. She seemed terribly sad. She said that since she'd been taking the medicine I got her she felt better. I hugged her and kissed her—almost willingly.

"A bachelor for a while again, eh?" I said to Dieter when I came home from the airport. Aminat was lying on her bed with her face pressed to the pillow. I couldn't help wondering why she loved Sulfia so much. She could get everything she needed from me.

Dieter sat down next to Aminat and put his hand on her head. I watched from the hall. I wanted to make sure he didn't forget who he had married.

I started working like a dog again. I had a goal. Only a blind person could fail to see how sick Sulfia was. I needed money for her treatment.

I had an address for a new client. He had a very nice name: John Taylor. I didn't like Dieter's name anymore. Just a normal German name. Sometimes I thought perhaps I shouldn't have rushed it with Sulfia's marriage.

Tutyrgan tavyk

John Taylor was just ten years older than I was, but already an old man. A widower. His wife had just died. It was a problem for him. His daughter had hired me because he couldn't do anything anymore. Not that he was physically incapable—he was still strong. But psychologically he just wasn't able.

He was an English teacher. He was out on medical leave for the time being because he was suffering from depression. I found him interesting because he was English and had a nice name.

He was an educated man and had a lot of books. Shelves from

floor to ceiling, and many of the books were old. The spines of the books were dusty. It would have made me depressed, too. I started to dust them immediately. John just said, "Please be careful with the books. I love those."

He had such a nice accent. It was a little hard to understand. I asked, "Who did you say you love—Rose?"

He looked seriously at me and said: "Not yet."

I didn't see much of him while I cleaned. He was in his bedroom most of the time. His daughter said he was afraid of people. Oh, yes, so am I, I thought to myself. People just didn't notice it in my case. I started going there two days a week, for four hours per day. The house had been neglected. John's daughter said I was worth my weight in gold. I knew that, of course.

At first I just cleaned up. There was enough work. John's wife had been sick for a long time. I was curious to know what she had looked like, but there weren't any photos. John's daughter said she had taken them all away because they made it more difficult for John.

One day John came out of his bedroom. He asked me if it would bother me if he sat in the living room. I said, "Not at all, it's your living room after all."

He sat down on the couch. I dusted and then wiped the wood flooring. It didn't bother me that John was watching me. But when I turned to him I realized he wasn't watching me at all. He had taken out a book without my noticing and was reading.

He didn't even look up from his book when the doorbell rang.

"Do you want to get that?" I asked.

When he didn't react, I went to answer the doorbell myself. In front of the house stood a young man. He handed me a tray with food on it—like on an airplane.

"Meals on Wheels," he said as he helped me balance everything. I must have looked pretty confused.

"Aha," I said, as if I understood. I wanted to go back inside to get money to tip him, but he was in a rush.

"John, Meals on Wheels is here for you," I said, placing the tray on a small wooden coffee table in front of him. He looked up from his book. I lifted the plastic cover.

"Here is . . . uh . . . soup, and here . . . um . . . looks like some kind of meat."

"What am I supposed to do with it?" he asked.

I didn't really know either.

Later I found out that his daughter had arranged it for him. She couldn't cook for him every day. And he needed to eat. Meals on Wheels, I surmised, was something like a pizza delivery service for old people in Germany. I shared my thoughts with John.

"Yes, except without the pizza and without the service," John said, laughing for the first time.

He never touched the yoghurt on his tray. I always took it home with me because Aminat loved it.

"If you'd like, I could cook something for you," I said.

"Not necessary," said John.

"You haven't tried my cooking yet," I said.

When I resolve to do something, I follow through. That's the way I am.

One Sunday at eleven, I stood in front of John's door with a sack of groceries. I rang the bell. Nobody answered. Then I jiggled the door. I had a key. I had told him I was coming. I knocked with my fist. Then I unlocked the door.

Everything was clean. I'd been there two days before. I went into the kitchen. Several trays of food were there. I lifted the tops and found them completely untouched. I put down my bag.

"John, Rosa's here!" I called.

Silence. I ran up the stairs and tore open the door to John's room. It was the only room I hadn't been in. Not yet. You could see right away: it was a dreadful space, full of books, papers, and garbage. An empty bed with sheets that were none too fresh. I should have had a look in here long ago.

"John!" I called.

Next I went to the bathroom. The door was locked. I shook it and put my ear to the keyhole.

"John!" I called into the silence.

Fortunately, nothing phased me. I'd been in a lot of houses and knew which ones had doors that could easily be opened even when locked. This was one of them, thank God. I found a coin in my pocket, put it into the slot, and turned. The door opened.

John lay in the bathtub. His long body barely fit. His head was above water, but it was hanging worryingly to the side. The water wasn't bloody. He didn't look good. I braced his head and tried to pull him out. Then, on the spur of the moment, I decided to hold his nose closed. That's how I woke him. John coughed, shook his head, tried to free himself from my grip, and cursed—first in English, then in German.

"What are you doing here?" he asked. "Are you a nightmare come to life?"

He still seemed disoriented. I felt the water. It was cold. I didn't expect any thanks for saving him.

"Why don't you get out," I said, looking around, finding a large towel, and offering it to him.

He slowly stood up. Yes, his face was the oldest thing about him. I couldn't resist looking at him. I hadn't seen a man in a long time. And an Englishman—never. He stood there and water streamed down off him. Then he stepped still dripping wet from the tub. A puddle formed at his feet. He ripped the towel out of my hands and wrapped it around himself.

"I fell asleep. Do me a favor and get out," he said.

"I need to mop up," I said.

I grabbed a cleaning rag and wiped the floor dry. John didn't wait around for me to finish. From his bedroom he asked, "What are you doing here anyway?"

"I told you I was going to cook for you today."

"You're a pain in the neck," said John. "Get out of here."

"After I cook."

He closed the bedroom door. I heard the key turn in the lock. He was stubborn, but his stubbornness was nothing compared to mine.

I ran the cold water and scrubbed the bathtub clean. And all of this out of the kindness of my heart.

I went to the kitchen and started to cook. It had been ages since I had a proper kitchen at my disposal. Today John's kitchen belonged to me. There hadn't been a woman in here for years. Everything was clean—I'd polished it myself—but it had been a long time since the kitchen's contents had been caringly handled and used. That was something I had in common with the kitchen. I wanted to warm it up again and bring it back to life with my hands.

I rinsed a chicken in cold water, took out the needle I'd brought, and sewed the body cavity shut. At the neck, I carefully separated the skin from the meat and blew into the gap. Anyplace air came whistling through, I stitched the hole closed. I beat eggs and cream with a little salt and pepper and poured that mixture between the skin and meat. Then I tied off the skin at neck of the chicken, wrapped the whole thing in a cloth, and placed it in boiling salt water.

This chicken was called *tutyrgan tavyk*, a dish that Kalganow's country relatives used to make. It had occurred to me today—at just the right moment. Not by accident, but because Dieter and I were discussing it. Or to be more precise, because Dieter reminded me of the recipe. He knew both what it was called and how to make it. The things he mentioned brought it to mind, and I realized I knew what he was talking about but had simply forgotten about the dish.

The chicken took an hour and a half and was a genuine traditional Tartar dish. I set the table in the living room. I already knew where everything was. I got out starched napkins and dusty glasses that I washed and polished by hand while the bird cooked. I turned off the stove and freshened up in the bathroom. My face was slightly flushed from cooking. I cooled it with water and applied fresh makeup. Then I knocked on the door to John's bedroom.

"Go away," said John.

I put everything back where I'd found it and left. Indeed, things didn't always work out on the first try.

Elegant and agile

It came to my attention that I still lacked a few skills. Everyone here knew how to swim, for instance—even the little kids. Even though you saw four-year-olds still in diapers, five-year-olds running around with pacifiers, and kids who started school unable to read or add. Even those spoiled children knew how to swim. They were taken by their mothers—my clients—to swim classes, the trunk of the car filled with bathing suits, towels, inflatable floatation devices, kickboards, and pool noodles. And in the summer they all drove to the beach.

I told Dieter he should take our child to the beach. Aminat could barely swim and I couldn't swim at all. That was a situation that had to be remedied. We shouldn't be any less skilled than the rest.

Dieter said maybe the year after next—there was no way he could do it on short notice. It was winter.

God consoled me: no sooner had I said this to Dieter than one of my clients asked whether I had time the following week to go with her family to the mountains. She wanted to take her husband and two kids to Switzerland. She had planned to take her mother-in-law to look after the pair of spoiled brats each afternoon. But the mother-in-law had intestinal polyps and had to undergo an operation.

When I was younger, Kalganow went cross-country skiing in the forest almost every weekend. Sometimes I went along, but for the most part I wasn't bothered with such idiotic pursuits. So I could ski, though I'd never been to the Alps. Aminat didn't know how to ski and also had never been to the Alps.

My client and her husband agreed to let Aminat come. They agreed to everything.

They drove there ahead of us and took our luggage with them. My client had given me a snowsuit she no longer fit into and a red ski jacket for Aminat. I bought a pair of sunglasses and two pairs of pants and we were all set. We took the train, transferring in Basel and getting out in Chur. There I caught sight of the mountains, very high, gray with snow-covered peaks. From Chur we got in a bus that wound its way up mountain roads. We sat directly behind the driver. It was the spot where you had the best chance of survival in case the bus fell off the edge of the cliff.

Aminat had turned all green beneath her pimples. She didn't do well on bus and car rides. She had inherited too much from her mother. We drove past forests, snowdrifts, and little villages. When the bus arrived at the next to last stop and we got out, Aminat threw up in the snow. Thankfully she was all finished before my client showed up to take us back to their vacation condo.

I had forgotten what it was like to be around so much snow. It glittered and smelled like watermelon, just like in my childhood.

The condo had two bedrooms. One had a double bed for my client and her husband, who was a senior government prosecutor, and the other had bunk beds. My client's children, Julius and Justus, slept next to each other on the top bunk. Aminat and I shared the lower bunk.

My employer was glad I was there. She didn't have her kids under control. In the morning, Julius and Justus went to skiing class. The senior government prosecutor plunked helmets on their heads, put their feet into ski boots, and pulled them on their skis to a little igloo, where other little brats were standing around on tiny skis.

It was my duty to pick up Julius three hours later, cook him lunch, and put him down for a nap. We picked up his older brother later. After naptime I put Julius on a sled and pulled him around. We went to the bottom of the ski lift and watched people swooshing down the hill. I couldn't get enough of it. They all looked so graceful. In this setting, Aminat's scowl suddenly bothered me. Her facial expression was ruining my stay, and probably that of my client as well. I told Aminat she had to wipe that look off her face.

The first night I made goulash and spaetzle. My employer and her prosecutor sat at the table with red cheeks, and the children were too tired to whine. Well-fed contentedness reigned.

"You're a jewel," said my client.

"I know," I said.

Now there was only one more thing I needed: to ski.

I was the first one up in the morning and made coffee and toast, and set the table. The children were difficult to wake. They slept soundly and were still tired, but they had to get to their skiing class. I executed all my duties flawlessly. By the time the parents emerged from their room, their kids, Aminat, and I were seated at the table.

"Do you know how to ski?" my client asked me.

"I'll be a quick study," I said in my unimpeachable German. "And so will Aminat here."

I didn't ask her for anything. She booked spots for us at the ski school on her own. We rented skis and went to meet our private instructor at the lift. In my jacket pocket I had the prosecutor's mobile phone. If the kids got into any trouble, I would get the call, not their parents.

I had already realized the men around here were good-looking and very healthy. These weren't men who sat around the office. They did lots of exercise out in the fresh air. Wiry, not too tall, with black hair and blue eyes. Our instructor was named Corsin. He led us to a kiddie slope and showed us how to ski. I mastered it immediately.

"You're talented," Corsin said to me. I found him charming. He took a very informal tone with me, which normally bothered me. He probably didn't realize how much older I was than him.

Aminat embarrassed me. All the other girls her age could ski very well. And they looked good. Aminat, on the other hand, was a clumsy beginner whose basic motor skills stood out for their awkwardness. She didn't have good coordination like me.

My employer was prepared to pay for three mornings of private lessons. I wanted to be able to ski like everyone else at the end of those three days.

On our last morning together, Corsin took us up the mountain on the lift. I shared a T-bar with Corsin; Aminat had one to herself. We could see her from behind. Several times she looked as if she was going to fall off the lift. I wished it would just happen. She clung with every ounce of strength to the lift, flailed with her legs, and got her skis tangled with each other. It was a wonder that she didn't fall. The way down was just as disastrous for her. I skied on ahead, elegant and agile.

After the final session Corsin gave me a piece of paper with his number on it. It looked like something a little kid had made in art class to look like a business card.

"Give me a call if you come back next year," he said.

I didn't let myself feel sad. In fact, I was happy—in the mountains, on skis, living very close to the way I felt befitted me.

The mountain didn't want me

The next morning Aminat refused to continue practicing. I was sorely tempted to smack her in the face, but my client and her prosecutor were still in the apartment and I didn't want to make a bad impression. I left Aminat in the apartment with a book.

I got dressed, took my skis, and went by myself to the lift. I was just as elegant and confident as the arrogant bitches that came here every year and wore their mirrored sunglasses pushed up on top of their heads.

Once at the top, I started down, gliding along behind the skier in front of me and matching his speed. Below me everything was white. Everything all around me was white, too. Then suddenly I realized that it was white above me, as well. I slowed and then fell down. I was taken by surprise by the snow. The flakes swirled around me and I could no longer distinguish the sky from the ground. The wind blew tiny pieces of ice into my face, making my eyes water.

I couldn't see a thing. The tears froze on my eyelashes, blinding me. The mountain didn't want me. I'd been too brazen for its taste, and now the mountain wanted to kill me.

I had stopped myself just in the nick of time at the edge of not just a drop but an abyss. My legs were shaking. I asked God whether my time had come and God answered with a flash of inspiration: Corsin!

That's right, Corsin, who could ski even better than I could, who said he knew every slope around here like the back of his hand. I stripped off my glove and pulled the prosecutor's mobile phone out of my pocket along with the piece of paper with Corsin's number on it. For a second, my fingers were too stiff to move. Then I pulled the antenna out. It was the first time I'd ever used a mobile phone. I breathed on my fingertips and then started to push the buttons with the number. Calling a Swiss number was probably going to cost a fortune, I thought.

There was a tooting sound in the earpiece and then someone answered. It wasn't clear whether the voice belonged to a woman or a child. I had forgotten for an instant that even though Corsin skied like a god, he spoke like a five-year-old.

"Help me!" I yelled.

I shouted the name of the slope I'd started down, but Corsin—if it was even him on the line—didn't understand. He just kept asking: "What? Who's there?"

The wind howled in the phone. It was probably difficult to understand me, but then again understanding wasn't Corsin's strength anyway. In any event, I was lost.

I shouted, "Drop dead!"

The mountain was saying the exact same thing to me.

I hung up on Corsin and tried to reach my employer. It was futile.

I shoved the phone back in my pocket, put my glove back on, and grabbed my ski poles. I looked down at the slick, ice-covered wall below. This must have been what they called a black diamond trail. I tried to calculate how many shifts in direction I'd have to make to get down the hill—or rather, how many I could survive.

Just as I was crossing myself with my cramped fist, a fleck of red appeared in the swirling snow. A person, maybe a man. I was just getting ready to start skiing, and had with superhuman effort positioned my skis parallel to the cliff edge. Now I shouted and waved my poles to draw attention to my precarious position. The person in red stopped just below me, hanging on the wall of ice like a fly on a window. I saw a flash of teeth through the snow soup, and Corsin's soft little-girl voice said, "Hold on to me, I'll get you down."

I was nearly paralyzed with happiness and relief. Corsin took the ski poles from my hands and tucked the ends into his waistband. He stood with his legs wide apart and reached out his hand to me. I slid toward the wedge Corsin had formed, my legs weak and shaking. The wind whooshed in my ears as I followed Corsin's broad shoulders, braking just enough to avoid planting my face on his red jacket. It felt as if it took an hour, maybe even two, and by the time we reached the parking lot at the base of the ski run, blood was dripping from my lips because I had bitten them so badly. Corsin smiled—he hadn't so much as broken a sweat.

"You're a brave woman," he said. "Going up the mountain alone even though you can't ski."

"How did you know it was me?" I asked.

He put his hand on the left chest pocket of his jacket and said, "I had a feeling."

I came out of the mountains like a conquering hero, slightly bronzed and with the bearing of a ski queen. The only problem was that I couldn't say the same of Aminat.

Corsin sent me postcards of bright, picturesque Alpine cottages. As a result I realized that what I had taken for an odd, childlike version of German was actually a completely different language. He and his entire village spoke the language of the ancient Romans, and he wrote in that language on his postcards.

He wrote, "*Gronda buna a mia amur e splendur al firmament,*" and "*vaiel tei fetg bugen,*" and "*far lamur in cun lauter, leinsa?*" I had no idea what any of it meant.

Corsin was like a Tartar in his country. He had other roots, other dishes, another language, and, importantly, a much more handsome look than the rest of the populace. In Russia, nobody would ever have considered sending out words someone else couldn't understand. But Corsin obviously thought nothing of it. I had tried to talk about it a few times with him. At some point I realized that his enthusiasm for talking about how different he was from normal Swiss people wasn't a flaw in his upbringing. It was just something deeply ingrained in him, something that couldn't be erased. Of course, he hadn't experienced a Soviet upbringing. His was somewhat more primitive. His urge to show off his roots reminded me of the way little children lifted their skirts to show everyone their underwear.

Once Corsin sent me a postcard written in German. He wrote that he missed me and that he was coming to visit the following Tuesday, driving the five hours from the mountains in his car.

His visit put me in a predicament. Fortunately one of my employers was on vacation. I took Corsin to her apartment in a nice old building, hoping not to be seen by the neighbors. It occurred to me only belatedly that beyond the ski slopes a man like Corsin was less a trophy than a joke. He was muscular, perhaps just a little too thin, and he looked around like a scared rabbit. Between the sheets my suspicions were confirmed: he only knew his way around the mountains.

The best daughters

I was pleased with myself. I was working a lot because I wanted to take Aminat to the beach that summer. Without Dieter, but with Sulfia—she needed to see a bit of sun, too. Then the phone rang one night and Kalganow was on the line. The same Kalganow Sulfia had been taking care of for four years now since his stroke. I didn't recognize Kalganow's voice. It was different than I remembered it. But it didn't matter whose voice it was once it said that Sulfia was dead.

"What?" I asked. "Why?"

I dismissed it as a tasteless joke and hung up.

The phone rang again. I looked at the display and saw a long number starting with the Russian country code. I didn't move. It rang and rang, until Aminat came out from her room still half asleep, looked at the number, and grabbed the phone.

"Mama?" she cried.

She had finally gotten over the ski holiday and was in a better mood. I looked at her, still hoping she would tell me any second that nothing I had heard was true. But I saw her face change as she held the phone to her ear. At first her face froze in a stiffly pensive expression. Then she frowned deeply, and I knew immediately that my powers of comprehension had not deceived me.

I flew to Russia and Aminat stayed at Dieter's.

I had to take care of the funeral. Who could possibly have handled it better than I could? When I arrived, I ran into people acting as hysterical as orphaned children. The biggest child was Kalganow, on whose conscience—I told him this immediately—Sulfia's death should have weighed very heavily. It was all because of him that she was kept far from my supervision and care. Now Kalganow was in a state of shock, which meant he was actually doing better. He was able to get out of bed and speak—his call with the news of Sulfia's death had been the first time he'd been able to compose a sentence.

His teacher of Russian and literature looked every bit the stereotype of an old teacher. She got on my nerves with her endless sobbing. I looked at her for the first time and had the feeling that she vaguely reminded me of someone. Every once in a while she clutched at her heart until finally I told her she should lock herself in her room and stop getting in other people's way.

"People like you live forever," I said. "And you kill the best daughters of other families."

A lot had changed in my old country. It had a new name. My city had a different name now, too. Everything was very dirty, and everybody was selling something. Stands and kiosks—some made out of nothing more than stacked cardboard boxes—stood shoulder to shoulder. Groceries, clothes, books, and empty Coca-Cola cans were all for sale.

People were dressed poorly and everyone looked miserable. All the girls looked like hookers. Most of them were hookers, too. Old women counted out coins with shaking hands. A decent woman couldn't contemplate entering a public toilet.

Kalganow's country relatives from outside Kazan suggested Sulfia be buried in the traditional Tartar way, wrapped in a cloth instead of a coffin. I didn't even react to that crazy idea. I had enough to worry about. They tried to convince Kalganow, but he just said, "Rosie always knows best." They gave up after that, but during the funeral they wore openly reproachful looks on their faces.

In the coffin, Sulfia had on a white dress and white silk shoes. I put flowers on her forehead and on the pillow her head was resting on and urged the funeral director to put real effort into her makeup. A lot of people came. It was news to me that so many people knew Sulfia. People who had gone to school with her, co-workers, neighbors, there were hundreds of people. Everyone could see what a beautiful woman she was: the long black hair, the white face, as symmetrical as a doll's, the fine, curved nose, the black eyelashes that cast shadows on her cheeks. I guess she had inherited quite a bit from me after all.

It emerged that Sulfia had not had her own room. She had a cot at Kalganow and the teacher's place. It was in the living room, separated from the rest of the room by a folding screen. Kalganow and his woman had a double bed in their bedroom, and they'd turned it into a double sickbed. Nightstands stood on each side, each covered with medicines.

After the funeral, I lay down on Sulfia's cot. It sagged, and the comforter on it was worn to tatters. I gritted my teeth. The bloodsuckers in the next room alternately sobbed and talked quietly to each other. I took off one of my shoes and threw it against the wall. Then it was quiet.

It was disgusting to lie in bed fully dressed and with one shoe on, but I did it anyway. I stared at the ceiling. At some stage the neighbor above must have had flooding because the ceiling was covered with stains shaped like exotic flowers. If someone had done that to me, I would have dangled them out the window by their feet until they agreed to pay for renovations and a new carpet—even if they had to pay with their gold fillings. But Sulfia was as gentle as a flower. If someone spat on her she took it for fresh rain and stretched out her petals to soak it up.

My head began to swell from within. It was probably just too full. The thoughts began to ball together, got tangled up with each other, pulled at others. My mind was an unimaginably crowded place. Everything pushed outward against my temples, pressed hard against my eyes and even my tongue. I held my head together with my hands. Sulfia, I thought suddenly. Sulfia always knew when someone was doing poorly. She could tell when someone needed her. You never had to say anything. She just knew where it hurt. She could tell from thousands of miles away. And she knew what she could do about it. She could chase the pain away. Sulfia, I thought to myself, had been a magician.

"Sulfia," I whispered with my lips stiff and unwilling to obey me. "Sulfia!"

My eyes burned and throbbed. The pressure was so extreme I worried they might pop. I held them in with my hands.

Then the pain let up. It happened so slowly and subtly that I didn't even notice it until I was able to open my eyes again, still worried they might pop out of their sockets. My thick, elongated eyelashes, from which I had yet to remove my makeup, tickled the palms of my hands as I pulled them off my eyes. I sat up. The room was dark, a streetlamp shone in the window. The headlights of passing cars crisscrossed the room and played on the pattern of the comforter.

"Sulfia," I said. "Sit down."

Sulfia sat down next to me, but not the one who had just disappeared into the crematorium. This was the Sulfia I had seen at our last meeting, exhausted but smiling, with tired but attentive eyes. So lifelike that I began to worry about her again. Then I stopped and grabbed the sides of the cot so I didn't give in to my urge to reach out to a ghost.

"Sulfia," I said. "I . . . "

Sulfia looked at me and smiled. She was too tired to speak. She was always working so much. She put her finger to her lips. And then I lay down in bed again, fully dressed, still in my makeup. Sulfia thought it would be okay for me to do so on a day like today. The second shoe, however, fell to the floor. The comforter, which smelled like Sulfia, shielded me from the emptiness and loneliness of this room and held the heartbreak at bay.

"Stay with me," I begged as I fell asleep.

Sulfia did as I asked. She always did. I couldn't compel her to do anything, but the things I simply begged her to do never went unfulfilled. Sulfia never left behind anyone in need. That wasn't her way.

When I woke up, my entire body ached. The fake lashes had fallen off and lay on the pillow. My face was encrusted in dried makeup and tears. The black dress that so flattered my figure did not smell too good.

I went into the kitchen. Kalganow and his teacher were there. She sat on a stool and he stood at the stove stirring something in a pot. I suddenly saw them as a unit, like two drops of grease on the surface of a bowl of soup that melt into one. Later I'd tell them what I thought of them.

I went to the bathroom and got myself together. I ran cold water through my hair so it would shine, and washed my face and refreshed it with cold water, too. I wrapped myself in a bathrobe that was hanging from the back of the door. It had no scent. But I could tell it had belonged to Sulfia and now it was mine.

Kalganow put a bowl of cream of wheat in front of me. I tried it. It was clumpy but I didn't say anything. I studied the kitchen tiles, each adorned with Sulfia's face. It was a wonderful portrait, an almost photographic likeness. I touched one of the tiles. It was warm and smooth.

"How did you do that?" I asked Kalganow.

"What?"

"That . . . the images on the tiles."

"What images?"

"Those," I said, pointing to Sulfia's face on one of the tiles.

"They're white," he said.

We had to sort out a few things. Material things. Sulfia's belongings. She didn't have much. She had two shelves in the bureau. She didn't have anything else—she had signed over the lease on her apartment to Kalganow.

"You took everything away from her!" I yelled.

"Rosie," Kalganow whispered. "It was her idea."

"But why? You're just a couple of old bags. She was young and . . . had her whole life in front of her."

There was nothing to be done at that point about the apartment. Unless I wanted to take the two of them to court. At first I planned to do that. I convinced myself to do it in Sulfia's name. But it was hard to commit to it—I just had no desire. I was exhausted. Normally I was never tired. I didn't sleep much as a rule—five hours was fine, and with six I was completely rested. But now I was sleepy. I covered my mouth with my hand so I wouldn't yawn directly in the bloated face of the teacher of Russian and literature.

"I'm tired," I said to the teacher.

She looked at me as if I were crazy.

"Then you might consider going back to bed," she said.

She was speaking in a more formal tone to me now, which I liked. During the funeral she had tried to speak to me in a very familiar way. I had thought it rude for her to try to ingratiate herself with me at a moment of weakness.

"I can't lie down," I said. "Unlike you, I have a lot to do."

I wanted to sort out Sulfia's things. Her few things—clothes, letters, documents.

But instead I went back to my cot and fell asleep.

As long as you're here

I didn't wake up until the next day. I had slept for nearly twenty hours. During that time, Kalganow—or so he told me—had kept checking to make sure I was still breathing.

"We thought you, too, were dead," he said.

But he'd gotten his hopes up in vain.

Then I realized that the teacher of Russian and literature had touched some of Sulfia's things. She had taken her few clothes and organized them.

I could barely breathe from indignation. "What are you doing, you old hag? And why are you putting your filthy paws on my daughter's things?"

"I was going to wash them," she said ruefully.

I pushed them out of the room. I sat down on the cot and picked up an undershirt. It was gray and threadbare. It had been washed too many times. It was almost small enough for a child to wear. I wiped away my tears with it.

As I pressed the undershirt to my face, I remembered that the teacher had a niece somewhere. This knowledge burrowed its way into the middle of my thoughts and I could see her in front of me—an unknown niece I'd never even seen before, a little slut with a child and no husband, in a one-bedroom with her old parents. Suddenly I understood why the teacher wanted to wash the laundry.

I sat there for a long time with my face buried in the undershirt. Then I got up and threw the laundry into an empty box. The dirty pieces I carried to the bathroom and piled in the bathtub. Then I knocked on the bedroom door. The teacher was sitting on the bed blowing her nose into a tissue.

"Sit up straight and . . . " I began and then clapped my hand to my mouth. Things were beginning to blur.

I shoved the box into their room with my foot.

"Take it," I said. "Give it to your niece."

The teacher took the tissue away from her face. I wish she hadn't.

"Sulfia doesn't need it anymore," I said and went back to the cot.

Sulfia had nothing. For all intents and purposes she had no worldly possessions. Any pants and sweaters I found I gave to the teacher for her niece. I didn't bother with the washing—it didn't hurt when someone like her lifted a finger once in a while. In the corner of a cabinet I discovered a little box with a cheap ring and a necklace and a smaller box full of letters. It was Aminat's letters, collected over the years. I put them in my suitcase.

Three days before my departure Kalganow picked up the urn. It was clear that I would take it with me. It was pretty. The sides were made of marbled stone and her name was on it in golden letters—just as it should be. She had a pretty name and it would no longer get mangled now.

Kalganow walked slumped over. He wanted to inter the urn somewhere nearby, actually, and he even had the audacity to tell me that. I wanted to hit him over the head with the urn, but I had enough respect not to do so. I wrapped the urn in a wool scarf and put it in a carry-on bag. I wanted to take it onboard with me. I wanted to get home, home to Aminat. I laid out the documents: my passport, Sulfia's death certificate, banknotes in an envelope. I had brought a lot of money, more than I needed in the end. I hadn't counted on Sulfia's friends collecting money—so much, in fact, that it paid for the funeral. I asked myself why they had done it. After all, Sulfia was dead, they didn't know me, and there was no reason to try to get in Kalganow's good graces. He was totally insignificant now.

The only possible reason was that Sulfia wasn't really dead. Others died, but not her. I was more and more sure of it.

I took the notes out of the envelope. Twenty 100-mark notes that I'd brought. A fortune. I held them up and spread them like a fan. They were new and smelled good. I went into the kitchen. Kalganow and his teacher sat opposite each other in silence. Oddly enough, they didn't seem to be pleased that I was leaving. They turned their faces to me—faces that in their hopelessness looked ever more similar. I laid the bills down on the kitchen table between them and left, this time for good.

There were no complications. Nobody was interested in my bags at the airport. They just waved me through at every point.

"See, Sulfia," I said. "And you were so worried."

But this wasn't true. Sulfia wasn't worried at all about the proper transport of the urn. She stood next to me and smiled. Why had I never noticed that her smile was so nice?

To my great surprise, Dieter picked me up at the airport. Aminat was next to him. I wasn't prepared for that. She had

THE HOTTEST DISHES · 227

lost weight. Before I saw who it was, I had thought, What a lovely girl—she could even be a Tartar.

Dieter gave me a quick hug. Aminat kept her distance.

"What is it?" she asked me while we were in Dieter's car.

"Everything's fine," I told her.

At home I took out the box of letters and gave it to her. I wasn't sure how she would react. She ripped it out of my hands, opened the top, and shouted: "You didn't read them, did you?"

"I had better things to do," I shouted back.

She turned and went into her room.

That evening as Aminat lay in bed, I grabbed a bottle of vodka and two glasses and sat down at the kitchen table with Dieter. He picked up the bottle.

"How much shall I pour you?" he asked.

"Can't you see the top of the glass?" I asked, taking the bottle from him and filling the glasses.

"Let's go," I said. "We're not going to clink our glasses."

He took a sip and grimaced.

"You have to just pour it down," I said. "Are you a widower now or what?"

Half an hour later he was crying bitterly. I didn't understand what was wrong with him. It just spilled out of him. He was pale and wrinkly. He spent too little time outside and did too little exercise.

I wanted to talk about Sulfia. I was sure he wanted the same thing. Perhaps he was just realizing how important she had been to him. He tried to tell me something, but for the life of me I couldn't understand what he was trying to articulate.

"Wait," I said, and went into my room.

The carry-on bag was on my pillow. I reached in and pulled out the urn, heavy and beautiful. I carried it to the kitchen and put it on the table between us. I winked at Sulfia and raised my glass.

"We're not going to clink glasses," I said, forgetting I'd already made that clear.

Dieter leaned his head sideways to read the golden writing on the side of the urn. Then he spilled his vodka.

"What is that?"

He pushed his chair back from the table.

"Is she in there?"

I leaned my head back. Looking at the white ceiling helped me gather my thoughts.

"In part," I said.

"Get rid of her," said Dieter. "You can't bring that into the house! How am I supposed to sleep tonight with that here?"

"Lying down," I said.

Now he looked at me with disgust. Hysterical men were divine retribution.

"That's . . . you can't just keep that around the house," he cried. "Take it to the basement."

I took the urn in my arms. I had the feeling that I had to protect her from him.

"Get rid of it," he begged.

"This is an urn with the ashes of your wife!" I screamed.

"That doesn't make it any better!" he shouted in response.

I held the urn in my arms and pushed past him. He jumped back, but in the wrong direction, so I ended up hitting his stomach with the edge of the urn. For a second I pondered whether to give him a hard, mind-clearing knock on the head. But Sulfia put her cool hand on my shoulder.

"Don't worry, dear," I said. "Not as long as you're here."

Dieter looked at me horrified.

"I didn't mean you," I said. "You can drop dead."

I went to my room, put the urn on my nightstand, and fell fast asleep.

The next thing I knew, I became aware of a burning smell. Things jumbled together in my mind. I thought of the ashes supposedly in the urn—unless they'd lied to me at the crematorium. I pictured Sulfia laughing while being engulfed in flames. And just before I awoke, I thought to myself that the flames suited her. Then I finally woke up and ran through the apartment following the trail of smoke. It was coming from the kitchen. Aminat was burning paper in the sink.

"Have you lost your mind?" I screamed.

I reached over her shoulder and lifted a charred corner of paper with a stamp on it. Aminat was burning her letters, the ones I had brought back from Russia. I turned on the faucet. She turned it off again.

"You can't do this!" I yelled. "You have to save these. What if you become famous?"

We hadn't spoken for a long time about how she needed to become famous—or at least successful, or at the very least rich.

"I don't want to be famous," she said.

"Then become a doctor," I said.

"Why me?" she asked.

"Sulfia would have liked it," I said.

Aminat looked into the sink. Scraps of paper floated among clumps of ash in the little bit of water that had streamed in.

"I'll clean it up for you," I said. "You go to your room and think things over."

"Think what over?" she asked.

"Think about how you can improve yourself in ways that would make Sulfia happy."

For a split second I felt uncomfortable as she stared at me. Then she turned around and left, and I could breathe more easily.

In Sulfia's voice

I was very busy at first. I called the offices of the cemetery and applied for a place for the urn. I called stonemasons about a grave marker. Sulfia needed to be properly interred with a nice gravestone. I made a sketch of how I wanted it. The money didn't matter but I still had everyone send me estimates. If an estimate took too long to arrive, I called the office and told them that this wasn't just any old job and that God saw everything. Whenever I got overly worked up or started yelling too loudly, I felt Sulfia's cool hand on my shoulder. I understood that my screaming disturbed her, and I settled down. Sulfia liked quiet, and I did everything I could to make her comfortable.

I wasn't going to be able to inter the urn. The idiots who designed graves just didn't understand what I wanted. Even for several thousand euros. I had the feeling that they didn't want to understand. It was the first time that I failed at something, but Sulfia said it didn't matter.

I had to admit she was right—the urn was beautiful and easy to handle. She didn't need a grave. I just left her on the nightstand next to a bouquet of white roses. I bought fresh roses every few days. Dieter said nervously that it was illegal. I told him where he could stick those regulations.

I kept working. I had to take care of my granddaughter. She was now an orphan and I had to replace her mother and father. Not that it was anything new for me. But something had changed. Before I had spoken only for myself, but now I was doing everything on Sulfia's behalf.

I spoke in Sulfia's voice. And what was even weirder about it was that I spoke with Sulfia's tone of voice. One morning when Aminat didn't want to get out of bed despite the fact that she had to go to school, I didn't say, "Go on like that and you'll end up in the gutter! Your German classmates got out of bed hours ago!"

Instead I said, "Sure, stay in bed, my child."

I bit my tongue as I soon as I said it. What would become of her if I continued to react like that—another Sulfia?

I started to form another sentence that would have featured the word "gutter," but before I got it out I realized I had no desire to say it. Instead I went to the kitchen and made a cup of strong, sweet hot chocolate and put it next to Aminat's bed. "Stay in bed, my child," I said. "You've been through so much in the last few years."

I practically choked on my words, and it took a tremendous effort of will not to let a few other things pass my lips before I went off to work.

John had adopted the habit of locking himself in his bedroom as soon as I arrived to clean his place. And sure enough, the first time I returned after my break, he hid himself from me. I didn't knock on his bedroom door. Actually I didn't even think about him. I didn't think about anything. I just mopped and wiped and felt quite peaceful. Which is why I jumped when he suddenly asked me with a furrowed brow where I had been hiding.

I continued to clean but told him as I did about the dress Sulfia had on in the coffin and the bouquet of flowers I had put in her hand so she would look like a princess. John followed me around the room. When I turned on the vacuum cleaner, he pulled the plug out of the wall complaining that he couldn't hear me over the noise.

When I was finished he asked whether he could drive me home. I figured I had talked enough, said "No thanks," and took the bus.

Obviously it wasn't good to spoil Aminat. I had always known that. And it was no good that Sulfia had convinced me to let the girl get away with everything. Now Aminat, whose life had been a rollercoaster ride, spiraled downward. But Sulfia held me back from doing anything about it. Instead I acted like Sulfia, watching and sighing pitifully.

Aminat was held back in school. My talk with the rector and my assertions about how gifted she was had no effect.

232 - ALINA BRONSKY

"Just leave it," said Sulfia. I could see the gutter before my eyes: dark, filthy, stinking. I told Sulfia that at this rate Aminat would never be a renowned doctor. Sulfia shrugged her shoulders in her own inimitable way.

I went in to see Aminat, who'd been lying in bed reading comics for days.

"Aminat, my granddaughter and daughter of your mother Sulfia, if you don't get up this very instant and try to fill in some of the gaps in your knowledge, you will never become a renowned doctor. You will never have a line of patients waiting to enter your gleaming practice that smells of disinfectant."

"I don't care," said Aminat.

I elbowed Sulfia aside.

"But I care, and I want you to be a doctor!"

"If it's so important to you, do it yourself," said Aminat, turning the page in her comic book.

I thought about it for two days and five hours. Aminat was right: my problem had always been that I undertook too many things for other people. Then they didn't do their part. Of course, I could follow through on anything I undertook on my *own* behalf. So I went to the basement and retrieved the old suitcase where I kept a lot of important documents. They were all in Russian and had all yellowed, but the official stamps were all still legible and in decent shape.

I took a blue plastic folder—labeled "biology"—from Aminat's desk and carefully put all of my credentials into it. I took this portfolio to the offices of the internal medicine specialist whose place I cleaned.

His receptionist couldn't understand what I wanted even after a long conversation. But then a side door opened and I saw the metal frames of my client's glasses. I walked into the room where he was, sat down, and was soon telling him about my plan. He was going to secure me a place at medical school.

He laughed for a second and then was serious again. He said I didn't have the educational qualifications. When I objected that I was a trained educator, he countered that we might as well put my old Russian credentials in a pipe and smoke them. I had to have a German high school diploma, and "at my advanced age" getting one would be "an ambitious challenge." I said I definitely wanted to work at a hospital.

He had an idea, he said, though he wasn't sure whether it was what I had in mind. He took his glasses off and polished them with a cloth, fidgeting around. Then he said he couldn't make any promises but that he would be willing to lobby for a job for me as a cleaning woman at the hospital where he was affiliated.

My women

It was a women's ward, and you had to start very early. That was fine with me, because Aminat was no longer going to school and otherwise I just sat around all morning stewing about it. The work would distract me. It wasn't much money, but it was a proper job—my first in Germany.

I signed a contract and received a white smock. I'd have to bring my own white slippers. I was extremely proud: I was a full-time employee of a hospital.

Some rooms housed three women, others were set up for just one per room. I cleaned quickly and well, and as my hands did the work I asked the women in the beds what was wrong with them. Some of them didn't answer at all. But a few talked. There were some with uterine myomas, others had cysts, a few were trying to conceive, and a few were already pregnant and had to be on bed rest in order not to lose the baby.

Soon I got to know them all—the talkative ones and the silent ones—because I worked very quickly. And because I also cleaned the offices and conference room, I saw all the patients' records, which were kept in large black folders in a rolling file cabinet. I knew all the women's names, their birthdates, and their addresses—some of the addresses were familiar because I'd cleaned somewhere nearby.

I read their medical histories, though the writing was difficult to decipher. I looked in the medicine cabinet, saw who got what and how much, and filed away all the information in my head. I have a good memory and an astute understanding. I spent all morning at the hospital. After I'd gone through all the rooms I'd be sent to change the sheets or take care of some mess or other that had happened during the course of the morning. I also pushed patients down to the OR if the nurses were too busy. Some of the patients were scared before their operations. I told them everything would be fine, and since I knew what was wrong with everyone I was able to be very precise about what exactly would be fine for each of them personally.

After three weeks I felt totally at home at the hospital.

I put off my plans to enter a medical training program. There was enough to learn here. I began to be able to read the doctors and nurses' writing more easily on the forms they filled out about the patients. I figured out where each type of medicine was kept. Then came the first time that a patient fresh from surgery was moaning in pain and I couldn't find anyone to help her. I went and got the right little vials and added them to her IV drip. I watched over her for a while to make sure I hadn't made a mistake and that she didn't die. A day and a half later her husband picked her up and she walked out leaning on his arm.

At home I chatted with Dieter about the medical histories of the women in my ward. I called it "my ward" and also soon referred to "my women." Sometimes Aminat came in and slouched down in a chair while we talked. She began to shower again, to iron her t-shirts, and to go to the salon to have her hair done. I continued to ignore her. She started going outdoors again. She never said where she had gone and I never asked. I ignored her. She began looking through her biology textbook again. I took care of my own business. I had taken a textbook out of a doctor's office and read it all the way through at home. Somehow I realized that Aminat had also paged through it. I let her. Perhaps she'd become a renowned doctor after all.

Just as I thought her life might be heading in the right direction, one that didn't lead to the gutter, she disappeared along with a large sum of cash from one of my drawers, money I had been saving for her education.

Dieter wanted to go to the police and register her as a missing person. Sulfia kept me from doing that, and I in turn kept Dieter from doing it. I should just leave Aminat alone, Sulfia said. It was no easy trick, since I figured I had lost her forever. I pictured her hacked up in the trunk of a car somewhere. But Sulfia laughed—as she often did at the most inappropriate times—and shook her head.

Aminat was eighteen and had run away from home. It was an embarrassment. Granddaughters didn't run away from good grandmothers. At first I reacted all through the night to any noise in the staircase and checked several times a day that the phone was working.

Sulfia took all the blame. She said she'd been a miserable mother and that there'd been no way for me to compensate for that. She was right, of course. But we were still in a pickle. Dieter blustered, but I told him that if he filed a missing persons report, I would go to the police to file a very different report. He quieted right down.

In order to keep from going crazy, I poured myself into my work at the hospital. I studied the new patients and tried to figure out what was wrong with them from their facial expressions and body language. I sketched out a clinical diagnosis of my own, and then I read what my scientifically trained colleagues had written in their files. At first I made a lot of mistakes, but the accuracy of my diagnoses soon improved. I began to immediately recognize women who were unable to have children. They all looked the same. But I also could tell whether the fallopian tubes were blocked, or whether the women were too masculine, too thin, or were with the wrong man. I was surprised nobody else could see these things. Then came a day when I approached a patient who was pulling on some antithrombosis stockings in preparation for surgery and said in her ear: "If I were you, I wouldn't let them remove my uterus. You might still need it."

Her fingers, fighting with a sock, suddenly froze.

"It's your body," I said. "Don't listen to their hogwash. You're fine."

I went into the hall and started washing a windowsill. I heard a door close. The patient had gotten dressed and run down the hall with her overnight bag. Her compression stockings lay on the floor next to her hospital gown. I picked them up and threw them in the trash, and began to strip the bedding.

The next morning I was fired.

Now I had time. Time I spent with Sulfia. I lay in bed talking to her. Then I got up and went searching. I went to the park. I usually avoided it because of all the homeless people loitering there. I talked to them now, asking their names and whether they'd seen my girl. I went to the train station and even took trains a little way to their next stop. I didn't know whether Aminat had left town and if so in which direction she'd gone.

Sulfia walked along behind me but she didn't participate in the search. Sometimes I thought I saw Aminat in the middle of a large group of people. I'd run to catch up, grab breathlessly at her arm—and a total stranger would turn to me. I carried photos around with me. Of Aminat somewhat younger, with nicely groomed hair and a smile that even then was unusual. And of Aminat as she had last looked, a disagreeable vision with straw-like hair and infected pimples on her forehead. Every day I removed her photo from my purse and showed it at least a hundred times.

After I'd been thrown out of the hospital, I also lost five important clients one after the next. Eventually I had just two cleaning jobs left, one of which was at John's place. Then only John was left. But I no longer did my work thoroughly. When I went to John's I had no desire to do anything. It would have been more honest just to quit.

I tried, actually, but he wouldn't allow it. So I showed up fifteen minutes later than arranged (me, who was always so punctual!), and instead of wearing my boots and changing into rubber slippers, I would wear normal street shoes and walk straight across his Persian rugs into the kitchen and sit down at the table. I didn't even bother to pick up the cleaning rags. He would just have taken them out of my hand.

As I sat there and read the Meals on Wheels menu that was stuck on John's refrigerator, he made tea with milk, following all the rules of tea-making that at one time I had paid such attention to. A heated teapot, loose tea leaves from an expensive-looking canister, boiling water, and warm milk that John poured into each cup before the tea. He served it with English cookies topped with sugar crystals. I dipped them in my tea. I drank two or three large cups while John told me about the goings-on in the world. He had begun once again to read the papers and watch the news on TV. I acted as if I were listening. I asked him to keep an eye out for Aminat's face or name, preferably in reference to someone who was alive. He promised me he would. I gave him some photos of Aminat. He put them on his refrigerator with magnets.

Once I had finished my tea, I got up from John's kitchen stool. He handed me the envelope with the usual fee for cleaning, but I pushed his hand aside. When I got home, however, I found the envelope in my purse.

It was, by the way, always quite clean at John's still. His daughter was happy with the way it looked. I asked him who was cleaning the place and he smiled a proud gentleman's smile.

"I am," he said.

The prettiest patient in the intensive care unit

The next few years went by quickly even though nothing really happened.

I kept looking for Aminat. What else did I have to do? But my searching had become half hearted. Now if I thought I saw her in line ahead of me at the bank, I didn't go running up and grab some stranger's sleeve anymore. I carried her photos around in my handbag still, but I no longer showed them to people.

John went to his brother's in England and stayed there. His house stood closed up and empty among the other houses like a dead tooth in a smile. I had a key. John had asked me to go by regularly, make sure everything was in working order, and dust, and for doing that he left me a nice sum of money. I did something I had never done before: I broke my promise and shirked my duties. It was just too much of a hassle to make my way to his house.

I didn't talk to anyone at all except Sulfia. Things happened that I wasn't sure had really happened. Perhaps I just thought they happened because it would have been good if they had. For instance, I wasn't sure whether Aminat had really called me during the first year after her disappearance and spoken three sentences over the phone: "I'm doing well. Leave me alone. You've done enough by killing my mother." Or whether she had wished me a happy birthday in the third year after her disappearance. Sulfia said I shouldn't make anything out of it. She assured me that Aminat still loved me, but in her own way, from afar.

Yes, that was Sulfia. She saw only the best in everyone. I took to doing something that had once been completely foreign to me—staying in bed. I locked my bedroom door and one night I even put a dresser in front of the door to guarantee I wouldn't be disturbed.

Dieter knocked on my door. I told him—from my bed—to go to hell. Sulfia convinced me that I should get out of bed and go have something to drink. I begged her to leave me in peace. I had earned it. She sat down on the edge of my bed and cried. It got on my nerves and I turned my back to her and faced the wall.

I prayed to God to bring Aminat back to my side because my final hour was approaching. I whispered it at the white wall as if God's ear was right there. Then I suddenly heard John's voice—outside the door. He called my name—loud, deep, hostile. He was asking why I hadn't gone over to his house as agreed. He was upset I had neglected my responsibilities. After all, I had been paid.

"Go away!" I called.

It was supposed to sound loud, but I didn't have any strength left. What came out of my mouth was just a weak hiss.

I had completely forgotten what a deep voice John had, a real teacher's voice. His voice filled my room even through the door. Dieter's croaking, on the other hand, barely registered.

I didn't move when the door broke down with a terrible crash and John fell into the room over the dresser—my attempt to keep the outside world at bay. Fleeting thoughts about what a bad impression this was going to leave John with ran through my head. Fortunately my silk nightgown was still fresh and its trim still nicely pressed—because I'd barely moved in bed. But

I certainly hadn't figured on a visit from a man. I hadn't put on any makeup before I laid myself down (I hadn't considered Dieter a man for a long time). Which is why I stayed in my original position, with my face turned to the wall, so John couldn't see my naked face. All he could see was my long hair, freshly braided before I had gotten into bed.

He shook me hard by the shoulder and asked if I was sick. Given how long it had been since we had seen each other, he was acting very familiar. Although I tried to stop him, he managed to roll me onto my back. He was shocked at what he saw. "She's deathly pale!" he called to Dieter. John had never seen me without my skillfully applied rouge. Dieter volunteered that I'd been in my room for two weeks without eating or drinking anything. Unless, of course, I had slipped out to the kitchen during his occasional absences. (Such impudence!)

John shook me as if he were fluffing a pillow. I groaned. I became painfully aware of my situation. I'd be unable to remedy the impression I had just made on him for the rest of my life (though, I forgot for a second, my life was about to end). Why did he have to show up now, of all times? Couldn't he have remembered me as the beaming Rosalinda I once was?

John disappeared into the hall, for which I was thankful. I didn't know yet that he'd called an ambulance that would transport me—lights flashing and siren blaring—to the intensive care unit at the municipal hospital.

I was the prettiest patient in the intensive care unit—and the loudest. It bored me to lie in bed with tubes sticking in me. The treatment seemed exaggerated. I had to go to the toilet and rang for one of the nurses in purple smocks. She brought me a bedpan. I screamed at her—I wasn't potty training! She looked at me totally shocked. Nobody ever screamed in the intensive care unit. At most maybe the occasional death rattle. I knew, I had worked at a hospital. The nurses spoke very slowly to me, in short sentences, everything repeated—as if I were brain damaged.

Two days later I was transferred to the normal ward. I walked there myself while a poorly shaved nurse's assistant pushed my things along behind me in a wheelchair. I lay down in bed. Here, fortunately, there were TVs. I wanted to see the news. Maybe Aminat would turn up. But I was also completely out of touch with what was going on. I also wanted to delay the talk with the doctor and call Dieter to have him pick me up.

A doctor came in. She was Asian, with flat black hair. She was very young, maybe even younger than Aminat was by now. Her white smock fit perfectly. She wore her stethoscope around her neck, as elegantly as a feather boa. On her chest pocket were a few syllables that sounded like bird calls. She was Chinese.

I sighed because this Chinese woman was not my granddaughter. She looked so hardworking that it was easy to see she would soon have her own practice. The Chinese always got what they wanted.

Now she was telling me I had to stay here because my kidneys were on the brink of failure. I laughed out loud and made a gesture that made clear how crazy I took this suggestion to be. She'd have to stay after school, this Chinese doctor. My Aminat would never have made such an error.

I told her I wanted to leave that night. The following morning at the latest. The woman in the white smock rolled her squinty eyes. Her eyes reminded me a little of Aminat's almond-shaped eyes. My mood was deteriorating.

The neophyte left, taking the results of my blood tests with her. I turned on the TV. There was an old lady in the other bed emitting a rattling noise. I turned up the volume so she could hear, too—and to drown out the rattling sound. I kept looking over at her. Someone should sit her up, I thought, so she can breathe more easily. I was about to ring for a nurse when I heard a voice on TV that made me forget the old lady.

On the screen was Aminat. At first I was surprised, then shocked, and finally ashamed. Aminat was on TV—it was more than I could ever have dreamed for. But my God, the way she looked! Why hadn't anyone told her what to wear? Why had they let her on TV with her hair like that? Why hadn't they made her up? Why would they let her go in front of German viewers and disgrace herself that way?

Aminat's black hair was pulled into a scrawny ponytail. You could see it because the camera kept circling around her. You could also see what bad posture she had. I was thoroughly ashamed of her. She wore a blue t-shirt on which my eagle eyes were able to spot tiny stains. Her jeans sat very low on her hips. At least she was slim. Very thin, in fact. She looked very young, as if the time since I had last seen her had never passed. She also looked as if she hadn't eaten since I last saw her. She was still a child, despite the fact that almost ten years had gone by.

And she sang. She sang on TV. And everyone could hear that she hadn't practiced enough. I should have sent her to music school. Maybe then she'd have sung a little better now and not have embarrassed herself. She sang a song in English, one I'd often heard on the radio. I think it was about love. In any event, it had a very melancholy melody to it.

Aminat sang a little softly. It was difficult to hear her. Now I noticed that in the room where she was being filmed, three people were seated at a long table. A woman and two men. They were listening to my little girl sing. And although the way she sang didn't appeal to me, it was clear how infinitely sad her song was. Even the old lady in the next bed stopped rattling.

Aminat was finished. Her bottom lip was swollen. Maybe she lived with a man who beat her. She must have lived off something for all these years. And since she couldn't do anything, she had probably found a man to take care of her— probably an old sad sack hot for some thin, young flesh. Just a shame he couldn't have bought her some nicer clothes. The camera focused on Aminat's eyes—black, nervously blinking in the close-up. Everyone could tell she had tried to apply eyeliner but had then wiped it off. Very sloppy.

The name they showed was hers: "Aminat K., 19 years old." It would have been nicer if they had written out her family name so everyone could read it.

We hadn't seen each other in nine years. She must have been nearly thirty, but it could stay her secret. Mine, too, I thought. She had every right—she looked very young. And anyway, who would put a thirty-year-old on TV?

"How old are you, Anita?" asked the bald-headed man at the table.

Aminat managed on the third attempt to say the number nineteen. She was so nervous because she was lying, it was clear. Pull yourself together, I whispered. And stand up straight! And as if she could hear me, she squared her shoulders and repeated: "I'm nineteen years old."

"And are you still in school?" asked the bald man.

She shook her head.

"And you want to become a famous singer?"

The camera caught Aminat's mouth. Anyone could see—she was missing an incisor. The mouth opened, the tongue licked dry lips, and Aminat said hoarsely: "Yes, I'm going to be a famous singer."

I clasped my hands as the three people at the table put their heads together. They didn't let Aminat out of their sight. She stood still, alone in the middle of the room.

"You're in," said the pretty woman with flat blonde hair and a glittering dress. She looked very fashionable, perfect for TV.

You're in, I whispered, as the camera started to rock and the bald man sprang up from the table. Then the entire TV-viewing country saw Aminat faint and fall to the floor.

I felt in perfect health after seeing Aminat on TV. I told the

244 · ALINA BRONSKY

Chinese woman and her two co-workers—two older doctors she'd brought in as reinforcements. They had all zeroed in on my kidneys. Maybe they needed donor organs. I let it drop that I'd just seen my missing granddaughter on TV, and that she was soon going to be a famous singer. The white-smocked doctors exchanged glances. Finally I signed a piece of paper that said I was leaving the hospital against medical advice.

I called Dieter and told him he needed to pick me up. He sounded weak on the phone—as if he had just gotten out of intensive care instead of me.

I went to the little sink in the corner of the room and looked at myself in the mirror. I went and got my bag and began to put my face in order. My colorless days were over. In the hospital I had worn just a little mascara and lipstick. I pulled out all the stops—it was as if someone had warned me that when the door opened John would be standing there instead of Dieter.

He was really there. This tall man with straight posture and gray hair, a real-life British gentleman. I was as bashful as a young girl.

"Where's Dieter?" I asked.

John shrugged his shoulders. He picked up my three travel bags and carried them along the hall of the hospital. I hurried along behind on high heels, and the nurses craned their necks. I saw for the first time what kind of car John drove. It was an old sand-color Mercedes. It suited him perfectly. He opened the door for me.

"Where are we going?" I asked, as he turned at the third intersection in a row and I no longer recognized the route.

"Home," he said.

"Aha," I said, and only when he carried my bags into the house did I realize he meant his home.

Mine is the prettiest

I never asked myself whether John had honorable intentions. I didn't care. I hadn't worked in a long time, I had no money, and John had a TV in the room where I now lived. I turned it on and searched all the channels for the show with Aminat. Once in a while John came in and took my blood pressure or brought me tea.

Sulfia sat on the edge of the bed and smiled. Aminat sang on TV and the woman with the long, gleaming hair told her she should dress differently. Aminat listened to her with a furrowed brow. I clapped my hands together—that was exactly what I had always told her. But Aminat shook her head. Stupid girl, she never listened to anyone.

John came in just then with a cup of green tea on a silver tray. I looked at him over the rim of my glasses. I wore glasses ever more frequently.

"What nonsense are you watching?" asked John.

"That," I said proudly, "is my granddaughter."

John sat down—not on the edge of the bed but in a chair in the corner. I was beginning to sense that I might be living in his dead wife's bedroom. I lay in a canopy bed with cream-colored sheets, all the furniture had curved legs, and all the upholstery was done in a pastel floral pattern.

"That's Aminat," I said. "She's very talented."

She was on TV all the time now. John looked silently at the screen. He didn't know anything—how I raised Aminat, how much effort I'd made, how time and time again she had spurned my good will, and how finally she had run away from me. He didn't know anything about me, and I didn't have any desire to tell him.

"Pretty girl," said John. "Though much too thin. Her voice is unbelievable."

"You think so?"

246 · ALINA BRONSKY

He didn't have any grandkids and was lonely. I thought it was gallant of him to watch the show—with Aminat struggling to hit the notes—without saying anything more. Not then and not the next day or the one after that.

Suddenly I had everything I needed, without having to fight for it. It was an unfamiliar feeling. I didn't need an alarm in the morning. I could sleep in. I didn't need to make breakfast. John took care of that. He did the shopping. It turned out he could cook. Simple Italian dishes, but they tasted good. He served the food in the living room and cleaned up himself afterwards. I didn't even go into the kitchen. I was mostly in my bedroom, occasionally in the living room (either eating at the table or sitting in the chair), and also sometimes in the garden. John's house had a magnificent garden—giant, with rosebushes lining the house, and softly sloping down to fruit trees that were already setting fruit.

"Why don't you plant vegetables?" I asked.

"I don't know how," said John.

I took off the rhinestone-bejeweled slippers with high heels and walked barefoot on the lawn. The lawn was his, too. He was a real English gentleman.

The grass caressed the soles of my feet. Behind the fruit trees I discovered a greenhouse. The glass was frosted with pollen. I ran my finger over it. I'd never been here. John's wife had probably raised tomatoes here.

"I do well with tomatoes," I told John over tea that afternoon. We were sitting on the terrace with our cups of tea in front of us and a tin of gingersnaps. "I have a green thumb."

John answered: "Go ahead and grow them for next summer then."

We went shopping in shops I'd never been in before. The saleswomen brought me clothing and lace underwear, John drank espresso on an upholstered bench in the corner, and he just raised his eyebrow occasionally when I came out of the changing room and walked around to see whether the clothes fit well.

John's face was inscrutable and I didn't ask his opinion. I knew that I looked good and that I had a nice figure. I also had great taste—I left the dressing room only in things that accentuated the delicateness and gentle curviness of my body. I could see in the merciless light of the dressing room itself that here and there some muscle and skin had lost its tautness. But I knew I'd soon have that back in hand. It stood me in good stead to be so slim just then. I had always had a healthy appetite, but it had left me of late. I was living primarily on tea with milk and ginger snaps.

I didn't say thank you when John paid with his credit card and carried the shopping bags to the car. I knew I had earned it all. At home I changed and we watched Aminat again. She looked better, too. She'd gotten over her constant trembling and the panic had faded from her eyes. Her hair was freshly washed and fell so naturally over her shoulders that I could tell immediately how much work had gone into it. She was now one of twenty girls being shouted at by three choreographers. Now and then they inserted scenes in which the girls sang individually and I thought to myself: Mine is still the prettiest.

John occasionally said: "What a horrible show."

And less frequently: "My God, what a voice."

I didn't think Aminat sang very nicely. I'd often heard her and I had never particularly liked the way she sang. Her voice wasn't powerful or melodic. But it did tug at your heartstrings. That much was true, I had to admit. And it was probably the reason they'd chosen Aminat. People liked it when someone tugged at their heart strings. I couldn't understand why.

I put on a silk pantsuit and new golden shoes and put my hair up. I bought a rotisserie chicken, peppers, marinated sheep's milk cheese, and a honeydew melon. I didn't ask John whether I could use his Mercedes, I simply said: "You needn't accompany me today."

He nodded.

How often I had taken this same route on the bus, transferring twice, waiting between five and forty-five minutes at the stop. I didn't feel a sense of triumph now, just a blessed peace.

I parked in front of Dieter's building. How long ago was it that I had moved out of here? How many years of my life had I spent here? I pulled out my key and walked past the burnt mailbox—someone must have put a firecracker in it. The place smelled stuffy, like stagnation and chronic sinus infections.

I went to open the apartment door with a familiar motion and felt a faint echo of the one-thousand-times-more-powerful worries the turning of this key had caused my soul in the past.

I fought a bit with the lock. It jammed and wouldn't let me take the key back out. Someone shuffled toward the door. It reminded me of a sound I'd heard while working at the women's ward of the hospital—when, after a stomach operation, my patients ventured into the hallway for their first steps, bracing themselves with their hand against the wall, they made a similar shuffling noise. A ghost now appeared in the doorframe. He was wearing a worn bathrobe that allowed a view of skinny legs and an equally gaunt neck poking out of the greasy collar. Dieter's face was no longer Dieter's face. Maybe it had something to do with the fact that his hair was also missing.

"Oh!" I said, trying to sound happy as I looked him in the eyes. "You look good, and I've brought something very nice!"

If I had ever permitted myself to talk to one of my patients in a tone like that, I would have despised myself for a week afterwards.

I put utensils on the table, cut up the vegetables, fished a couple of plates from the sink, and washed the dried food bits off of them. Then I brushed the crumbs off the table and put down a clean tablecloth.

"Food!" I called.

Dieter sat down at the table and lifted a piece of roast chicken to his mouth. I had already removed the skin for him. He chewed on it and swallowed it. I could see it make its way painstakingly down his throat.

"And?" he asked. "What's the story?"

He meant with me and John. I shrugged my shoulders. I ate the entire chicken by myself. Along with fresh organic peppers and crunchy chunks of bread torn from a baguette. Dieter wasn't hungry and chewing caused him pain.

"Everyone has left me," said Dieter. "Everyone, everyone. Even you."

I chewed thoroughly and looked past him.

But there was nothing about me

I didn't tell John that Dieter was going to die soon. The good thing about John was that you didn't have say much to him and yet he knew everything. He always handled the bare necessities. That may not sound like much, but it was. John did the things that were absolutely necessary—and without ever needing to be asked. Everything else he ignored. But everything else was superfluous.

Sulfia came less often now. She didn't like TV, and I didn't want to monopolize her. I let her peel away. Together with John I watched the show featuring Aminat. John didn't offer any more commentary. But I talked nonstop.

"Look, John, what an outfit they've packed her into this time. You can't even recognize her. But maybe it's better that way. She's moving much more confidently onstage than last time, don't you think, John? The dance lessons really helped. She'll show them all, my Aminat. That baldheaded judge must be sleeping with her—he loves her even when she doesn't hit a single note. And that pretty woman, the other judge—why did she have tears in her eyes when Aminat sang? It was obvious to everyone. And the voting—the viewers deciding who stays and who goes . . . surely that's all rigged, right? Otherwise she couldn't possibly still be in the competition. John, why does everyone still call her Anita and Alina—is it really so difficult to remember her name? The main thing is that they all continue to believe she's really that young. When I was her age . . . "

John rarely said anything. But one day as we sat eating breakfast, he excused himself, got up, and came back a few moments later with a stack of newspapers. He put it down in front of me and before I could ask him the point of it all, I saw the photo on the top page. Aminat. All these papers had written articles about her and published photos of her.

"Tartar Orphan Causing a Stir," "Anorexic Abuse Victim Sings Circles Around Competition," "Descendent of Genghis Khan—Most Beautiful Eyes on German TV," "Childhood Stolen, Girl Sings Her Way Into Viewers' Hearts," "Is She Really nineteen? Ten Pieces of Evidence That Suggest Aminat K. Is Still a Minor."

I spread the papers out on the table in front of me so I wouldn't miss a single column. I started to read. My Aminat was in the papers—and not just one paper, she was apparently in every paper, over and over. The photographers couldn't get enough of her narrow face and mysterious eyes and shiny hair. Yes, she was beautiful, even though some of the shots didn't capture her in the most flattering light. She looked so much like me.

I read how Aminat had grown up in a Soviet ghetto without a father, just her mother's ever-changing men. How she had starved and had been beaten for being such a disobedient child. How finally she had been sold to a German pedophile

THE HOTTEST DISHES · 251

by her grandmother in exchange for him marrying her mother, and how she landed in Germany as a result. I read and read, but there was nothing about me. Typical.

"Look, John," I said. "Nothing but lies. The papers always do that."

John nodded.

"She'll be the best. She'll make it big and earn lots of money," I said. "All the work and love I put into her won't have been for nothing. She's going to be someone. She's going to be famous!"

"She's already famous," said John.

He was right. Though I normally noticed things right away, I'd missed the fact that my Aminat had become famous. I guess I'd been talking too much with Sulfia. Everyone was talking about Aminat. The papers wrote contradictory things about her. She couldn't have grown up in Kazan and Sverdlovsk simultaneously. She couldn't be both fluent in Tartar and not speak a word of it. She couldn't possibly be a virgin, have AIDS, and be pregnant. It was obvious from all the lies—Aminat was a star.

Lena

I discovered that I missed Aminat. I thought I'd gotten used to her absence, that it didn't hurt anymore, that I was doing well. Until, that is, I realized I couldn't stand being without her. On the one hand I could see her round the clock. I saw her constantly on TV and had bought magazines with posters of her in them. I'd bought a compilation CD of her and the other competitors on the show. That was even before she won. Her song was being played all over the radio.

"I want to see her," I said to John. "I want to see her before I die."

252 · ALINA BRONSKY

I also realized that all the requests I would earlier have held God responsible for I now put to John. Whether I wanted something big or small, I simply turned to John. It was uncomplicated and had quick results. Unlike God, John had yet to misunderstand anything. I also didn't have to constantly apologize to John or promise him anything in return the way I always felt obligated to do with God. It made things easier.

"I have to see her," I said to John.

He nodded.

I wouldn't have been surprised if an hour later the doorbell rang and Aminat was standing there in the sequined dress from her last show with a bouquet of flowers in her hand for her beloved grandmother. But nothing happened. Not that day or the next. She didn't call. And John just trimmed the roses in front of the house. I didn't pressure him—he was after all no God.

The phone hardly rang at our place anyway. Sometimes John's daughter was on the line and sometimes Dieter, for whom I bought groceries and whose apartment I cleaned. He, too, collected newspaper clippings of Aminat and doused them in his tears. He watched the same shows, though he seemed to see something completely different from me. He saw her as a victim of all the media attention.

But then one day the phone rang and there was a young woman's voice on the line speaking somewhat shyly in broken Russian.

"Aminat!" I cried, hardly able to believe it was her. "Aminat, has your polished Tartar completely displaced your Russian?"

"I'm not Aminat," said the girl. "I'm Lena."

Lena. Who was Lena again, I asked myself, but then hit upon the answer. I remembered it like it was yesterday—the ugly, chubby-cheeked baby, Sulfia's daughter with Rosenbaum. Lena! The one who'd been kidnapped and taken to Israel by Rosenbaum, breaking Sulfia's heart. That Lena was on the line now. She'd probably heard that Aminat was a star and wanted money. I decided to play dumb.

Lena had called Dieter—Rosenbaum had that old number—and Dieter had given her my new number. She said she was coming to Germany and, if possible, hoped to get to know her sister and her mother—the whole family. Lena didn't even know that Sulfia accompanied me in an urn now, and she acted as if she had no idea about Aminat's success. I acted as if I believed her.

"How's your grandmother?" I asked, assuming that not only the grandmother but both old Rosenbaums were long since dead.

"Very well, thanks," Lena answered cheerfully.

On the day Lena's plane landed, I had a migraine. John drove to the airport in his sand-colored Mercedes. I gave him Lena's mobile number and described her to him, at least the way I remembered her: big head, short legs, small eyes, fuzzy hair.

John nodded and drove off.

Less than two hours later, he was back. He carried a little rolling suitcase into the house. Then he stepped to the side to let the girl behind him through the door. I was stunned. Before me stood Sulfia incarnate, an eighteen-year-old Sulfia in flesh and blood, slightly stooped and with a shy smile. This Sulfia had brown hair and light brown eyes—the copy had somewhat different coloration, but the rest was a perfect facsimile. She even dressed like Sulfia—the loose jeans created the suspicion that the person in them was overweight in the most inopportune places. She had on a dark-blue t-shirt with writing on it I couldn't read, and not a single piece of jewelry beyond her gold earrings. Neither John nor Lena understood why I was frozen in place. Then Lena wrapped her arms around me. She was apparently a very impulsive girl.

I sat down on the sofa while John showed Lena around the house. They chatted away chirpily in English, which I couldn't understand. I decided I needed to ask John to teach me. It bothered me that Lena could speak it and I couldn't. I also wanted to speak English with John.

They came back to the living room and Lena kneeled in front of me and said with a shy smile, "And where is mama?" She wasn't a baby anymore, and I didn't like her smile. Others might say it was charming, but I refused. I stood up and gestured with a wave of my hand that she should follow me. Lena traipsed happily along behind me as I led her into my bedroom. I took her by the shoulder (she was shorter than me, just like Sulfia), pointed to the urn, and, relishing this moment, said, "In there."

At first she didn't understand. Then she approached the urn and read the golden lettering on the marble—the name and date. Her lips began to quiver and she turned to me.

"Why didn't anyone tell us?"

"Because none of you would have given a shit," I said.

Germany is a small country

I was happy that John decided to take care of Lena. He gave her a tour of the area, driving her around in his Mercedes. She had evidently coped well with the urn incident and squealed happily around the house. She was thrilled by how clean and green everything was in Germany. She had brought Russian books for me, and a poppyseed cake from a Tel Aviv bakery. She was a somewhat different Sulfia, lighthearted, with a gleam in her eyes. She was almost always in a good mood and she didn't get upset about things or hold grudges. She asked me a thousand questions about me and her mother. But I didn't feel like answering. John didn't know anything about our history so luckily he couldn't help her, either.

About Aminat I said only that she was away.

I found out from John why Lena had suddenly landed on our doorstep. She had a boyfriend who was a little bit older and who had a job that revolved around mass-produced Chinese copies of well-known paintings by Van Gogh, Rembrandt, that kind of thing. Lena's boyfriend sold the copies in Germany. Why, of all things, an Israeli was selling Chinese forgeries wasn't clear to me. It all sounded downright crooked to me. Lena said he wasn't making much at it but that it allowed him to fulfill a dream—living in Germany. She'd been to visit him in Hamburg and now she was here with us. Finally, she said. And as she did she took my hand. I took it back.

John said she could stay at his house as long as she wanted. I gasped silently. I tried to talk to him about it and he said: "It's no problem, I like your family."

"This little whore is not family and never will be" were the words that came to me, but I swallowed them as I heard Lena's laugh waft in from the garden, where she was talking on the phone. Sulfia had never laughed like that. Maybe she would have if she had ever had something to laugh about.

I was still waiting for Aminat. But who should ring? Kalganow.

I recognized him from the wheezing on the line long before he spoke a word. He had snored in exactly the same rhythm.

"Kalganow," I cooed pleasantly. I was in a good mood because Lena was out somewhere and John had brought home some new kind of cookie. "Kalganow, are you calling in your sleep?"

"Rosie," said Kalganow, choking back a miserable cough. "Rosie, my most beloved."

It turned out his teacher of Russian and literature had died.

"When?" I asked mistrustfully.

"Two weeks ago," he said.

The time that had elapsed since then was sufficient for him to realize he could no longer live without me—that, in fact, he never had been able to.

"Kalganow, I have a man!" I yelled. "I have an English gentleman with a big garden and twenty kinds of tea in the pantry."

"It doesn't matter, Rosie," said Kalganow. "We're still married for all eternity."

"You wouldn't even survive the plane ride," I said.

"Then you can bury me, which would suit me just fine," he answered.

I didn't say anything to him about how expensive funerals were in Germany. I went straight to John. I said that Kalganow was an old relative of mine and didn't have long to live. John kissed my hand. At that moment I wished very much that he would ask me to be his wife. I even thought about telling him how much I wanted it. After all, he had fulfilled all my wishes up to now—with the exception of seeing Aminat. But I was too proud. And besides, it was true: I was still married to Kalganow.

I sent Kalganow a plane ticket and the formal invitation necessary for a visa. With John, I picked him up at the airport. He had gone completely gray, still wore his old work jacket, and walked with a cane.

Kalganow wet my cheeks with his kisses and said that everyone around him was old or dead, and I was the only one who was still as fresh as in the days of our youth. And that was true, of course. John shook Kalganow's hand and took his luggage— an old suitcase with holes in the leather and wire wrapped around it to hold it closed, and a big plastic bag. Kalganow leaned on me as we walked to the parking garage. Using all of our strength, John and I managed to help him into the backseat and balance him upright. We put his cane in the trunk.

Kalganow pressed his face to the window. He liked the autobahn. He kept letting out cries of excitement. It reminded me of my arrival in Germany. I felt ashamed—both for him and because of my memories.

"You are so beautiful, Rosie," muttered Kalganow from the backseat.

I looked at John out of the corner of my eye. And although his face was as placid as always, I had the feeling that somewhere in the corner of his mouth a smile was hiding.

When we entered the house, Kalganow's feeble eyes played a mean joke on him. Lena came down the steps calling "Grandpa!" loudly, and Kalganow opened his arms wide, barely keeping his balance. As he did, however, he cried out the name of our daughter. They fell into each other's arms and said silly things to each other. I couldn't stand it any longer and went to my bedroom, turned on the TV, and cheered on Aminat.

"Show them what you can do, my child. Don't let me down."

The four of us sat together on John's leather sofa as Aminat was crowned the most talented young singer in Germany, having won the final round of viewer voting. Kalganow cried, I sat there frozen with excitement, unable to move. John's face was as clear as a cloudless sky. Lena had her hands squeezed between her knees and shook her head.

"What is it?" I hissed at her, for in her ability to annoy me, she exceeded even Kalganow.

"Poor, poor thing," whispered Lena.

I attributed the distressed look on Lena's face to pure envy.

Aminat stood on the stage with a stone face as glitter rained down on her and white doves circled above her head. She now had a record contract. All the cameras were pointed at her and all the microphones awaited her words. The audience was giving her a standing ovation and she lifted one of her stiff, thin arms and waved. I just hoped the viewers wouldn't realize what a mistake they had made in choosing her. But anyway, I thought, the first step to fame has been accomplished. She still had a lot ahead of her. Germany is just a small country.

Tartar cuisine

Dieter died the day after Aminat was crowned.
It would be blasphemous to suggest that it actually suited
me. But the timing really wasn't bad. I had to take care of
everything, and I was happy to get out of the house. Lena and
Kalganow somehow managed to be in every nook of the house
at every moment—her giggling, him wheezing—and I couldn't
just lock myself in my room all day. John trimmed the roses,
looked at the clouds, and made tea. I didn't ask him whether
the company of a poorly raised Israeli and a slobbering old
Russian suited him. The smile I'd always thought I detected
lurking in his face had recently come tentatively to the surface.
To keep myself occupied, I organized Dieter's funeral and
cleaned up his apartment. When I went into his bedroom, in
which the stench of sickness and fear still hung, I opened a
drawer and found a pile of handwritten notes.

The label on the first notebook said: "Tartar Cuisine." I
opened it. "*Pechleve*—a layered dessert," I read. Dieter's writing was small, curvy, and the letters were rounded—if I didn't
know better, I would have taken it for a woman's handwriting.
The neat script was easy to read. After the first few sentences,
images of my old life flooded my mind. I had up to that day
never believed that Dieter had really been travelling around
the Soviet Union to research ethnic cuisines. But now I held
the proof in my hands. Descriptions of his wanderings through
half-derelict villages, sketches of landscapes, and, first and
foremost, recipes. "*Kystybyi*, also called *kuzikmak*, is a sort of
pierogi made out of unleavened dough." "*Katyk* denotes cur-
dled milk that the Tartars heat for a long time in a clay pot. It
is sometimes finished with the addition of cherries or red
beets." "For the filling of *gubadia*, a baked layered pie made
for festive occasions, they sometimes use *qurut*, a uniquely
processed dried yoghurt."

In one of the notebooks I found the angelic photo of Aminat that I'd sent Dieter many years ago, in another life. Tartar words were sprinkled in among the notes. He had tried to learn the language and maintained a kind of vocabulary book:

Bola—child
Singil—little sister
Oschyjsym kila—I'm hungry
Sin bik sylu—you're very pretty
Schajtan—demon
Ischak (as in, you're as stubborn as an *ischak*)—donkey

And then the note: "It is proving practically impossible to write a cookbook about Tartar cuisine."

I shoved all the notebooks into a large duffel bag that I found on top of the dresser, gray with dust and cobwebs.

I would like to have left Dieter's apartment and forgotten it forever. But I wasn't one to run away. I bore a share of the responsibility—after all, I'd lived here, and Dieter had no next of kin aside from me. I worked quickly, sorting, stuffing nonessential things into plastic bags, taking them downstairs. I arranged for the removal of the bulky items, sold Dieter's leather sofa and matching chairs to the Turkish neighbor, and washed the windows.

I'd always thought Dieter's dishes were appalling, but I found some real treasures in his kitchen cabinets—two heavy cast-iron woks, a genuine copper kazan, various African clay pots, all apparently unused, covered with cobwebs. I wrapped it all in newspaper and put it in a box to take with me. The kitchen furniture I sold very cheaply to the landlord, who as a favor then agreed to help me carry my box down to the car.

From that point on, Lena and Kalganow didn't bother me at all. I stopped asking when they planned to leave. I trembled with curiosity about Dieter's notes.

I sat on a silk cushion on the floor and read. I had no idea

260 · ALINA BRONSKY

that Dieter had written so many things about Aminat—the story of her life, beginning long before her birth, beginning, in fact, with my story. I had no idea Dieter knew so much about my life. I couldn't remember telling him about my family. Maybe it had been Sulfia who told him about things I hadn't even talked about with her. Maybe talking with her hadn't been necessary—maybe she had the stories in her blood the same way Aminat had Tartar words in hers.

I came across Aminat's drawings, which Dieter had carefully taped into a notebook. I ran my finger along sentences that Aminat was supposed to have said as a child. I read about Dieter's efforts to distinguish—with German precision—Tartar cuisine from other ethnic groups' national cuisines and his failure to be able to do so. About his exasperation when he realized the subject of his interest was influenced by the surrounding Bashkir, Kazak, Uzbek, Azerbaijan, and Yakut cuisines and that the boundaries blurred. It must have been something very difficult for him to deal with.

I pored over sketches and maps in which he had tried to track the spread of various Tartar offshoots during bygone periods about which nobody cared anymore. I suspect he may have just made some of it up. And as usual, he had devoted the most energy—not to mention ink—to the least important things.

John entered the room and sat down on a chair nearby. I didn't hold it against him that he hadn't been able to bring Aminat to me. It was the only thing so far that he hadn't pulled off—and he still had a better success rate than God.

All the time in the world

One evening John and I were driving to the opera because I had bought myself a new dress and John had gotten hold of tickets. I was caressing the silk in my lap and the leather of my new handbag when John stopped at a traffic light and I looked to the side. I saw an open door that led to a dimly lit room. It was a bar called Istanbul. The windows facing the street were filthy. There were a few tables and chairs out on the sidewalk. I tugged on John's sleeve and said, "Can you pull over?" He parked in front of the bar. We had some time to kill. I took my handbag, hooked my arm through his, and we went into the place and sat down at a table. The table was covered with a layer of grease and I refused to touch it. John leaned back in his chair and said nothing.

From a side room came a stocky man with a bushy black moustache and the eyes of a beaten dog.

"Closed," he said.

I could tell from his nose that he was no Turk. He was an Azeri.

"Closed," he repeated.

I didn't move, and John asked for the wine menu.

"CLOSED!" yelled the man. "NO WINE MENU! RESTAURANT CLOSED FOREVER!"

We remained seated.

He left, rustled around loudly in the next room, and finally returned with a bottle and three glasses.

"You're my last customers," he said. "I'm broke."

We lifted our glasses and drank them down without clinking them together. We respected his sorrow. His moustache was already soaked. Then I stood up and went into the kitchen. It smelled like burnt oil and a spice that reminded me of the childhood I had never had. I found a rag and a nearly empty bottle of dishwashing liquid. I squeezed the last drops out of it and began to clean the cooking surfaces. The bar owner came and stood in the kitchen doorway. I heard him breathing but I didn't turn around.

He left me alone again and continued talking with John in

the other room. I didn't listen—accounting didn't interest me. I moistened crusty stains and thought about Aminat. I'd read in some paper that she was pregnant by a Canadian who was actually an Indian whose tribe lived in Toronto. I didn't believe anything anymore—but that I believed straight away. Aminat had never listened to me. She always did the opposite of what I wanted of her. Now, barring any unforeseen complications, she was going to give me an Indian great-grandchild. So be it, I thought—as long as they didn't name the child Jacqueline.

I had all the time in the world to wait for Aminat, and I wanted to make good use of that time. John always kept his word in the end. Pressuring him was unnecessary. Besides, I was a little afraid to ask him when Aminat would be coming back to me. I was afraid to hear that she had already been there and that I hadn't noticed. I much preferred freeing metal countertops from encrusted bits of food and sending silent thanks to God, mechanically, out of courtesy—I mean, so he wouldn't feel totally useless.

ABOUT THE AUTHOR

Alina Bronsky was born in Yekaterinburg, an industrial town at the foot of the Ural Mountains in central Russia. She moved to Germany when she was thirteen. Her debut novel, *Broken Glass Park*, was nominated for one of Europe's most important literary awards, the Ingeborg Bachmann Prize, and was published by Europa Editions in 2010.

Europa Editions publishes in the USA and in the UK. Not all titles are available in both countries. Availability of individual titles is indicated in the following list.

Carmine Abate
Between Two Seas
"A moving portrayal of generational continuity."
—*Kirkus*
224 pp • $14.95 • 978-1-933372-40-2 • Territories: World

Salwa Al Neimi
The Proof of the Honey
"Al Neimi announces the end of a taboo in the Arab world: that of *sex!*"
—*Reuters*
144 pp • $15.00 • 978-1-933372-68-6 • Territories: World

Alberto Angela
A Day in the Life of Ancient Rome
"Fascinating and accessible."
—*Il Giornale*
392 pp • $16.00 • 978-1-933372-71-6 • Territories: USA & Canada

Muriel Barbery
The Elegance of the Hedgehog
"Gently satirical, exceptionally winning and inevitably bittersweet."
—Michael Dirda, *The Washington Post*
336 pp • $15.00 • 978-1-933372-60-0 • Territories: USA & Canada

Gourmet Rhapsody
"In the pages of this book, Barbery shows off her finest gift: lightness."
—*La Repubblica*
176 pp • $15.00 • 978-1-933372-95-2 • Territories: World (except UK, EU)

Stefano Benni
Margherita Dolce Vita
"A modern fable...hilarious social commentary."—*People*
240 pp • $14.95 • 978-1-933372-20-4 • Territories: World

Timeskipper
"Benni again unveils his Italian brand of magical realism."
—*Library Journal*
400 pp • $16.95 • 978-1-933372-44-0 • Territories: World

Romano Bilenchi
The Chill
120 pp • $15.00 • 978-1-933372-90-7 • Territories: World

Massimo Carlotto
The Goodbye Kiss
"A masterpiece of Italian noir."
—*Globe and Mail*
160 pp • $14.95 • 978-1-933372-05-1 • Territories: World

Death's Dark Abyss
"A remarkable study of corruption and redemption."
—*Kirkus* (starred review)
160 pp • $14.95 • 978-1-933372-18-1 • Territories: World

The Fugitive
"[Carlotto is] the reigning king of Mediterranean noir."
—*The Boston Phoenix*
176 pp • $14.95 • 978-1-933372-25-9 • Territories: World

(with Marco Videtta)
Poisonville
"The business world as described by Carlotto and Videtta
in *Poisonville* is frightening as hell."
—*La Repubblica*
224 pp • $15.00 • 978-1-933372-91-4 • Territories: World

Francisco Coloane
Tierra del Fuego
"Coloane is the Jack London of our times."—Alvaro Mutis
192 pp • $14.95 • 978-1-933372-63-1 • Territories: World

Giancarlo De Cataldo
The Father and the Foreigner
"A slim but touching noir novel from one of Italy's best writers
in the genre."—*Quaderni Noir*
144 pp • $15.00 • 978-1-933372-72-3 • Territories: World

Shashi Deshpande
The Dark Holds No Terrors
"[Deshpande is] an extremely talented storyteller."—*Hindustan Times*
272 pp • $15.00 • 978-1-933372-67-9 • Territories: USA

Helmut Dubiel
Deep in the Brain: Living with Parkinson's Disease
"A book that begs reflection."—*Die Zeit*
144 pp • $15.00 • 978-1-933372-70-9 • Territories: World

Steve Erickson
Zeroville
"A funny, disturbing, daring and demanding novel—Erickson's best."
—*The New York Times Book Review*
352 pp • $14.95 • 978-1-933372-39-6 • Territories: USA & Canada

Elena Ferrante
The Days of Abandonment
"The raging, torrential voice of [this] author is something rare."
—*The New York Times*
192 pp • $14.95 • 978-1-933372-00-6 • Territories: World

Troubling Love
"Ferrante's polished language belies the rawness of her imagery."
—*The New Yorker*
144 pp • $14.95 • 978-1-933372-16-7 • Territories: World

The Lost Daughter
"So refined, almost translucent."—*The Boston Globe*
144 pp • $14.95 • 978-1-933372-42-6 • Territories: World

Jane Gardam
Old Filth
"Old Filth belongs in the Dickensian pantheon of memorable characters."
—*The New York Times Book Review*
304 pp • $14.95 • 978-1-933372-13-6 • Territories: USA

The Queen of the Tambourine
"A truly superb and moving novel."—*The Boston Globe*
272 pp • $14.95 • 978-1-933372-36-5 • Territories: USA

The People on Privilege Hill
"Engrossing stories of hilarity and heartbreak." —*Seattle Times*
208 pp • $15.95 • 978-1-933372-56-3 • Territories: USA

The Man in the Wooden Hat
"Here is a writer who delivers the world we live in…with memorable and moving skill." —*The Boston Globe*
240 pp • $15.00 • 978-1-933372-89-1 • Territories: USA

Alicia Giménez-Bartlett
Dog Day
"Delicado and Garzón prove to be one of the more engaging sleuth teams to debut in a long time." —*The Washington Post*
320 pp • $14.95 • 978-1-933372-14-3 • Territories: USA & Canada

Prime Time Suspect
"A gripping police procedural." —*The Washington Post*
320 pp • $14.95 • 978-1-933372-31-0 • Territories: USA & Canada

Death Rites
"Petra is developing into a good cop, and her earnest efforts to assert her authority…are worth cheering." —*The New York Times*
304 pp • $16.95 • 978-1-933372-54-9 • Territories: USA & Canada

Katharina Hacker
The Have-Nots
"Hacker's prose soars." —*Publishers Weekly*
352 pp • $14.95 • 978-1-933372-41-9 • Territories: USA & Canada

Patrick Hamilton
Hangover Square
"Patrick Hamilton's novels are dark tunnels of misery, loneliness, deceit, and sexual obsession."—*New York Review of Books*
336 pp • $14.95 • 978-1-933372-06-8 • Territories: USA & Canada

James Hamilton-Paterson
Cooking with Fernet Branca
"Irresistible!"—*The Washington Post*
288 pp • $14.95 • 978-1-933372-01-3 • Territories: USA & Canada

Amazing Disgrace
"It's loads of fun, light and dazzling as a peacock feather."
—*New York Magazine*
352 pp • $14.95 • 978-1-933372-19-8 • Territories: USA & Canada

Rancid Pansies
"Campy comic saga about hack writer and self-styled 'culinary genius' Gerald Samper."—*Seattle Times*
288 pp • $15.95 • 978-1-933372-62-4 • Territories: USA & Canada

Seven-Tenths: The Sea and Its Thresholds
"The kind of book that, were he alive now, Shelley might have written."
—*Charles Spawson*
416 pp • $16.00 • 978-1-933372-69-3 • Territories: USA & Canada

Alfred Hayes
The Girl on the Via Flaminia
"Immensely readable."—*The New York Times*
164 pp • $14.95 • 978-1-933372-24-2 • Territories: World

Jean-Claude Izzo
Total Chaos
"Izzo's Marseilles is ravishing."—*Globe and Mail*
256 pp • $14.95 • 978-1-933372-04-4 • Territories: USA & Canada

Chourmo
"A bitter, sad and tender salute to a place equally impossible to love
or leave."—*Kirkus* (starred review)
256 pp • $14.95 • 978-1-933372-17-4 • Territories: USA & Canada

Solea
"[Izzo is] a talented writer who draws from the deep, dark well of noir."
—*The Washington Post*
208 pp • $14.95 • 978-1-933372-30-3 • Territories: USA & Canada

The Lost Sailors
"Izzo digs deep into what makes men weep."—*Time Out New York*
272 pp • $14.95 • 978-1-933372-35-8 • Territories: World

A Sun for the Dying
"Beautiful, like a black sun, tragic and desperate."—*Le Point*
224 pp • $15.00 • 978-1-933372-59-4 • Territories: World

Gail Jones
Sorry
"Jones's gift for conjuring place and mood rarely falters."
—*Times Literary Supplement*
240 pp • $15.95 • 978-1-933372-55-6 • Territories: USA & Canada

Matthew F. Jones
Boot Tracks
"A gritty action tale."—*The Philadelphia Inquirer*
208 pp • $14.95 • 978-1-933372-11-2 • Territories: USA & Canada

Ioanna Karystiani
The Jasmine Isle
"A modern Greek tragedy about love foredoomed and family life."
—*Kirkus*
288 pp • $14.95 • 978-1-933372-10-5 • Territories: World

Swell
"Karystiani movingly pays homage to the sea and those who live from it."
—*La Repubblica*
256 pp • $15.00 • 978-1-933372-98-3 • Territories: World

Gene Kerrigan
The Midnight Choir
"The lethal precision of his closing punches leave quite a lasting mark."
—*Entertainment Weekly*
368 pp • $14.95 • 978-1-933372-26-6 • Territories: USA & Canada

Little Criminals
"A great story...relentless and brilliant."—*Roddy Doyle*
352 pp • $16.95 • 978-1-933372-43-3 • Territories: USA & Canada

Peter Kocan
Fresh Fields
"A stark, harrowing, yet deeply courageous work of immense power and magnitude."—*Quadrant*
304 pp • $14.95 • 978-1-933372-29-7 • Territories: USA & Canada

The Treatment and the Cure
"Kocan tells this story with grace and humor."—*Publishers Weekly*
256 pp • $15.95 • 978-1-933372-45-7 • Territories: USA & Canada